I0678852

JUDAH

IRVING A. GREENFIELD

ALSO FROM BLUEBERRY LANE BOOKS

Books by
Irving A. Greenfield
ONLY THE DEAD SPEAK RUSSIAN
A PLAY OF DARKNESS
SNOW GIANTS DANCING
BEYOND VALOR

Ken Altabef
WAY OF THE SHAMAN: Touching The Mystery
WAY OF THE SHAMAN: Discovering The Way
WAY OF THE SHAMAN: The Hidden World

Ben Parris
WADE OF AQUITAINE
MARS ARMOR FORGED

Anthologies
DRASTIC MEASURES
WASH THE SPIDER OUT

Judah

Irving A. Greenfield

Blueberry Lane Books

New York

2014

JUDAH

Irving A. Greenfield

All Rights Reserved. Copyright © 2001, 2013, and 2014 Irving Greenfield

No part of this book may be reproduced or transmitted in any form or by any
means, graphic, electronic, or mechanical, including photocopying, recording,
taping, or by any information storage or retrieval system, without the permission in
writing from the publisher. This is a work of fiction. Names, characters, places, and
incidents either are the product of the author's imagination or are used fictitiously,
and any resemblance to actual persons living or dead, business establishments,
events or locales is entirely coincidental.

This edition was produced by Blueberry Lane Books
Published in the United States of America
Cover © Copyright 2013 and 2014 Blueberry Lane Books

ISBN 978-0-930064-8-0
Blueberrylanebooks.com

This book is dedicated to my grandchildren,

Ann-Sophie Pascale Greenfield and Nicholas Greenfield.

NAME USAGE

While the hero of the Maccabean revolt is generally known as Judas, the Hebrew name, Judah, is used in this book [to avoid confusion]. The Book of Maccabees was not included in the Old Testament, and the original Hebrew text in which it was written was eventually lost. It had, however, been translated into Greek, and it is that version that is now preserved in the Apocrypha. It seemed appropriate to revert here to all of the original Hebrew names where they differ from the Greek. The Hebrew names of the five sons of Mattathias, in order of seniority, are Johanan, Simon, Judah, Eleazar, and Jonathan. That is how they will be referred to in this book.

PROLOGUE

There was rioting in Jerusalem against the High Priest of the Jews, Menelaus. More Hellene than Jew, he had been appointed by Antiochus, King of the Seleucid Empire, of which Judea was only a small province.

The Seleucid garrison in Jerusalem could not control the Jews, and its commander appealed to Antiochus for help.

In a rage over his unsuccessful Egyptian campaign, Antiochus would not tolerate any opposition to Menelaus. He ordered additional troops into the city to quell the violent demonstrations. These troops were under the command of Sostrates. His orders were to destroy all opposition, reduce the walls around the city to rubble, and, once his authority was reestablished, have the soldiers commence the building of a huge fortress, the Citadel, adjacent to the palace on the hill opposite the Temple.

Sostrates rode north with ten thousand men. When they came to the city of Jerusalem, they found its massive gate shut. Sostrates ordered the city stormed. The Seleucid soldiers flowed over the walls like the waves of a storm-driven sea, and they submerged the city in an epidemic of killing, burning, looting, and raping.

The Seleucids came in the morning, when the sun was halfway up the eastern sky. By nightfall, every street in the city was stained with the blood of Jews.

Many of the soldiers pulled infants from the breasts of their mothers and bashed the heads of the screaming children against the walls of the buildings. Others raped and sodomized the weeping women they had dragged from the houses. The men were butchered wherever they were found. All through the afternoon and well into the night, the screaming continued.

The Jews called upon their God for His help. They cried for His hand to come between them and the Seleucids.

When night came, the soldiers lit several large fires and, skewering two, sometimes three Jews on their long spears, they slowly roasted them to death, laughing and drinking, while the dying men screamed and screamed.

Sostrates gave his men license to do what they liked and to take whatever they wanted. No house, no matter how stout the door, was safe from their invasion, no man was safe from their sword and no woman was safe from their lust. But soon even they exhausted themselves in an orgy of destruction and killing.

By morning, the surviving Jews prayed for someone to help them, for someone to take up arms against their tormentors. But their prayers were in vain. Hundreds of them were rounded up by the Seleucid soldiers to be sent to other cities, where they would be sold into slavery to pay for the cost of the troops.

The riots were quelled. Menelaus continued in his position of High Priest at the Temple. The soldiers of Sostrates began the task of pulling down the walls around the city. Later they would begin construction of the Citadel.

Jerusalem and the Jews seemed now to be forever in the firm grip of their Seleucid overlords. With this accomplished, Antiochus triumphantly entered Jerusalem.

CHAPTER I

A storm was raging in Mattathias. Its signs were openly visible to the members of his family. Each one of them could read his silences and distinguish angry silences from all the others.

With dismay, they noted the appearance of the two vertical ridges that always came to his brow when he was angry with one of them, or about something that happened in the village, or even in Jerusalem, where there was enough happening to put him in a sullen mood. They watched the gray of his eyes change to the color of dark smoke. Even his stance was different. He was taller now because he pulled his shoulders back and stood up as straight as his three-score years would permit.

Mattathias was not nearly as tall as his sons, though he could easily look down at the tops of his wife's and daughter's heads. To everyone in his family and in the village of Modin, where he was the Priest, no man could equal his stature, especially on the Sabbath or on the holy days, when he donned the white robes of his office and led the people in worship and prayer.

Mattathias faced his family. He held them in the fell clutch of his power that had its beginnings with the Hasmoneans, those warrior priests who had fled Egypt with Moses.

Mattathias stood off to one side of the hearth. The flames bathed him with a reddish light. His large shadow was cast against the far wall, brooding over all of them the way the dark clouds of summer hover over the land before the advent of the storm.

He began to pace.

Almost by the ritualistic demands of the situation, the children of Mattathias gathered together along the wall opposite the hearth, where Miriam, their mother, stood. Though all of them were adults, they still remained absolutely silent. The room, though it was the largest in the mud and stick house, was small and filled with the diffuse smells of chickens, goats and Miriam's cooking.

Still pacing, Mattathias made several circuits between one end of a large wooden table and the wall, where there was a window that overlooked his terraced field to the east. That field and the one to the north, beyond his vision, were the chief means of his sustenance.

His sweat and the sweat of his sons had made it yield a bountiful harvest year after year. But now, because the King, Antiochus-Epiphanes, needed money for his army, he would have to give a greater share of his crops, or the equivalent in gold, to Dion, the Seleucid tax collector for the district.

Mattathias sighed deeply and looked at his family.

Jonathan, his youngest son, made no secret of his admiration of things Greek, not the least of which was Iphegine, the widow of a wealthy Seleucid merchant whose house was in Jerusalem. Mattathias knew his son was sorely tempted to give up his God and go whoring after the false gods of the Greeks that were brought to Judea by Alexander the Great more than one hundred and fifty years before.

He glanced at Judah. If Jonathan would be willing to give up his God for the sake of the delights he found between the thighs of a Greek whore, then Judah would be equally ready to do the same for the love of fighting, no matter if it was wrestling naked in the gymnasium whenever he went to Jerusalem, or fighting in the town's tavern. Judah loved to fight; it meant more to him than the pleasure given by a woman to a man.

Mattathias feared that one day his middle son would tell him he was going off to join the Seleucid Army, some of whose phalanxes were completely made up of Jewish mercenaries, God forgive them!

Judah was physically different from his brothers. He was the tallest of them, and where their hair and beards were the color of copper, Judah's was the color of ripe wheat. Their eyes, like their father's, were gray but Judah's were blue, very blue, like the sky of a summer's day.

Mattathias scanned his three remaining sons: Simon was the only one of them who was really clever. He could read and write Hebrew, Aramaic, Greek and some Latin. Johanan, the eldest, was a farmer and more concerned with his coming marriage to Sarah, a girl from a neighboring village, than anything else. As for Eleazar, he would follow Judah through fire to be with him.

Finally, Mattathias looked at his daughter Rebecca, a dark-eyed, raven-haired woman of seventeen, who, if God granted it, would soon be married.

Miriam suddenly stepped away from her children and said, "My stew will burn." She started toward the hearth where a large pot hung suspended over the fire.

Mattathias waved her back. "The stew will wait!" he told her in a low but commanding voice.

She stopped, but did not return to the children.

"We must give more to Dion," Mattathias said, pausing at the window. He motioned toward his field. "We must give him a third again as much as we already give, or its worth in gold."

"Oh, my God!" Miriam exclaimed.

His sons immediately groaned. They knew the land would not yield any more than it already did. To meet Dion's demands they'd have to take the tribute from their own food, or sell less.

"There isn't any choice," Mattathias said. "The penalty for refusing this new demand is death."

"Death," Miriam repeated in a choked whisper.

"If we give Dion this," Johanan questioned, "will he ask for more after the next harvest?"

Mattathias scowled. He couldn't answer the question truthfully.

"Dion is only doing what Antiochus orders," Simon said. "The monies paid by Antiochus to the Romans for having dared to invade Egypt is enormous."

"We had nothing to do with invading Egypt," Eleazar commented harshly. "Why should we have to pay for it?" He looked at Judah, expecting him to voice his wrath as he himself had done.

But Judah was silent. The expression on his face betrayed nothing of what was in the man's heart, or the direction of his thoughts.

"Dion might be bribed to take less?" Jonathan asked. Mattathias shook his head.

"Not this time. He won't take less than he asks for."

"Perhaps," suggested Simon, "a deputation of priests from the villages and towns could go to Menelaus and beg him to intercede with Antiochus on the behalf of all of the farmers?"

Mattathias spat into the hearth. "I think no more of him or the help he might give us than that," the old man said, his voice cracking with anger. "He'd see us all Greeks!"

Another silence came to the room until Jonathan whispered, "We're like mice in the mouths of cats. Our Seleucid overlords devour and devour and are never satisfied, no matter how much they have devoured."

Mattathias nodded and, gesturing again to the field beyond the window, he said, "The Seleucids know what they ask for can't come from the earth but must be taken from our mouths to be put in theirs, or we must forsake our small profit and give it to them."

"If we do nothing to stop them," Judah said, "then why do we talk about it?"

"What would you have us do?" Jonathan questioned.

Judah did not answer. His eyes stayed riveted to his father. As far back as he could remember there was a special bond between them. Not that Mattathias loved him more than the others. For each of them, even Jonathan, who cared less for God than he did for his whore, Mattathias had a deep affection.

"We must endure," his father answered.

"How much and how long?" Judah asked.

"God will be merciful," Mattathias said.

"Then let Him show His mercy," Judah responded, "before we are ground into the dust by those who take tribute from us. Let Him . . ."

"Silence!" Mattathias thundered. "How dare you speak that way in my presence. He is the Lord, your God. How dare you speak of Him as if He were accountable to you or any other man!"

The rebuke meant nothing to Judah. Though he did not speak again, his eyes never left the old man.

"Father," Simon said, speaking softly, "Judah meant no disrespect to the Almighty. He only asked what every Jew must be asking at this—"

"He did not ask," Mattathias replied. "He demanded. He ordered."

"Judah, even to God," Simon said, "must be known as a blunt man."

Mattathias considered Simon's words. Then with a nod, he commented, "Judah is fortunate to have you for a brother."

Simon ventured a smile and answered, "No more than I am for having him for *my* brother, or for that matter having the others."

The tension in the room suddenly dissipated.

Simon understood their father's anger was not directed against them, but rather at their impotence. The Jews of Judea were truly no more than mice in the mouths of the Seleucid cats. For a man like Mattathias to know that and not be able to do anything about it was a burden whose weight and dimension were beyond reckoning. In that sense, Mattathias and Judah were more similar than either of them realized. Both were men of action. Both commanded and received the respect of other men. Both were full of rage.

"To keep peace," Mattathias told them in a much softer voice, "We must give Dion what he asks."

"And if we are to eat," Miriam interjected, "that pot should be taken from the hearth before everything in it burns."

Mattathias moved aside to let her pass. Then he motioned his sons and daughters to take their places at the table. Before they ate, he gave thanks to God for the food Miriam placed before them.

During the meal, Mattathias mentioned that he was planning to go to Jerusalem to visit his old friend Eleazar, for whom he had named his fourth son. "And I want to see what is happening in the city with my own eyes," he said.

Simon glanced at Judah. "I will go with you," Judah said.

"I don't need anyone to guard me," Mattathias responded. "It's no strange city I go to. It's mine, as it is every Jew's."

Judah rolled his eyes upward and with his hands he made a gesture of helplessness.

"I'll go in the morning," Mattathias told them, "and return the following evening."

"Eleazar can't put you up for the night," Miriam said. "He only has a small room for himself given to him by his son-in-law."

"I will stay at an inn."

"That is all the more reason for you to take at least one of your sons," she cautioned. "The city is filled with cutthroats and . . ."

"Mother is right," Johanan said. "The city is no longer safe. Even in daylight people are robbed and murdered, and the worst offenders, the very worst are the soldiers; they stop at nothing."

"Please, Father," Rebecca pleaded, "take someone with you."

Mattathias stopped eating and looked up from his bowl. "Do all of you think I'm no longer able to take care of myself?" he asked in a gruff voice, though he was pleased by their concern, very pleased indeed.

"Hardly, Father," Simon answered. "Think of yourself as the protector of the one who goes with you rather than the one who is being protected."

"Tell me that again."

Simon repeated what he had just said.

Mattathias felt the urge to laugh but instead made himself look very thoughtful. "And who will I protect?" he asked.

"I said I would go with you," Judah responded.

"I will tell you the day before when we leave."

"Yes, Father," Judah answered.

Mattathias nodded, drank some wine and continued to eat the hearty stew Miriam had prepared.

CHAPTER II

Oblivious to the three men behind him, Antiochus stood at the window of the palace and looked out over Jerusalem. All day the threat of rain had been in the air, and now with the rapid coming of twilight, a fine rain was falling. In the square below him, people were hurrying in every direction. Many carried torches to light their way, while others held small oil lamps.

In the distance, Antiochus could see the Citadel. It was on the hill in the western section of the city. He moved his eyes from the Citadel to the Temple in the East. Even from where he was he could see the flicker of torches and the steady yellow glow of oil lamps.

The Temple was no more than a series of inner and outer courts and a few buildings, one of which was used as a sanctuary for sacred writings of the Jews. It was small compared to the temples of Zeus that he had seen in Athens in his youth and later in Rome, where he had been held as a hostage.

The holy Temple of the Jews was made out of ordinary red bricks. But what it lacked in size and beauty, it held in wealth. Every Jew in the land, no matter how rich or how poor contributed to the upkeep of the Temple and its priests. From such loyalty grew a fortune reputed to be worthy of a king.

To make his acquisition of that wealth easier, Antiochus had given the position of High Priest to Menelaus, indeed he had even arranged for the murder of one of Menelaus' predecessors, Onias.

A sudden shift of wind brought a torrential downpour. In an instant, the city seemed no longer to exist. There was nothing except the stygian darkness, the sound of the wind and the rain.

Antiochus moved away from the window. He was tall and broad shouldered with the muscular body of an athlete. Black curly hair with a hint of gray emphasized a handsome face that, even at the age of forty-six, made it easy for him to bring young women to his couch.

He motioned a slave to the window and told him to close the shutters. Then he extended his hands toward the fire in a tripod-mounted brazier.

"Suppose," he said suddenly, addressing the three men who were in the room with him, "you were in my place. What would you do after you heard your own doom prophesied? Tell me. Especially you, Menelaus, since he is one of your prophets?"

"Surely, My Lord, one of your prophets would be able to nullify anything a Jew said," Tyropus offered, before Menelaus spoke.

"The Jews would not believe him. Besides, theirs having spoken first has already dulled the edge of whatever ours might say."

"My Lord," Apollonius said, "I'd mount a search for him, and when I found him, I'd make his dying such an agony that to be done with it, he'd gladly recant what he wrote."

"And do you think, General, that a recantation under such conditions would be believed by the Jews, or for that matter anyone else?" Antiochus asked. "It would be a waste of time. But we still have not had an answer from Menelaus. Come tell us. You're from their line. Tell me what to do?"

"My Lord," the High Priest said hesitantly, "it is not at all certain that the man Daniel is a Jew, though in his writings he claims to be one."

"From what ill-begotten people do you think he might have come?"

"He could be a Roman or even an Egyptian."

For several moments, Antiochus remained silent. Then slowly shaking his head, he told them, "An Egyptian would not dare, and a Roman would not have to. No, it was the work of a Jew."

"Even if it was," Menelaus said, sensing a disaster close by and hoping to avoid it, "he lived when the Jews were held captive by Nebuchadnezzar, the King of Babylonia."

Antiochus pointed to the small bundle of papyri in the hand of the High Priest. "Am I to suppose that you place no value in what is written there, or perhaps you prefer to be blind to the meaning that others might gather from the words set down, regardless of when they were written. The book of Daniel is seditious, but to openly declare it so would only call more attention to it. We will initiate other measures to protect ourselves against it. I can no longer risk having an alien people in my midst."

Apollonius nodded vigorously.

"I might have tolerated those Jews who stupidly cling to their unseen God, but with that kind of writing in circulation, I would be a fool not to see the danger, and I am not a fool. Am I?"

Immediately the three men praised the King's wisdom.

"I must strengthen what I have," Antiochus said.

"Make it strong enough," Apollonius commented, "and the Romans will never dare to attack it."

"That is my intent." Then, looking at Menelaus, Antiochus said, "You will provide me with an example for the others to follow."

"My Lord," the High Priest answered, "I am already more Greek than Jew. I dress as a Greek. I eat at your table. I take part in the games at the gymnasium. I even exhort all Jews to give up their old God, their old laws and to embrace your faith and your ways."

"To your credit," Antiochus said, "many have heeded you, especially here in Jerusalem and in some of the smaller cities in Judea."

"Thank you, My Lord," Menelaus responded. "I am only sorry there are those of my people who reject your gift."

"I can no longer wait for them to accept it," Antiochus said harshly. "There must be one people here in Judea. Only then will we be strong enough to defend ourselves against the Roman dream of conquest. Carthage is theirs, as is Macedonia and . . ." Still suffering from the humiliation he had suffered at the hands of the Roman legate, Caius Popilius Laenas, Antiochus could not bring himself to mention Egypt.

Just as Antiochus was about to undertake the siege of Alexandria, Caius had come. After having drawn a circle around him with a stick in the sand of the desert, the emissary from Rome had said, "You must decide on the spot and not go out of the ring until you give me an answer as to whether you would have peace or war with Rome." Antiochus chose peace and, turning his army around, he marched it out of Egypt.

"You are my first example," Antiochus said. "But now I must have a second example, a man whose reputation and background harbor none of the doubtful shadows that are in your own."

Menelaus was about to object. Though not descended from a priestly line, he knew the law and carried out the rituals as well as his predecessor had.

Antiochus held up his hand to stem anything the High Priest might say to defend himself. "Permit me to clarify my words. The doubtful shadows are only in the minds of those who do not understand you, or the reasonableness of your actions."

"Thank you, My Lord," Menelaus said.

"We live in new times," Antiochus said, "and are obliged to do new things so that we might grow and prosper. The God of the Jews was sufficient for them once, but in the face of Zeus and our other gods what can he offer his people? His way and his law are not our way and our law."

"I think I would die," Tyropus offered, "if I had to live with such an unforgiving god. Zeus is bad enough in his rage but their God does not allow his followers much joy."

"Well," Antiochus said with a slight smile teasing his sensuous lips, "all that will soon change. When it does, all my people will rejoice during the feast days of our gods." Then, turning his attention to the High Priest again, he explained, "That is why I need a second example. Preferably an old man, a priest of some lesser degree than yourself. Someone who the people will follow."

"Yes," Menelaus answered. "But where will this venerable old man lead them?"

"Why, to me, of course," Antiochus chuckled. "To me and hence to Zeus, since I am the God . . . Manifest."

Menelaus nodded. He dared not question the King any further. In truth, he did not want to know what Antiochus intended to do with the old man. "On an appointed day in the near future," he said. "I shall dedicate the Temple to Zeus."

The sudden rustling of the papyri in Menelaus' quivering hands sounded like the whisper of dry leaves when the wind moves among them. But he found his voice. "Lord, you yourself dedicated our temple to Zeus just about this time last year."

"Then we will have two such edifices dedicated to him in Jerusalem," Antiochus responded with a pleasant smile "He, I am sure, will be most appreciative and shower us with good fortune in all our enterprises."

"But the other temple . . ."

"Since none can be built in time for the occasion," Antiochus said, "we will use yours."

Despite the chill in the room, Menelaus' forehead glistened with beads of sweat.

"Have you any objection?" Antiochus asked.

"None, My Lord," the High Priest stammered.

"Soon I will issue a number of edicts that will help the Jews become more assimilated in our Greek way of life. To me, it is perfectly reasonable that if I deny them their holiest of holy places, then I have removed their God from their midst. And further, if I make it a crime punishable by death to worship Him in any manner they will soon find their way to Zeus."

"My Lord," Menelaus said, "they are not reasonable about their faith and their God. They are . . ."

"I care not what they are," Antiochus shouted. "I will make them into Greeks. In time, they will laugh at the days when they were foolish enough to want to be a separate people with an outlandish God, who demands so much and gives so little in return."

Menelaus fell silent.

"I will have my old man for a second example," Antiochus told him.

"You will have him, My Lord."

"If there is a way to avoid bloodshed," Antiochus said, "I will take it. But if I must kill a few to save the many, I will do that. Apollonius, I want you to bring in as many troops as you think will be necessary to keep the city under tight control."

"Yes, My Lord." "And you, Tyropus," the King said, "go with Menelaus, take several other men from the court, and make an accurate tally of the gold, silver and other things of worth in the Temple."

"Yes, My Lord."

"And Menelaus," Antiochus said, "I am eternally grateful to you for having brought the writings of Daniel to my attention. You might yet become my satrap for all of Judea. But before that can happen we must make Greeks of all the Jews."

"Yes, My Lord."

CHAPTER III

A cold driving rain was falling on the morning Judah and his father began their journey to Jerusalem. It had rained now for three full days and nights without letup and intermittently for ten days before that. They left their village of Modin just as the coming of dawn began to gray the day. Each wore a thick hooded cloak of wool over their other clothing and boots of soft leather coated with tallow to keep the insides dry.

Mattathias held a staff of cedar in his right hand and Judah carried one of oak, along with a leather pouch containing bread, cheese and a small bottle filled with wine.

Until the walls of Jerusalem materialized out of the rain, the two men did not speak. Then it was Judah who said, "We might be wise to find an inn before you visit your friend."

"I'm anxious to see him," Mattathias answered.

Judah knew it was his father's way of being contrary. But rather than try to change the old man's mind, he agreed to go directly to Eleazar's house and then go alone to seek lodging for the two of them.

"Be sure it is clean," Mattathias cautioned. "I don't want to return home full of vermin."

"Nor I, Father," Judah responded.

The old man made a low guttural sound but said nothing more.

Despite the hard downpour, the road to the city was uncommonly crowded with soldiers, who looked as if they had been on the march for several days. They were bearded, weather-beaten men who slogged along the muddy road in sullen silence.

Judah scanned the troops. Their battle standards were unfamiliar. He guessed that they had been brought down from the East, since he knew the standards of those troops who had been with Antiochus in Egypt.

"Where will he put his soldiers and how will he feed them?" Mattathias asked. "We can't take any more bread from our mouths for Antiochus to put into theirs."

"They might be coming here for another reason altogether," Judah answered.

"Another war?" the old man asked.

"I don't think so," Judah answered. "The last one cost too much. But tomorrow is a special day for their god, Zeus. It has something to do with the celebration of the end of winter. He was born then, so they say."

Mattathias spat and in a deep, passionate voice, he said, "There is no God but our God, blessed be His name."

To quell his father's wrath before it flared into an ugly rage, Judah repeated the same words. But in truth he did not feel passionately about his God. He did not, on the holy days in the small synagogue in Modin, or during those times he had cause to be in the Temple, feel humble before Him. He did not, like his father, see the order of the universe as stemming from His hand. But because He was the God of his father, Judah saw no reason to abandon Him for Zeus, though there were many, many things he admired about the Grecian way of life, not the least of which was their acceptance of man's sensuality and his need to satisfy his appetites.

Judah's friend, Glacon, an officer in the army of Antiochus, had recently told him, "The real difference between your people and mine is that we have fashioned our gods in our own image, whereas your God has fashioned you in His image; your God holds you, but it is *we* who hold our gods."

Regardless of the rain, people and soldiers thronged the narrow, twisting streets. There was nothing splendid about the city. It was gray and filthy; garbage and human waste were everywhere.

Hawkers lined the streets. The smell of food and spices filled the sodden air. Spitted pieces of lamb, kid, and pork were sold on every street. Pork was a favorite with the soldiers.

The city was divided by a central valley. The house of Eleazar's son-in-law was in the middle of a street that made several sinuous turns up the eastern slope of the valley and eventually opened onto the square in front of the Temple.

Mattathias pointed to the Citadel. "Antiochus wasn't just satisfied to build a fortress in the city, but to spite the Jews he built it higher than the Temple."

"He may fear us more than we realize," Judah answered.

"It was he who ordered our slaughter, not we his," Mattathias fumed. "It was he who took our High Priest from the Temple and put his there. It is he who holds against us the swords and spears of one hundred thousand soldiers."

They were in sight of the street where Eleazar lived, when suddenly people came running down from the direction of the Temple. Some were weeping. Others shouted for God's help. Many were wide eyed with terror, as though they had witnessed a terrible slaughter.

Then from other parts of the city, people surged toward the Temple. With shouts and cries of despair, they jammed the narrow streets, overturning the stands of the vendors, trampling underfoot anyone who was unfortunate enough to lose his footing.

Judah attempted to wrest his father from the stream of people, but strong as he was, he could not. The two of them were no more than flotsam swept along by the tide of screaming people.

The cries coming from the people were against Antiochus, whose soldiers had surrounded the Temple, preventing the Jews from entering. They poured into the square in front of the Temple, where there were soldiers standing in close ranks, with their heavy shields ready and their spears pointed at the Jews.

A Seleucid officer barked an order. Instantly the troops moved. The Jews fell back.

Another order was given and the soldiers stopped.

Except for the drumming of the rain on the stones of the Temple, the square was absolutely silent.

A second Seleucid officer, Sostrates, arrived on a white stallion.

He was a short, lean, dark-complexioned man whose hands were already drenched with the blood of Jews who had been slaughtered during the recent uprising. He brought his mount to a halt in the open space between the troops and the Jews. Though a long black cloak protected him from the rain, he was dressed for battle, complete with a short sword at his right side and a leather helmet on his head. He took his position in the center of the first line of troops. In a loud voice, he said, "The Temple and all that is in it now belongs to Antiochus-Epiphanes."

A moan rose like the sound of the wailing wind.

"It is decreed by our sovereign King, Antiochus-Epiphanes, that henceforth all Jews will worship Zeus and no other god. Any Jew found guilty of violating this decree will be put to death."

The people in the square were too stunned to cry out.

"Furthermore, it is also decreed that no male child will be circumcised. Jews are forbidden to congregate for prayer, observe the Sabbath, or any of their religious festivals. Any violation of these decrees is punishable by death. And furthermore," the officer shouted, "any Jew having in his possession the sacred writings of their false religion or any Jew practicing these dietary laws that sets him apart from other peoples will suffer death."

Abruptly, from the very front rank of the Jews a tall, dark-haired man stepped away from the people on either side of him. "Hear, oh Israel, the Lord is our God, the Lord is one!"

From a thousand throats the ancient battle cry broke like the crash of thunder over the square.

In an instant, the air trembled with the whir of a single spear. With a dull thud, the spearhead struck the man in the chest. He dropped to his knees. The spear shaft quivered. He tried to grasp it and pull the head free from his blood-soaked chest.

"The Lord is Our God, the Lord . . ."

Sostrates galloped toward the man, forced his horse to rear, and with a swift slash of his sword, severed the man's head from his body. The head dropped into the mud, while the remainder of the body pitched slightly forward spouting blood from the neck; then it, too, fell sideways into the mud.

"Zeus is your god," Sostrates yelled. Pointing to the severed head with his bloody sword, he ordered the head to be mounted on a spear and placed on the left side of the Temple for the vultures and crows to eat.

Then he said, "By order of Antiochus-Epiphanes all Jews will assemble at noon tomorrow in front of the Temple. Those found in any other part of the city will be killed." He turned his horse and rode away.

Silently the Jews and the soldiers faced each other.

"So, now we know why we saw so many troops entering the city," Mattathias whispered to his son.

Judah said nothing. He looked around him. Everywhere, people were weeping.

"The Temple," Mattathias groaned, "the Temple has been taken from us."

"Come," Judah told him, "I'll bring you to Eleazar's house." "We're nothing," the old man sobbed, "without a place for our God, for our laws."

"Come father," Judah said gently. "Come. We can't undo what has been done here today."

"To make Greeks of us all . . ." He bowed his head as tears rolled down his weathered cheeks.

Judah led him down the narrow, twisting street.

"We are being tested," the old man wept. "Our God is testing our faithfulness to him."

Judah shrugged. If God was testing His chosen people, He could have found some other way, one that at least matched them equally with their adversary.

CHAPTER IV

Judah brought his father to the house where Eleazar lived. The two friends embraced and with tears in their eyes spoke in choked whispers of what had happened a short time ago in front of the Temple.

Eleazar was too frail to go out any more unless the day was bright and warm with sunshine and then only with the aid of a stout oaken staff blackened by age.

"I stood in the opened doorway," he told Mattathias and Judah, his voice cracking with emotion, "and the crowds reached from the valley there, up this twisting street to the square in front of the Temple." He paused and wiped his eyes. "Even without seeing them, I know all the streets were filled with people. And whatever happened there in front of the Temple, whatever laws were announced against us, came down in a low, throbbing murmur to those who were here in the street. Never in all my life have I witnessed anything like it. Each movement of the soldiers, every word, every act. It was spoken from man to man."

Judah stood apart from the two old friends. Their business did not concern him. He was anxious to leave. He still had to find an inn for the night, and now that the Jews in the city were in a state of ferment, he doubted whether it would be an easy task.

The death of the man in the square had whetted his appetite for drink and for a woman. The drink would brace him, and the woman . . . he almost smiled . . . the woman would soothe him. In most circumstances, it would be as good a combination as any man might hope to experience, but now it seemed only the best temporary escape that a few coins could buy and a troubled life could offer.

Eleazar cocked his head to one side and studied Judah. The eyes of the old priest were set deep in his skull but they were bright and alert, almost like those of a falcon, or some other bird of prey. For all his age, his bent body and wispy white beard, there was definitely something hawkish about him, albeit of an old one, whose wings could hardly bear him aloft.

The piercing look in Eleazar's eyes dug deep into Judah, making him feel ill at ease.

"This one," the old priest said, moving his eyes from son to father, "is more rock than flesh."

Mattathias was about to object, but Eleazar said, "Take no offense old friend, but consider, where would we stand if the stone of the earth were not there to support us?"

As if to brush away the old priest's comment, Judah made a vague gesture with his hand and said to his father, "I must go and find lodgings for us."

"But the house of my son-in-law is open to us," Eleazar said and called to his daughter, who came and with little enthusiasm supported her father's invitation.

"There is not enough room for the three of us," Judah lied. "Three?" the old man asked.

"My brother Jonathan will join us," he answered, glancing at his father, who did not know his youngest son was also in Jerusalem.

"Yes," Mattathias said, "there are three of us." But he was clearly struggling to keep a tight hold on his temper. That Jonathan was in the city meant only one thing, he was whoring with that Seleucid bitch Iphegine, who held him between her legs as surely as a carpenter's vice grasps the piece of wood he seeks to shape.

"I will be back here for you," Judah said, "before the midnight watch calls the hour." He embraced Eleazar; then hurried to the door and let himself out into the rain.

* * *

Eleazar beckoned to Mattathias to follow him into his room. It took a few minutes for the two old men to settle themselves comfortably.

The room was no more than a small shed-like appendage to the house. There was a pallet for sleeping, a brazier that provided some heat, a table, piled high with scrolls of parchment, sheets of papyri. Off to one side, a small oil lamp provided a feeble light that was scarcely enough to illuminate the rest of the chamber.

Mattathias was glad to be free of his wet cloak and sat in the one chair in the room, while Eleazar apologized for the meanness of his quarters. "But what does an old man like me need if I have my God. I cannot eat much and the years have robbed me of my sleep, preparing me for the eternal one that is soon to come."

For a while the two men discussed the new proclamations and their effect on the Jews.

And Eleazar said, "From the time we were in Egypt until the present, we have asked nothing more than to be allowed to worship our God, to honor the Covenant made between Him and Abraham and refined between Him and Moses." Eleazar sighed, "He has given us the laws which make it possible for each of us to live with other men and for these people to hate us. Mattathias, I have spent a good part of my life trying to understand why we are hated, and I still do not know the answer."

The conversation continued in the same vein for a while longer. Eleazar did most of the talking, and then he said, "But there is a change coming, a change that will bring Antiochus to his knees. Yahweh will find the means to do what He has done to so many others who sought to wrest from Him His dominion over us."

"He must move quickly," Mattathias answered, "or those of us who remain Jews will surely perish."

Eleazar took several sheets of papyri from the table. "The Book of Daniel," he whispered. Then in a low, but steady voice he read them to this guest. When he was finished, Eleazar said, "The little horn is Antiochus and he has already been defeated by Rome. Soon he shall be utterly defeated. Not only will the Jews rise up against him, but other kings will bring him down. That is the prophecy, my friend, that is how our God has said to His people it would come to pass."

"And to whom did He say this?" Mattathias asked.

"Daniel."

Mattathias repeated the name.

"You do not believe it is the word of Yahweh?" Eleazar asked.

"Would it was His word," Mattathias muttered. His thoughts scurried back and forth from the agony that once again had befallen the Jews and the promise of future deliverance offered by Eleazar's prophet, to the obscenities being committed by his youngest son between the thighs of a Greek woman. "Do you know this Daniel?" he finally asked.

The old priest nodded.

"Could I know him?"

"Not the way you know other men." Eleazar said. "Should you have need of him, he will seek you out."

"And will he say, 'I am Daniel ... '"

Eleazar laughed. "He will come to you by whatever name he chooses to use, Mattathias. He is one of God's chosen, a man to bring His promise to us as He has always done from the time of Moses."

"It would take an army to defeat Antiochus."

"Then an army will be raised."

Mattathias did not answer. He did not know what to think of the prophecies. They could be false. Daniel might be another false prophet. The history of the Jews was studded with so many men who claimed to have been given God's word. But because Mattathias loved his friend, he nodded and said, "God would not put the words of such a great hope into the mouth of a man unworthy of being His messenger."

Eleazar nodded enthusiastically and added sadly, "But now we are a people who have nothing beautiful to put before their God. All that we possessed has been stolen from us."

Neither one dared mention what new torment might be visited on the Temple tomorrow, but each was sure it would be something transcending what had already been done.

"Does the past still stand between you and Judah?" Eleazar questioned after a few moments of silence.

"Yes," Mattathias answered sorrowfully.

"And you have never spoken to him about it?"

"No," Mattathias answered.

"It is a pity," Eleazar said. "It haunts him as it does you. It is buried in his eyes. I could almost see it there when I looked at him. But he loves you, Mattathias."

"Not with the warmth of my other sons," he answered. "His love is there because I am his father."

"He protects you even while you're here in the city."

"Judah would die for me, Eleazar," Mattathias said, "not because he loves me; but because he loves himself less for not being able to love me the way my other sons do."

"Do you love him?" the old priest asked.

"More, oh, so much more than my own life!"

A silence fell over the room, and after a while Eleazar stood up from the pallet and put some charcoal into the brazier. Then without looking at Mattathias, he said, "My time will soon come and when it does, will you pray for me?"

"Yes," Mattathias said, "I will pray for you as we have always prayed for each other."

Eleazar turned from the brazier. There were tears in his eyes. "I weep not because I fear death. I have lived a long and useful life, but life, even with all its attendant struggles, Mattathias, is beautiful, so very beautiful."

Mattathias nodded, stood up and embraced his old friend.

* * *

With a murmuring sound of satisfaction, Judah pushed deeper into the body of the woman under him. A riot of colors burst against the insides of his closed lids. Brilliant reds. Bright yellows. Vivid purples and greens. They came and passed like the great sheets of rain that swept across the land of Judea in the spring. When the spasms of orgasmic pleasure no longer shook his loins, the colors melded one into the other and then began to fade, then left him altogether. A warm physical lassitude spread through his body and he became aware of the woman, whose round, firm breasts filled his hands.

"It was strong for me, too," she laughed.

Judah opened his eyes and looked down at her. She was dark skinned, a shade or two lighter than some of the women slaves the traders brought from Egypt. She had high cheekbones, black, kinky hair and sloe eyes that even in the meager light of the crib showed a touch of purple. Her teeth were very white. When she smiled, as she was now smiling, she seemed to possess a certain childlike innocence. Her name was Ismene, and whenever Judah came to Jerusalem he lay with her.

"Are you going to stay the night?" she asked.

He shook his head. "I brought my father to the city to see an old friend."

"I never mind sleeping the whole night with you," she said, moving her fingers over his face and beard.

"Nor I with you," Judah responded.

For a while neither one of them spoke. Judah was content to luxuriate in the sensual aftermath of their ecstasy. He took pleasure from the press of her nipples against the palms of his hands, from the now-loose hold of her thighs on the broad of his back and from the rose of attar scent on her body.

"Some of the other women are jealous that you prefer me to them," Ismene said in a low voice.

Judah rolled away from her and stood up.

She raised herself on her elbows and said, "They say I must be a Jewess for a Jew to always want me. They say that all Jews possess a magic power enabling them to immediately know a Jew from a non-Jew."

"Are you a Jewess?" Judah asked, as he dressed.

With a toss of her head that made her naked breasts roll, she said, "I was taken from my parents when I was a little girl, no more than five or six, until I was old enough for a man to enter me." Dressed, Judah sat down on the edge of the pallet and placing his hand on her cheek, he asked, "Do you mind what they say?" Then without giving her a chance to answer, he said, "I don't know who your people were and I don't care. I come to you and none other. I'd buy you, if I had the money."

She kissed the back of his hand.

"Come now," he said, "put your gown on and we will go downstairs. Maybe Glacon will join us."

"I heard what happened at the Temple this afternoon," she told him as she dressed.

Judah nodded. "I was there."

"Some of the soldiers who came here afterwards," she related, "claimed Jews threw themselves down and wept like children, while others grew wings and like giant bats flew away."

"Many wept," Judah responded. "But none grew wings and flew away."

"The soldiers," Ismene continued, "said that soon everyone will be Greek and there won't be Jews anymore."

Judah's features clouded over with impatience. How could he answer that, when he had never thought about the possibility? Yet, he had heard Antiochus' decrees and knew, as did every Jew, that to follow them would mean the end of the Jewish people.

"Judah, do you believe in your God?" Ismene asked, looking straight into his eyes.

"He's the God of my father," Judah responded.

She seemed ready to ask another question, but for some reason or other, she changed her mind. And instead she said, "I'd take your God for my own, if He'd have me."

With the hint of laughter in his voice, Judah replied, "I'm not even sure He has *me.*"

"But you said He's the God of your father."

"He is."

"Then I don't understand."

Judah shrugged. Suddenly he began to laugh: here he was discussing Yahweh with a prostitute, a woman who from childhood on had been used by men for only one purpose, and yet she was trying to understand what he himself did not, and perhaps she was even willing to believe what he merely accepted only because it had been given to him.

Ismene cocked her head to one side. "Is my question foolish?"

"No," Judah answered, "only my answers are foolish." He put his hands on her arms and, drawing her to him, he said, "I meant what I said about wanting to buy you."

"I know you did," she replied, pressing herself against him.

He held her very tightly. Then hand-in-hand they left the room, walked along the dimly lit, musty-smelling hallway and down the steps into the large room filled with men eating and drinking on crude wooden tables. On the walls there were burning torches held by iron brackets. The floor was covered with filthy straw, and the air was filled with the heavy odors of food, beer, and wine. The men and women smelled of sweat and the women of perfume.

Many of the men they passed ogled Ismene, or made some obscene comment about her. A few even called out the price they would be willing to pay for her services. But a dark, menacing glance from Judah made them quickly turn away. None was willing to risk a fight with the blonde giant, who held an oaken staff in his hand in a way that left no doubt in the mind of any man who saw him that he knew how to use it with great skill. No prostitute was worth a broken head!

Threading his way through the crowded floor, Judah led Ismene by the hand to the table off to one side near the hearth, where it would be warm.

Judah ordered a chicken to be shared between them, beer for Ismene, because she preferred it to wine, and wine for himself.

He looked around. The Jews there were more Greek than Jew. They dressed and ate like Greeks and often spoke in Greek rather than in Hebrew, Aramaic, or the local dialect of Koine. All of the conversations, even those of the soldiers, were about what had happened in front of the Temple that afternoon. He even heard a man at a nearby table repeat the story about the Jews who sprouted wings and flew away like bats.

The soldiers, from what Judah could hear, were worried about what might happen the next day. They did not want to be caught in the midst of a bloody uprising. Those with any sense realized they would be hard pressed to defend themselves in the narrow, twisting streets of the city.

An old woman brought the mugs of wine and beer to the table. She bared her toothless gums and cackled, "Soon all the Jews will be Greeks." Her brown eyes rested on Judah, and then she commented to Ismene, "But some whores prefer a dirty Jew to a good Greek."

"Some good Greeks might some day wish they were Jews," Judah said. "Now go about your work old hag, or I'll put you in your grave before the night is out."

The woman scuttled away.

Judah drank all of the wine from his mug, and he immediately called for more. For a moment or two, something dark and ominous passed through his brain. Something like a warning . . . but then someone called out his name. He turned toward the door and saw Glacon coming toward him.

"No sooner I enter this den of Hades," the Seleucid officer laughed, "than who do I see but you."

Glacon found a chair, brought it to the table and sat down. He looked at Ismene. "She positively glows when you come here. I envy you, to be able to do that to a woman. The best I can manage is a groan or two, and those I'm never sure are for my benefit or the woman's."

Glacon was not as tall as Judah, but he was as broad and as strong. Born in southern Greece, he was educated in Athens. He became a soldier because it gave him the opportunity to make a name for himself, to say nothing of wealth that came his way from the booty taken by the army. He spoke and read many different languages, including that impossible tongue used by the Romans.

When the old woman brought the roast chicken to the table and saw Glacon, her eyes went wide with surprise.

"Anything wrong, Granny?" Glacon asked.

She shook her head and rushed away from the table.

Judah explained what had happened before Glacon arrived. "Someone put her up to it," he said, glancing around. "These mongrels will do anything for a fight."

Using his hands, Judah tore the chicken into thirds and handed part to his friend.

"I saw you in the square in front of the Temple," Glacon said.

"Who was the old man with you?"

"My father."

"If my father had lived," Glacon said, "he might have looked like that. He was rock, through and through."

Judah laughed. "My father is just as hard."

"And you, Judah," Glacon questioned, "are you any softer?"

Ismene reached across the table and putting her hand on Judah's, she said, "He can be."

"Now that's a compliment," Glacon said, "worthy of a woman . . ."

Suddenly, shouting erupted. Someone came at Judah, calling him a Greek-lover. But Judah bolted up and struck him down with a blow in the chest. In an instant, tables were being overturned and men were grappling with each other.

A melee had started. A whirlwind of anger roared in the tavern.

Seleucid soldiers used their spears and swords to cut their way out. Many fell with smashed skulls. Bloodstains blossomed on the straw-covered floor.

The staff was wrenched from Judah's hands, and he used his fists.

"Take a sword," Glacon shouted above the din, "or we will never get out of here."

Judah dropped to the floor and grabbed a fallen soldier's weapon. As he came up, he drove it into the belly of a soldier who was about to thrust at him. The man staggered back, clutching his stomach, and fell to the floor.

Judah glanced up. Some of the soldiers had gotten hold of Ismene. That was what the fight was all about. The soldiers were angry with her for having lain with him.

She shouted his name again and again. They tore the clothes off her body.

Judah tried to cut his way through to her but, even with Glacon fighting at his side, there were too many of them.

Abruptly, the fighting and shouting ceased, except for one terrible shriek that clawed its way to the very darkened roof timbers.

One of the soldiers had thrust his spear into Ismene's sex. She screamed again as she was lifted high above the soldiers. The blood poured out of her body, drenching the soldier's hands and the top of the table on which he stood.

Judah could see nothing except a red haze and the dark forms in it. He started to rush forward.

"They'd just as soon kill you," Glacon said, grabbing hold of his friend's arm. "There's nothing more you can do." He put his arm around Judah's shoulder. "Best come with me."

"One more thing," Judah shouted as he broke free and rushed forward. "One more thing!" Using the sword as spear, he hurled the weapon into the throat of the soldier who held Ismene's writhing body above the crowd. The man staggered and let go of the spear. Ismene fell into the straw.

Glacon tossed another sword to Judah, and together they fought their way to the door and into the narrow street.

"Judah," Glacon called, "Judah, stay close to me."

"No," Judah shouted, "I'll go my own way." He ran until he felt his lungs would burst, and still he continued to run.

When he finally stopped, he knew he was somewhere near the Temple. He sank down on a large rock. Looking up into black sky, Judah shouted, "You knew I loved her! You took her from me! You took her from me!" Then he bowed his head. His salt tears mingled with the rain that beat against his face.

CHAPTER V

Mattathias lay on his pallet, which was softened by a ticking filled with straw. The room in the inn was clean. The owner, a wizened old man with rheum in his eyes, was kind enough to provide a ewer of water and a basin for the following morning's use.

Mattathias looked across the small space separating him from Judah. From his son's disheveled look and the fact that he no longer had his staff, Mattathias knew Judah had been brawling again. He had refrained from mentioning it, for fear they might have become embroiled in yet another futile argument. The events of the day sorely troubled him. The gravity of Antiochus' decrees and actions outweighed his concern for the waywardness of his son, who, with God's help, would eventually come to his senses.

Mattathias suddenly sensed a difference in the tone of his son's voice. It seemed harder than usual, but at the same time mixed with a low, sustained note of sadness he had never heard before. Again he raised himself up. Looking over at his son, he wondered if Judah had been moved closer to God by the events he witnessed in the square that afternoon.

"Greeks, rejoice. Therefore, we have a double reason to honor him, and we have dedicated this Temple . . ."

Before Antiochus finished, a cry of despair rose from the Jews in the square. It was wordless at first, just a long drawn out expression of agony. Then it took form and the people cried out to God for help.

Antiochus glared at Menelaus and ordered him to silence them. "They are your people. Silence them, or I will have my soldiers do it."

41

Menelaus moved slightly forward and holding up both his hands, he turned first to the right and then to the left. He repeated this movement several times.

Gradually the cries ceased. All that could be heard was the low sobbing of a grief-stricken people.

The High Priest said to the Jews, "Listen to Antiochus-Epiphanes; he is offering a new life."

"He is offering us death!" A man shouted from somewhere deep in the ranks of the crowd. Many took up that cry and it was repeated until Antiochus roared out, "Your God has no place here. Zeus now dwells where your Yahweh did. This Temple belongs to Zeus, the god of the Greeks. I have sacrificed a swine to him and given burnt offerings to him. Your God has fled. He has deserted you!"

The people in the square looked at one another and shook their heads. They were totally confounded by what they had just been told. "The swine," Antiochus told them, "is sacred to Zeus."

"In the eyes of our God," a man cried out, "it is an abomination, an unclean beast."

Antiochus turned to Menelaus and said, "Now give me my second example."

With his eyes, the High Priest searched among the members of the lesser priests until he found the one he wanted. Then he said to Antiochus, "His name is Eleazar; he stands there, between the tall blonde man and the one with the long white beard."

Antiochus spoke to Apollonius, who in turn relayed the King's request to his subordinates. Before anyone realized what was happening, four soldiers had pulled Eleazar away from Mattathias and Judah and were marching the old man to the King.

Mattathias started after his friend, but Judah grabbed him by the arm and stayed his movement. "It will do no good," he said.

Antiochus motioned the soldiers away and for a long time he looked at the old man. Then he took several steps back. "Menelaus," he asked, "why did you choose this particular man?"

"The prophecy of your downfall came from his hands," the High Priest answered.

"Is he the author?" Antiochus asked, glowering at the old man.

"Only the recipient," Menelaus answered.

Antiochus nodded and stepped back to confront Eleazar, who was leaning on his staff.

"I understand," the Seleucid king said, "that you are held in great respect for your learning and your devotion to your people."

"And also, I should hope," the priest said boldly, "to my God."

"Yes, I was told that. But since He no longer exists, you must hold Zeus with the same devotion that you held . . ."

Eleazar drew himself up on his staff and cried out, "Hear, oh Israel, the Lord is our God, the Lord is one!"

Antiochus's face flushed with anger. "Your God is dead," he shouted, "and this I will tell you; eat of a swine's flesh and save yourself, and lead your people to their new god. I respect your age, Eleazar, and above all I respect your courage."

The old man silently shook his head.

And Antiochus said, "I cannot think you to be a philosopher, when you have so long been an old man, and still cling to the religion of the Jews." The last few words the

King uttered with unabashed hatred. Then he asked, "Why do you refuse?"

Eleazar looked about him, and then with a nod, he spoke for all the Jews there and he said, "We, Antiochus, out of conviction, lead our lives in accordance with Divine Law . . . therefore under no circumstance do we deem it right to transgress the Law. Nay, even if our Law were, as you suppose, not divine, even so, it would not be possible for us to invalidate our reputation for piety. You mock at our philosophy ... yet it teaches us temperance, so that we rule over all pleasures and desires; and it inures us to hardship, so that we willingly endure any difficulty." The old man paused; his breathing was shallow, and he was clearly frightened. "I shall not violate the sacred oaths of my ancestors in regard to keeping the Law, not even if you cut out my eyes and burn my entrails." And then, after a momentary pause, Eleazar added, "Unsullied shall my fathers welcome me."

The Jews remained silent; but they knew that their old priest spoke for all of them, and they loved him for what he had said.

Antiochus, too, remained silent. He admired the man's courage, though he could not understand its wellspring. He could not understand what bound the Jews so tightly to their God, to their Law and to each other. But whatever those bonds were, he must now begin to cut them apart. He could not afford the risk of having such an obdurate people in his midst. They must be made one with his people, or suffer destruction.

He nodded at the old man. "I asked for a second example and Menelaus has presented me with a martyr. You still have the chance to save yourself."

"Can you not," Eleazar asked, "do what you set out to?"

Antiochus shook his head. With a gesture of his hand, he signaled to his soldiers. They rushed to Eleazar and threw him to the ground.

Shouting his friend's name, Mattathias again started toward Eleazar, but Judah still held his father's aim. "Fool," he hissed, "it is enough that *one* must die."

With tears in his eyes, Mattathias said, "I shared everything with that old man, even what you saw happen."

"Enough!" Judah exclaimed, cutting him short. "Honor him. He deserves more than your tears."

The soldiers tore the clothes from the old man's pitifully thin body. Then at a nod from Antiochus two of them scourged him.

As they snaked through the air, the whips made a whirring sound that suddenly changed to a slapping hiss when they struck Eleazar's back. Each lash made the old man's body jump, but he did not cry out. A half a dozen strokes of the whip stained his back with blood. He lost control of his bowels.

Abruptly, the whipping ceased and one of the soldier's cried out, "Obey the word of Antiochus . . . Epiphanes."

Eleazar shook his head.

Instantly the bloodstained whips began to bite into the old man's back. He tried to stand, but the soldiers kicked him to the ground. The earth around the fallen priest was spotted with blood and the whips raised founts of it. Bits of raw flesh were stripped from the old man's back.

Once more, Eleazar tried to stand and, again, one of his tormentors kicked him down.

Then Menelaus himself intervened and, obtaining permission from Antiochus, he approached the blood-soaked body on the ground. Kneeling, he said, "You still can save yourself."

Gasping for breath, Eleazar answered, "I am but a short distance from death. It stands closer to me than you are now. If I pretend to eat pork to please Antiochus, I will betray my God and my people. I would lead my people astray and not be worthy of being a Jew."

Menelaus stood up. The hem of his priestly robes were stained with blood. He looked toward Antiochus and shook his head.

A rack was dragged into the square and the naked priest tied to it. The wheels were turned until even Eleazar could no longer stand the pain and loosed a piercing scream. Every bone in the old man's arms and legs were pulled out of their joints. There were great bloody rents in his body, exposing bone and raw flesh.

A brazier was placed near the rack. Pincers were heated until they glowed with a cherry red color. With these the soldiers took hold of Eleazar's manhood.

The priest screamed and pleadingly shouted for death to claim him.

Oil was boiled and poured into his nostrils. It was too much for him to stand and, filling his lungs with air, the old priest again shouted, "Hear, oh Israel, the Lord is our God, the Lord is one."

In an instant, that same cry came from the people. They shouted it over and over again.

Antiochus turned to Menelaus and said, "He was a brave man, a very brave man. See that his body is given to his family for burial."

"Yes, My Lord," the High Priest answered.

"If that old man is an example of the will of the Jews to keep their God and follow His Law, then indeed I might have to kill all of them who refuse to adopt our ways."

Then he became aware that the Jews in the square had fallen silent. He turned toward them and saw the man with the long white beard, who had stood next to Eleazar, cradling in his arms the broken body of the old man and silently weeping. And over the two stood the tall blonde man. In his right hand he held the blackened staff of the priest.

Antiochus nodded and said, "I have seen the same thing done by soldiers many, many times on the battlefield. And this square for the Jews, as well as for us, is a field of battle, the first, I fear, of many."

The soldiers started for Mattathias and Judah, but Antiochus motioned them back, commenting to those close by, "It is enough for today, enough . . ."

CHAPTER VI

By turns, the days were either sullen with a cold, windblown rain coming off the sea to the West, or filled with the warmth of a resplendent sun in an intensely blue sky. It was on such an afternoon, when the outer chamber of Antiochus' apartment was bright with huge shafts of mote-filled light, that he summoned several of his priests, generals, and ministerial counselors to discuss the situation of the Jews in Jerusalem, since, whatever happened there would have a telling effect everywhere else in Judea.

Those present quickly noticed the absence of Menelaus, the High Priest. It was further confirmation of the rumor in the palace that he had fallen out of favor with the King. But they were also aware of the young blonde woman reclining on the couch where Antiochus sat. She was totally naked. Antiochus smiled at his guests. By this small but powerfully voluptuous exhibition, he would keep their attention from wandering. And, since they were all virile men, they would be caught in a web of erotic tension, making it easier for him to manipulate their wills to his own. He had to have a clear indication from them about what to do with the Jews. He could not dally much longer in Jerusalem.

The Persians on his eastern flank, having heard of his expulsion from Egypt, were beginning to defy the satraps he had installed there and were even sending their troops against his own. The Jews were no more than a swarm of gadflies he had to do something about, or suffer the disrespectful jibes of his own people and the open ridicule of other potentates.

His spies had informed him that people in the streets of the city were whispering insults against him. Some claimed the Roman Legate, Popilus Laenas, had him cast bodily out of Egypt. Others were saying his phallus had shrunken to the size of a child's thumb, making it impossible for him to give pleasure to women.

Yet the most insidious calumny against him he had himself heard the previous night when, as he was often wont to do, he had moved about the city disguised as a merchant from some nearby county. In that role, he frequently learned more than his spies could ever tell him. In a tavern he overheard a conversation between two men that deeply distressed him.

One man asked the other, "Have you heard about the new name for the King?"

The second man answered that as far as he knew the King was named Antiochus-Epiphanes.

And the first said, "Oh no, you are wrong my friend, since he has been booted out of Egypt and has spent all his time having his army chase Jews, he is called Antiochus-Epimanes."

The two men roared with laughter. The slight alteration in the orthography of the word Epiphanes, drastically changed its meaning. Instead of being referred to as Antiochus . . . the God . . . Manifest, he was now being called Antiochus . . . the Madman.

Not wanting to hear any more slander, for fear that he would kill the men and thereby reveal himself, he fled from the tavern...

The King was so involved with his own thoughts that he failed to notice the officer standing close to Apollonius, until he realized the young man was staring more intently than the others at the movement of his hands over the woman's body.

Noticing Antiochus' questioning look, Apollonius explained, "My Lord, I took the liberty of bringing my aide, Glacon, with me. He has many friends among the Jews."

Antiochus held up his hand and repeated Glacon's name several times. Then with a smile, he pointed to him and said, "Yes, yes, I remember him. He was the officer who cut his way through the Egyptian ranks to one of their generals, and that night in my tent we had a long discussion about Sophocles. I seem to remember, we had some interesting questions about his attitude toward the justice of the gods."

"Yes, My Lord," Glacon answered, unable to take his eyes off the woman. He guessed she was from a country far to the north of Greece.

The King nodded and courteously said, "Perhaps on some future evening, we might resume our discussion."

"I would be honored," Glacon replied.

"But now," Antiochus informed them, "we have another matter to be decided. We must reach a reasonable answer to the Jewish problem." His minister and generals chorused their agreement.

"We must Hellenize them," the King said. "It is not only from a military necessity that it must be done, but it will insure our national cohesion."

"The public executions . . ."

Antiochus waved his minister silent. "My decrees are not being followed. The Jews are artfully concealing their sacred books and they are surreptitiously continuing to practice their religious rituals." He paused and, carelessly extending his caresses to the woman's pubis, he said, "You,

Glacon, tell me why they insist on circumcising their males?"

"It is continuing renewal, so I have been told, of the Covenant between them and their God," the officer answered.

"But their God no longer exists," Antiochus said, continuing idly to stroke the woman. "Yahweh, as they call him, has been driven out of the Temple by Zeus. Zeus is now there. They can see him; his statue is there."

The woman began to moan; her eyes were closed and her breath became shallow and rapid.

Antiochus took his hand away from the slave's body and told them, "If they cannot believe in Zeus, then surely they can believe in me: I am his manifestation."

"Their God is unseen," one of the ministers commented.

Antiochus uttered a loud exclamation of disdain.

"I cannot understand it either," the same man said, "but that is what they believe."

The King's eyes found Glacon. "Apollonius said you have many friends who are Jews. Do they believe that their God, or any god, can be unseen?"

"For them," the officer answered, "their God is unseen. Even Moses, who led them out of Egypt never saw Him."

"What then did he see?"

"A burning bush that was not burning."

Antiochus began to play with the woman again. After a long pause, he said, "I cannot give them that, but nonetheless I must make them Greek."

"Suppose," suggested Dryas, one of the Greek priests, "you give them yourself. That is to say, My Lord, you have statues made that resemble you and have them brought to every village in Judea by soldiers, who then make sure the

Priest of the village bows to you and eats the meat of a swine, Zeus' sacred animal, since as an infant he was suckled by a sow. That way, they would be joining their body with that of Zeus."

The idea put forth by the priest of Zeus was definitely flattering to Antiochus. He already had his likeness on the coins of the country. Why not in the Temples of all the towns and villages?

"That way," Dryas expanded, "the people will be aware of the incarnation of their god."

Though Antiochus did not mention it, he believed that the rulers of other nations would very quickly learn through their spies that even those stiff-necked people, the Jews, worshiped him. Such a situation might give Rome pause and dampen some of their eagerness to conquer his country.

The woman started to move. Her eyes were closed. She made low throaty sounds of pleasure.

Antiochus looked at her and smiled. Still smiling as he stood up, he said, "And those who do not accept Zeus and eat the meat of the swine will instantly be put to death."

"That would seem the most logical way of dealing with them," Apollonius said.

"What do you think, Glacon?" Antiochus questioned "That is, if you can take your eyes off Helen long enough to think."

Glacon stammered.

"It is all right," Antiochus laughed, looking down at the woman who was in the throes of climaxing. "This is the first time you have attended one of my conferences. Sometimes I provide some diversion, especially when the matter is weighty. But tell me what do you really think of the plan put forth?"

Glacon hesitated. He tried to imagine how Judah would react to making obeisance to Zeus in the likeness of Antiochus?

"You seem to be weighing your answer most carefully," the King chided.

"My Lord," the officer responded, "I only know a few of these people, and those I know are different from the others."

"Different in what way?" Antiochus asked. He moved closer to where the officer was standing.

"It is not easy to explain. Some Jews would be willing to die, but some would not."

"They will have no choice, if they do not accept me . . . I mean Zeus, of course."

"Some might choose to fight."

"Jews do not fight," one of the ministers said. "You have seen them in the square go to their death without so much as raising their hands in their own defense."

"My Lord," interrupted Apollonius, "Glacon is right."

Antiochus shifted his eyes from the young officer to the weather-beaten face of his General.

"Even now, My Lord, there are several thousand Jews in the hills to the southeast of the city. From what our spies tell us, they are armed and are willing to fight. They call themselves the Hasidim, or the pious ones."

In an instant, Antiochus' whole manner changed. His face became flushed with anger, and he shouted, "Why was I not told about this sooner?"

"I myself," Apollonius explained, "received this information only this morning."

"Destroy them!" Antiochus fumed. "Show no mercy; I want all of them destroyed. Spare none, not even the women or children!"

"Yes, My Lord," Apollonius answered.

"If they are true to their precious Law," a minister said, "they will not fight on the day of their Sabbath."

Again the Seleucid king looked at Glacon and he asked, "Will they fight on that day?"

"No, My Lord."

"Then we will do our killing on that day," Antiochus told them. "Use Sostrates against them; he takes a great pleasure in killing Jews. Tell your men they have my royal permission to use the Jewish women as they please before putting them to the sword. We will end this rebellion. Then we will bring Zeus to all of them. They will have him in every village and town in Judea."

The men agreed with him.

"As for the woman here," Antiochus said, "Glacon, you take her. But in a few days return her to Suidas, keeper of the palace slaves. She will be auctioned off with several others who were sent as gifts to me." The King shook his head and, with a wave of his hand, he dismissed the group. "Jews," Antiochus muttered to himself. "I have an empire to hold together and I have to waste my time with Jews and their unseen God!"

* * *

Jonathan rushed into Iphegine's open arms. "I need you," he said, pressing her body hard against his.

"If you're to have me," she chided, "I'll have to have my ribs. With them crushed, I'll be unable to satisfy your needs, or my own longing."

Jonathan eased his hold on her. She was exquisitely attired in a light blue gown that revealed a portion of her left breast. He touched the soft whiteness, first with his fingers, and then almost reverentially pressed his lips to it.

"I was so afraid you would not come," Iphegine said, taking hold of his hand. "We will eat and drink. You must be very hungry."

They entered a small room, made warm by two braziers and sunlight that streamed through a window overlooking a garden not yet colored with flowers.

"I prepared everything myself," Iphegine announced proudly. "Lamb, bread pudding, and a soup with vegetables."

"A feast!" Jonathan exclaimed. He poured wine into a cup for himself, while Iphegine went into the kitchen.

"Meat first or soup?" Iphegine called from the other room. "Soup," Jonathan answered. Though at her table he ate meat that had not been slaughtered according to the Law, he only ate enough of it to avoid giving offense.

Iphegine carried a large, steaming black iron pot to the table. Neither one of them spoke very much, though Iphegine asked, "Do you intend to spend the night with me?"

"Yes."

She nodded but refrained asking if he intended to honor his word and accompany her to Aphrodite's Temple. She did not really know the extent of her hold on him; whether it was strong enough to eventually pull him away from his father and make him her husband. But she knew how strong the ties were that bound him to his family. Yet, she did not despair. She was an artful woman and knew the value her young lover placed on the pleasure she gave him. From her first marriage she had learned much about how to wheedle out of a man what he might be reluctant to give.

"There are troops everywhere in the city and on the roads leading to it," Jonathan said.

She shrugged. "I mind my business and they mind theirs." Jonathan laughed.

"It is true," she told him.

"For you it is easy because you are a Seleucid," he answered, "and for me . . . it is the same, because I look like a Greek and when I come here I dress like one."

She filled her own wine cup and waited for him to say more; then she would remind him of his pledge to go to Aphrodite's Temple and she would speak about several other things that she had hesitated to tell him.

Without looking at her, Jonathan whispered, "It goes hard with my family."

'That you lie with a Seleucid woman?" she suddenly flared. "More than one man would pay a small fortune to be where you've already been, and you've paid nothing, not one piece of gold, not one small gift."

For a few moments they glared at each other. Then Jonathan said, "Yes, my father anguishes over my love for you. But, nonetheless, I come to you."

"Am I to be thankful for that?"

"As I am to be here," he responded, in a much softer tone. "But my feelings for you do not blind me to whatever else is happening. Antiochus doesn't realize he's asking us to do the impossible."

"But so many have already turned from your God ..."

He nodded. "I envy them, Iphegine; I truly envy them."

"You can do the same thing," she replied excitedly. "It is nothing, absolutely nothing. You are already halfway there; each time you lie with me, you move closer and closer. You're not like most of the other Jews, even those that have renounced your God. They care nothing for beauty, for the things that are truly Greek."

"I'm a man who lives through his senses," Jonathan said. "Those things that are beautiful move me."

Iphegine was on her feet and quickly hurried to the other side of the table where Jonathan sat. She took hold of his hands and pressed them to her breasts. "I've given you what a woman can give a man," she told him passionately, "except for a child. I want you to father mine, to be my husband and father to my children. What difference does it make whether you believe in Zeus or in your own God, when, by believing in one, you would be allowed to live like a man among men."

The warm softness of her breasts quickened his blood and in her dark eyes he saw the bright glow of passion. He stood up and drawing her close pressed his lips to hers.

"Come with me now," she whispered, "to Aphrodite's Temple. Let Aspasie, the High Priestess, seek the help of the goddess to keep our love from dissolving."

"But I am a Jew . . ."

"No," she said passionately, "you only think you are."

He shook his head.

She pulled away from him. "You are willing to forget you are a Jew when you are between my thighs. Or should I say," she challenged, "you're willing to forget not only that I am a Seleucid woman but that I also have had a husband and lovers … yes, lovers ... you are willing to forget all of that, as long as you can put your phallus inside of me?"

"I forget all of it because I love you," he answered, without attempting to bring her close to him again. "But I was in the square when Antiochus ordered Eleazar to be tortured and then slain. I cannot forget the old man's words or the look on my father's face when he held the broken body of his friend in his arms." And shaking his head, Jonathan continued, "If I did what you asked, I would not be a man, Iphegine, I'd be something else, and whatever that something else would be, I'd hate, and you would also come to hate me."

Even as he spoke, Jonathan realized something in him had been stiffened by what he had witnessed in the square.

Iphegine's heart began to race. The color drained away from her cheek and, forcing the words out of her throat, she asked, "Are you trying to tell me that . . ."

Jonathan put his finger across her dry lips and with a shake of his head, he told her not to put words in his mouth. "Let my words be my own," he said. "I love you as much as any man can love a woman. You know that. But to keep that love, I can't do what you ask. I'll live with you; I'll eat at your table; I'll do things that according to the Law of my people are an abomination to Yahweh. But I won't surrender Him for any other god; there is no other one but Him. No, listen to me, Iphegine, and then you make up your mind. I'll even go with you to Aphrodite's Temple, if that is what will please you. But I'll do nothing to deny Yahweh."

"Then you'll not have me for a wife?" she asked in a whisper.

"I cannot have you according to the Law of my people, and I will not have you by the Law of your people.

Trembling, Iphegine tried to speak but could not find her voice. He was only asking her to let him lie with her and use her body to pour his fluid into her. "Like your God, Jonathan, you ask much and give so very little in return."

"I'm only a man," he answered. "I ask the woman I love to love me in return."

"It is too much to ask when you offer only your body and not your name, when you offer physical love and not the protection of your house, when you offer children and not even the food to feed them."

He did not answer.

"I didn't think you to be such a hard man," she told him.

"I'm not hard," he said. "But I must hold fast to what I have, to what I've been given and to what I am."

She moved to the sunlight and for several moments studied him. Then she asked, "Tell me what will happen to you and those like you who will not embrace Zeus?"

Jonathan pursed his lips and rubbing his hand over his small beard, he admitted that he did not know. "Perhaps," he continued somewhat wistfully, "Antiochus will change his mind and let us live in peace." Iphegine faced the window.

Though she realized she had just suffered a setback, she was not willing to relinquish her hold on him and in a low voice she said, "Come with me to Aphrodite's Temple."

"Yes, I said I'd go."

"Then, for now I am content," she commented. "Perhaps the goddess will succeed where I have failed?"

Gently, Jonathan turned her to him. "You haven't failed," he told her, "and I haven't won." Then he kissed her passionately on the lips.

* * *

The breath from men and horses steamed in the predawn darkness. To steady his mount, Antiochus patted its neck. "The horses sense what is to come," he said to Apollonius.

"Always, My Lord," the General answered, shifting slightly in the saddle to look at his king.

Antiochus gestured toward Menelaus and his brother Lysimachus, who were there at his order and were wrapped deep in their heavy woolen cloaks to protect them against the cold. He had not allowed any fires to be made, for fear the light from them, however feeble, would betray their intentions to the Jews and allow some of them to escape.

Again the King's horse nervously pawed the ground.

Leaning forward, Antiochus spoke gently into the animal's ear, telling him he would not have to charge into the fray. "We're here as spectators," the King said. "We won't do any fighting today." Again he directed his attention to the High Priest. "What did you say the name of their leader is?"

"Ruben, My Lord."

Repeating the name three times, Antiochus shook his head. He was about to comment he did not like the sound of the name, when his attention was diverted by the arrival of Glacon, who reported to Apollonius. "All of the troops are in place; and Sostrates has managed to bring up several machines to hurl Greek fire into the gaps between the rocks where the Jews might take refuge."

"Where are the machines?" Antiochus questioned.

Glacon, who was the only one amongst them dressed for battle, not only pointed with his sword to show the King, but he also said, "There on the high ridges. It's still too early to make them out, but with the first light you'll see they command everything from their base to the ridges behind us, to the West."

Antiochus followed the movement of sword's point and nodded with satisfaction. "I wouldn't have thought of using Greek fire here. I must remember to give my compliments to Sostrates for his cleverness." Then looking at Glacon, he asked, "Are you going to take part in the action?"

"I've two squads of cavalry to lead," Glacon answered. "But they won't be in the initial assault. That'll be left to the infantry. We'll go in to mop up and herd any of the Jews that are left toward the infantry."

"I wish you well," Antiochus said.

Raising his hand, Glacon saluted the King, wheeled his horse around and trotted off to join his men.

"His attitude impresses me," Antiochus said, speaking to Apollonius about Glacon. "Glacon is one of the best officers we have, I shouldn't be in the least bit surprised to hear that he one day commands an army."

"From you," Apollonius said, "that is indeed a high recommendation."

"Given by one soldier who appreciates the qualities of his subordinates," Apollonius responded.

Antiochus accepted his General's response without further comment. He kept straining to see the darkness of the eastern sky dissolve into the first gray of dawn.

As Glacon rode away, Lysimachus leaned close to his brother and whispered, "He is the one I told you about."

Menelaus looked questioningly at him.

"The one who has been bribing Suidas, the keeper of the palace slaves."

It was inconceivable to Menelaus that, at a time like this, his brother's thoughts would be of sexual intrigue, yet they were; they most definitely were.

"He does not want to see her auctioned off," Lysimachus explained. "Suidas himself told me that. He thinks the woman has cast some sort of spell over the soldier."

"You no doubt want to see if she can do the same to you?"

Menelaus asked in disdainful tone.

"Am I no less a man than he?" Lysimachus responded. "The woman is a rarity, a blonde from somewhere to the north of Greece itself. I'll have her. I have money to buy whatever I want."

Menelaus shook his head. "Take care Glacon doesn't catch wind of your scheme, or he might cut away that part of your body you're so anxious to use on the woman."

Lysimachus chuckled softly. "It wouldn't come to that—if you happened to tell the King that his officer was defying him. I don't think the King would take too kindly to that, at least not in his present frame of mind."

Menelaus made a slight gesture to encompass the darkened landscape in front of them. "Let this bloody business be settled this morning, and then perhaps the King will once again see me and my efforts on his behalf in a more favorable light."

"Glacon won't be able to continue bribing the keeper much longer," Lysimachus said. "I have a small arrangement with the keeper so that his demands increase every few days. If Glacon cannot meet them, then he must surrender the woman, and that very day I have the keeper's word he'll sell her to me. But if that doesn't work, a word to the King at the right moment will make it possible for me to buy her."

"I'll try to help you," Menelaus said.

"Believe me, brother," Lysimachus responded, "it never entered my mind that you would not."

"What are you two whispering about?" Antiochus asked, looking at the High Priest and his brother.

"My brother," Menelaus quickly answered, "has never seen Greek fire being used."

"Have you?" Apollonius questioned.

"No," the High Priest replied, "but I've read about it, and in truth I have a better imagination than my brother."

Neither the King nor his General pressed the matter any further.

A few more moments passed; then suddenly the sky in the East became perceptibly lighter. The escarpment was black against the gray. The morning star was still bright in the sky.

The four spectators were very conscious of the immense silence that hung over the land.

"Do you think they know?" Antiochus whispered.

Apollonius stuck out his lower lip; then, realizing he had not answered, he said, "Menelaus would be better able to answer that than I."

The King turned to Menelaus and put the same question to him.

"I wouldn't think so," the High Priest responded. "But even if they did, it wouldn't matter. Today is the Sabbath and they won't tolerate it."

The gray light became brighter. The black escarpment quickly revealed details: giant cracks, ledges, and many caves where the Jews were known to be hiding.

"How many men are we going to use?" Antiochus asked his commander.

"Twenty thousand," Apollonius said.

"Imagine," the King commented, "there are twenty thousand men whose hearts are quickening, whose mouths are dry and whose hands are sweaty with anticipation of the fight or, more correctly, for the slaughter."

Pink began to slide over the escarpment, and then the first flash of yellow sunlight leapt off the rocks. That was the signal for the Seleucid troops! In an instant, a wild shout rose from the base of the cliff, a single insane scream from an army on the move.

Men rushed forward, brandishing their spears. Others ran toward the rocky enclaves with their swords at the ready.

As soon as the last echo of the blood-lust cry had died, the terrible wailing of the Jews took its place.

The soldiers ran up the slopes of the cliffs and the Jews came out of the caves.

Spears flew and many Jews fell. Like some giant bugs, they writhed in a hopeless effort to free themselves of the agonizing pain in their chests.

To escape, Jews ran among the rocks. But the soldiers caught them with their short swords. Some died quickly from a single thrust in the heart, or a slash that severed their head from their body. Others were chopped to pieces by one soldier hacking at a leg, while another was severing the arm.

The children were torn from their mother's sides and put to death quickly. If the victim was an infant still suckling at its mother's breast, it was hurled aloft and caught on the point of a spear or sword. But most babies had their brains bashed out against the sides of the cliff.

Jews were scurrying like rabbits. Now here; now there. But there was no escape from the Seleucids. Their swords and spears were everywhere!

Like some demonic sound from the nether world, the screaming rose and fell. It was commingled with calls for God's help. And, over and over again, came the cry of "Hear, oh Israel, the Lord is our God, the Lord is one."

Women were pulled down to the ground; held secure by two soldiers and were raped by a third. Each man had his turn. The younger women were raped by one soldier and sodomized by another.

Mothers were made to watch their daughters being defiled and then killed, after which it was their own turn to be ravished and slaughtered.

The rocks and the entrances were slippery with blood. The vultures had caught the scent of death and were circling slowly above the hills.

A brazen trumpet sounded and Glacon and his two squads of cavalry galloped into the fray. Here and there they drove Jews directly before them onto the spears of the infantry. Then they dismounted and tried to find women for themselves. But most of the women had been used and killed. Those they did find, no matter whether the woman was old or not yet old enough to have begun her monthly bleeding, they raped and killed.

By the time the sun was completely up over the escarpment, there was not a Seleucid soldier whose hands and arms were not covered with the blood of Jews.

Again the trumpet sounded. As quickly as they had rushed to the slaughter, troops now ran from it.

Within minutes the huge machines at the top of the escarpment began to hurl globular buds of Greek fire that burst like crimson flowers on the bloodstained rocks below. The air quickly became filled with the stink of burning flesh.

A third blast from a trumpet signaled that Sostrates had finished the bombardment.

"My Lord," Apollonius said, "the action is over"

"Shall we see how successful it was?" Antiochus asked. Without waiting for an answer, he spurred his mount to a gallop.

The others came racing behind him.

The bodies of Jews were strewn everywhere along the slope and at the base of the escarpment. Some were slowly burning, while most of them lay in grotesquely twisted positions.

Menelaus paused and vomited.

All of the women were left naked. Most were gutted after they had been used, and some, even before they had been killed, had to suffer having their breasts cut away.

Nothing was alive, except the vultures that came down from the skies in droves to feast off the flesh of the dead.

"A harsh lesson," Antiochus said, "to those who would rebel against me. I would have preferred not to give it. But I have no doubt that Zeus meant it to be this way."

"Nor do I," Apollonius agreed.

Antiochus looked toward Menelaus for additional confirmation of his statement.

The High Priest nodded. "I don't think Jews will ever forget what was done here this morning."

"But will they do my bidding?" the King questioned.

"From this," Menelaus responded, encompassing the entire grisly scene with a wave of his hand, "they will know that the alternative to obeying, even for them, is too great a price."

Antiochus was pleased with the answer. "I have seen enough," he said, and turning his horse around, he rode back to Jerusalem...

CHAPTER VII

From refugees, news of the slaughter came to the village of Modin. Many fled the city immediately after they had heard about the annihilation of the Hasidim. Others took flight only after they had gone into the hills and had verified for themselves the results of the Seleucid butchery.

Mattathias listened to all of the people who came to Modin. Every family in the village had taken in refugees. His own family was no exception; it increased in size by three distant cousins from his wife's side; two young women; Naomi and Ruth; and Joseph, a young man about Judah's age. The three children had been sent into the country by their parents.

Mattathias, already agonizing about what he had witnessed in Jerusalem, found this new honor a dark, dimensionless void into which he could almost not bear to look. But he forced himself to face the reality of what had happened and what would happen.

He spoke about the situation most often with Simon, who appeared to be more aware of his suffering than were his other sons. Indeed, Simon seemed to take some of the heavy burden off of his father's weary shoulders and to carry it himself.

When they spoke, they walked to the highest reaches of the terraced fields. Usually, they picked a place to sit from where they could look down on the village.

"It's ours," Mattathias would frequently say, gesturing down at the forty-odd dwellings clinging precariously to the side of the hill. The village was so small it had only a narrow ill-defined roadway running through it from either end to the square in the center. And there were only footpaths between the houses.

Simon would nod and answer, "Yes, Father, it is ours." Then he would wait for Mattathias to speak again. Sometimes he would say nothing more, and they would sit in silence for a long time before his father would say, "It's time for us to return home."

But, now and then, his father did speak, telling his son that the Covenant between Yahweh and the Jews bound each one to the other until time would be no more. "You see," the old man said, "if He is to be our Lord, we must obey the laws He gave to us through Moses. If we do not follow His Law, He will not protect us. He has given the Law and we must keep it."

"We will follow it," Simon told him. "We will not break the Covenant."

"And will my sons Judah and Jonathan also keep the Covenant?" "Each in his own way, Father," Simon said.

"With Jonathan between the thighs of a Seleucid whore," the old man commented harshly, "and Judah fighting, always fighting?"

"They will keep it," Simon responded stubbornly.

"For their sake," Mattathias said, "I hope and pray they do."

Simon was aware of the subtle shift in his father's relationship with Judah that had taken place since their visit to Jerusalem. Judah somehow had acquired the look of a man who was suffering intensely. And, more significantly, he carried Eleazar's age-blackened staff with him wherever he went.

Simon's efforts to discover the reason for his brother's suffering were unsuccessful. Judah would not speak about anything that had happened in Jerusalem. But one night when everyone else was asleep, he found his brother standing at the window looking up at a star-splattered sky. He went to him and asked if he were ill. Judah did not answer for such a long time that Simon thought his brother had not heard him.

"I am filled with longing for something I can never have," Judah said with a sigh. Then turning to him he added, "But do not press me, Simon. Perhaps some day I will tell you."

Simon nodded.

"Come, let us sit down, Brother," Judah told him, "and drink some wine."

"One will be enough for me," Simon said, as they approached the table.

Judah poured the wine and both of them toasted to long life. "What do you think will happen to us?" Simon asked.

Judah cocked his head to one side and, filling his cup a second time, he said, "I'm not gifted with foresight; I seem to lack hindsight and I'm almost totally blind to the present. Considering these three grievous shortcomings, I should be the last man you would ask that kind of question."

"If that's your way of saying you won't answer," Simon chuckled, "then so be it." Then, his eyes became clouded, "But Father is . . ."

"Yes," Judah said, the tone of his voice tightening considerably, "yes, I can see what's happening to him; he has become gaunter, and his eyes have the look of a man possessed."

Simon nodded and realized that, though Judah had described their father, he had also given an accurate description of himself.

"There's something that bums in the old man," Judah said. "Perhaps he's concerned about our family?" Simon offered. "What you're really trying to say is that he's worried about me and Jonathan."

"The two of you give him more to worry about than the rest of us."

Judah laughed and said, "I can't answer for Jonathan, but I'm a Jew; my father should know that. Oh, yes, there are many, many things about the Greeks I find attractive. And, for that matter, so must you, but we are Jews."

"Yes," Simon answered, "I understand."

"I can't frame the difference between those people and ourselves any better than Eleazar did for Antiochus before he died," Judah observed. "That difference is what all these killings are about."

"Father says," Simon told his brother, 'that if we bow to Antiochus, that within a few years there will be no Jews left anywhere. Our people and the God that brought them forth will vanish from the face of the earth." Judah took a third cup of wine before he asked his brother whether he agreed with their father.

"He is right," Simon answered.

"Not much of a future to drink to," Judah said, lifting his cup, "but nonetheless, I'll toast it: to the future, may it prove all our predictions wrong."

"Will you answer a question before you go back to sleep?" Simon asked, suddenly becoming very bold.

Judah nodded.

"Do you love Father?" Simon questioned.

"He's my father," Judah said.

"That isn't much of an answer."

"Of all my brothers," Judah said, "you should know that what's between our father and myself has nothing to do with the rest of the family."

"You're wrong, Judah; you're very wrong."

With a look of dismissal, Judah commented, "It won't be the first time or the last, will it?"

"He needs you," Simon said, "more than he needs any of us."

"I can't give him anything," Judah responded. "I've already given." He left the table and returned to the window. For a few moments he remained silent; then he said in a choked voice, "Stay where you are Simon. Don't come close to me."

"As you wish my brother," Simon answered. But he knew that Judah was weeping quietly.

* * *

Alone, Glacon sat at a small table in a tavern.

For several days now, he had listened to the boasts of his men about the number of women they had raped and the many Jews they had killed. Some of the soldiers had not even bothered to wash the blood from their hands, and it had dried to the dull red of sandstone.

Again and again, his men complained that there had been no sport in the killing. Many agreed it would have been more to their liking if the Jews had resisted. Several said they liked it just the way it had been, and some laughingly added that if all their future battles were the same way, they might live to a ripe old age.

Finishing his wine, Glacon tossed several coins on the table and left. It was late afternoon. The sun was warm and bright, but the stink of death hung over the city, while flocks of vultures rode the air currents above it, in the hope that below them there would soon be more carrion on which to feast.

Glacon had drunk too much wine, and he staggered toward the Citadel, where his quarters were. His intention was to bathe and then have Helen oil his body. Perhaps he would sleep for a while and then make love to her, or maybe he would do it before he slept.

He passed through the huge wooden gate and received a salute from the guards. He did not return it.

Seeing the officer stagger, one of the guards called out, "Too much wine and Bacchus will numb your brain and steal your wit."

"Too much killing," Glacon responded with a wave of his hand, "too much killing numbs my brain and steals my honor."

Shrugging, the guard turned away.

Glacon's quarters were in the northwest section of the fortress, which was a city, albeit a small one, within the greater city of Jerusalem. It consisted of several small villages, complete with their fields, wells, and even wooded areas. Within its walls lived several thousand troops and most of the Jews who renounced their God for Zeus. It was designed to be self-sustaining and to endure a siege for a very long time, years if necessary.

"Years," Glacon mumbled to himself. He stopped, looked at the battlements, nodded, and repeated, "Years . . ." before continuing.

A short while later, he came within sight of his small house. Suidas, the keeper of the palace slaves was there and with him was Lysimachus, the brother of the High Priest.

Suidas, a huge man with powerful arm and leg muscles, called out, "I was beginning to worry about you, Glacon. We have been waiting for most of the afternoon for you."

Looking at Lysimachus, Glacon answered, "Since our brilliant victory a few days ago over the Jews, I have been with my men listening to them boast of their heroic deeds."

"Celebrating, naturally," Suidas laughed.

Glacon was directly in front of them. Fixing his eyes on Lysimachus, he asked, "Tell me, do your people celebrate death or do they mourn?"

Lysimachus caught the barb of Glacon's anger, and he suggested that he and Suidas return at a more propitious time. "It is easy to see," he commented in an all-too-obvious tone of solicitude, "that Glacon is still tired from his hard fight and . . ."

"Slaughter you mean. You were there. We did no fighting, but, by Zeus, we did do a great deal of killing." He sniffed and with a faint smile, he said, "The air now stinks of what we have done."

"A soldier's duty . . ." began Lysimachus, but he fell silent under the young officer's withering glare.

"We did not come to speak about military matters," Suidas said. "I did not think so," Glacon responded. The moment he saw them, he had known why they were there.

"The King's slave would not unbolt the door," Suidas told him, "and since you have paid for her until sundown today, I did not want to call the soldiers to break the door down."

Glacon nodded. The effects of the wine had cleared as quickly as if a strong wind had blown through his brain. "We will talk inside," he said and called to Helen to open the door for him.

The wooden bar was removed, and a few moments later the door swung open. Glacon nodded and bid his two guests enter before him. Then he stepped across the threshold and closed the door.

Helen drifted off to the far side of the room, where the sleeping couch was.

Glacon made a broad sweeping gesture and said, "Not the luxury of the palace, but I have a roof over my head, a place for my bath, and as you can see, a hearth, and sleeping couch. I assume the regular troops are not nearly as fortunate as myself."

Suidas looked at Helen and asked, "Have you had the need to beat her?"

"No," Glacon answered. He had made his decision and now was waiting to see if he would have to carry it out.

"And she obeys you," Suidas questioned, "in all things?"

"Yes."

Suidas nodded and, going to Helen, he said, "Glacon, I can no longer allow you to keep her. Unless, of course, you can match the offer Lysimachus has already made."

Helen gasped.

"Let her disrobe," Lysimachus said, starting to move toward the woman. "I would like to examine her before . . ."

Glacon slipped his sword free of its scabbard. He'd seemed ready to kill anyone who would try to take Helen from him. That he might be killed never entered his mind.

His arm shot forward and down. The blade opened Lysimachus' stomach, spilling his bloody guts onto the floor.

To defend himself Suidas lifted a chair and thrust it at Glacon, who leaped nimbly to one side.

With knees drawn up, Lysimachus lay in a pool of blood. He moaned pitiably.

Suidas circled around Glacon, trying to get past him to the door. "You will die on the rack for this," the keeper of the palace slaves panted. Glacon did not waste his breath answering.

"I am dying," Lysimachus wept. "I am dying."

Suidas paused. "You can have the girl," he cried. "You can have the money Lysimachus paid me for her."

Silently Glacon shook his head.

"I will tell the King that Lysimachus tried to kill you and you killed him in self defense. He will believe it."

Glacon said nothing.

Without warning, Suidas lifted the chair and hurled it at him. He rushed toward the door. Glacon came up in front of him. Suidas ran straight into the point of the sword. The blade entered his chest. He screamed.

Glacon drove his foot into the man's stomach, pulled his blade free and then plunged it into Suidas' heart.

Lysimachus was still whimpering. He begged to be killed.

"No," Glacon responded, "I want you to die slowly, very slowly." He sheathed his bloody sword and, going to the terrified woman, he told her, "We must leave immediately."

"But where will we go?" Helen sobbed.

"Trust me," he said, "trust me."

She nodded and whispered, "I love you. I love you, Glacon." "Come," he said. Taking hold of her hand, he led her past the dying Lysimachus and the dead Suidas. They left the small house and hurried to the stable for the horses.

"But where can we go?" she asked.

"We will find a place," Glacon said. "Perhaps even Greece or Rome."

CHAPTER VIII

It was late morning. Antiochus sat with his eyes closed. His head felt heavy and a sour taste filled his mouth. He had drunk too much wine the previous night. The stink of the dead Jews was still in the air.

Slowly he opened his eyes. The hard light of the sun against the opposite wall of the room was painful for him to look at. He squinted at the people standing before him. Tyropus, his friend, was near the window. Apollonius and Sostrates were also there, so was Menelaus. Lycurgas, his soothsayer, was also present, and not too far from him was Dryas, the priest to Zeus.

Antiochus focused his bloodshot eyes on Menelaus. The man was distraught. There were dark crescents of grief under his eyes and the gaunt expression of mourning on his face. No doubt he, too, had a difficult night.

The King cleared his throat. "Your brother's death grieves me," he said to Menelaus.

"My Lord, I ask that the persons guilty of his murder be punished."

Antiochus looked toward Sostrates. "Now, tell me once again what your men found."

Sostrates took a step toward his king. He was a lean man with a dark complexion and green eyes. He saluted and said, "The smell attracted some of the guards. When they went into Glacon's house they found the bodies of Suidas, the keeper of the palace slaves, and Lysimachus, brother of the High Priest, Menelaus."

The King moved his eyes to Apollonius. "What do you know of this matter?"

"Nothing, My Lord," the General answered, "until I heard about it here."

"Have you seen Glacon these past few days?"

"No, My Lord. But that is not unusual," the General explained. "He generally does not come to me, unless he has something that must be brought to my attention."

"Has anyone seen that woman slave I gave to Glacon?" Antiochus questioned.

"My Lord," Sostrates offered, "I think the two murders are the work of the Jews."

Antiochus did not respond. He closed his eyes and moved his hand over his forehead to ease the ache. The meeting was taxing his patience. He would have much preferred to retire to his chamber and drink something prepared by his physician to settle his stomach and to ease the throbbing in his head.

"My Lord," Apollonius ventured, "Glacon was much taken with the woman."

"I could see that from the way he looked at her the first time he saw her," Antiochus said, still keeping his eyes shut.

"If it please My Lord," Menelaus offered, "my brother arranged to buy the woman from Suidas."

Antiochus opened his eyes, stood up and took several steps back and forth in front of the chair. He stopped and, looking at his General, he said in a voice filled with disappointment, "I fear we have misjudged Glacon."

With a silent nod, Apollonius agreed.

Tyropus stirred from his place at the window and, walking languidly toward the King, he asked permission to venture an opinion of the matter under discussion.

"It would be most welcome."

"Our concern," Tyropus commented, "should be wholly centered on apprehending Glacon, who obviously slew Suidas and Lysimachus. When we find him, no doubt the woman will be with him or close by. By Menelaus' own admission, we have it that his brother wanted the woman. I would guess Lysimachus was . . . forgive me, Menelaus, for stating it so bluntly for I know you grieve for your brother ... Lysimachus was imprudent or perhaps impatient enough to accompany Suidas to Glacon's quarters."

"Are you saying," Antiochus questioned, "that Glacon never had any intentions of returning the woman as I had ordered'?"

"That is a logical assumption, My Lord," Tyropus responded. "He already had kept her for more than the few days you so magnanimously granted him."

A dark red suffused Antiochus' face. He took several deep breaths before he said, "According to what you have just told me, Glacon had defied me even before he killed Suidas and Lysimachus."

"Yes."

"Have you any proof?" he asked angrily.

"None, My Lord," Tyropus said. "But I am sure you know that, for a sum of money, Suidas would not have been above postponing enforcement of your wishes."

Antiochus nodded; for sometime he had heard whispers about the special arrangements Suidas made with those willing to pay the price he asked for a woman or a young boy in his care.

"This time," the King said, "the price was death; I am sure it was not what he expected to be paid."

"But my brother—" Menelaus began.

Antiochus waved him silent. "When we find Glacon and the woman, they will pay in long suffering for having killed your brother. Glacon, I will have flayed and exposed for the vultures to eat him alive. As for the woman, I will give her to some of my soldiers to use in whatever way they please, and when they are finished with her she will be tied to a stake and be available for any man to use. This will continue until she dies. Are you satisfied, Menelaus?"

"Yes, My Lord. But I have one request."

"Make it."

"Before you give the woman to the soldiers," Menelaus petitioned, "would you send her to me?"

Antiochus raised his eyebrows questioningly.

"I want to use her as my brother had intended," he said, "and then I want to tell her what will happen to her; I want her to anticipate the torment that will await her. And if it is possible, My Lord, I want her to witness Glacon's agony before her own begins."

"You will have her, and she will watch what we do to officers who defy the King."

"Thank you, My Lord."

Antiochus returned to the chair and sat down. He was feeling very much better. He pointed to Lycurgas, his soothsayer, and asked, "What are the signs for me?"

Lycurgas, a small reed-like man, with a white beard and white hair, answered, "They are not the best. I would counsel against undertaking any vast enterprises for the next several weeks, at least until we have passed through the equinox."

"Dryas," Antiochus asked, "have you made the necessary sacrifices to Zeus?"

"Yes, My Lord," the priest said. "Just this morning, I personally slaughtered a young ram, and then I carefully examined its entrails and liver."

"And what did you read in them?"

"All that My Lord sees for himself," the priest said, "will come to pass."

"Excellent!" Antiochus exclaimed brightly. Then he asked, still smiling, "There was nothing in what either you, Lycurgas, saw, or you, Dryas, that indicated I would have more trouble with the Jews?"

"Nothing," the two men responded in unison.

"Then I am free to get on with my work," Antiochus said. "Sostrates, I am leaving you in command of Jerusalem. You will see that every village and town pays homage to Zeus in my likeness. In each, the village head or priest must eat the meat of a swine. All my decrees must be upheld. The Jews must not be allowed to practice any part of their religion. Those who disobey must be killed."

"It will be done," Sostrates replied, saluting his lord.

"Apollonius," the King said, "prepare the army for marching. In two days' time we will leave Jerusalem and move to Samaria and eventually to Antioch on the Orontes Rivet I have a great longing to see my city again."

"Yes, My Lord," the General answered.

"Tyropus," Antiochus said, "I want you to remain here and aid Sostrates. Lycurgas, you accompany me, and as for you, Dryas, stay here and serve Zeus. And before I forget, Sostrates, you will offer gold for information about Glacon and Helen. Also, issue a decree to the effect that anyone found aiding them will be put to death. Have I left anything out? I do not think so." Satisfied with himself, he nodded; then he said, "I must rest now. All of you may leave."

Antiochus remained in the chair until he was completely alone. Then he summoned a servant and told him to bring a woman to his chamber.

"Any particular one?" the man asked.

"The woman you brought to me last night," Antiochus answered. "She has an artful tongue."

"Yes, My Lord," the slave answered.

Antiochus stood up and, nodding, said aloud, "By the great god Zeus, I will be happy when I leave this city and happier still to be away from the Jews." He turned and walked slowly to his private chamber. The ache and heaviness in his head had miraculously vanished; even the sour taste in his mouth was greatly attenuated. The thought of the pleasure he would soon experience brought a smile to his lips.

* * *

Though spring was still several weeks away, the afternoon was bright with sunlight. The air was so seductively warm, that Mattathias ordered the shutters on the windows in the main room to be opened while he was negotiating Johanan's marriage contract with Nashon, the bride's father.

The two fathers sat across from each other at a large table. Nashon was much younger than Mattathias; his beard was just beginning to gray. Though he came from a venerable family and could trace it back to the days of Moses, he was no more than a farmer, albeit a wealthy one. He was a broad-chested, sturdy looking man with bright green eyes. His daughter, Sarah, was his female counterpart. She was big-chested and wide-hipped. She sat to her father's left, while her mother, Esther, was to his tight.

Johanan sat on Mattathias' right and Simon, acting as scribe and arbitrator for the proceedings, was to his father's left.

At the far end of the table was a large pitcher of wine, cups, a bowl of fruit, one of nuts, and a platter of sweet cakes baked for the occasion by Miriam. The people facing each other across the table ignored the food and drink. Before any food or drink would be offered by Mattathias or accepted by Nashon, all parts to the marriage contract would have to be agreed upon by them.

After Nashon recited the list of physical items Sarah would bring to her groom, such as the number of sheets, pots, cooking utensils and the like, the negotiations became more intense and quickly came to an impasse.

"I'll give Johanan one-fifth of my land," Mattathias said.

Nashon raised his eyebrows. "As your eldest, he should receive more."

"I have five sons," Mattathias said. "No one merits more than the other."

"And I have one daughter," Nashon responded, "and no sons."

"Yahweh gives what He gives," Mattathias commented.

Nashon leaned toward his wife and whispered something into her ear. She nodded but did not speak.

"I've had offers from other sources," Nashon said. "Some came from men with more land than I own."

Mattathias ran his hand over his beard, considering how to answer him. He glanced at Johanan. His first-born was a man of the soil, even more than he himself. He glanced at the bride. Her eyes were cast down. Her hands were clasped together and rested on the edge of the table. From the rapid rise and fall of her breasts, he knew she was very agitated, perhaps even frightened that the negotiations would be terminated.

"Suppose," Simon said, breaking the silence, "I give my brother my share of the land?" He had thought many times in the past year or two about leaving Modin. If the Seleucids had not started to persecute the Jews, he might have taken the step. He hadn't the love for the soil the way Johanan did. His interest lay elsewhere. For better or for worse his education had taught him to think and by thinking, he had arrived at the conclusion he would make a better *anything* than a farmer.

Mattathias regarded his son but did not question him.

"I don't want to be a farmer," Simon explained. "Other things interest me."

Johanan leaned forward and, looking at his brother, he asked, "You'd do that for me?"

"You'll be a better farmer than I," Simon answered with a smile. "That's still not much land," Nashon grumbled.

"It's what I offer," Mattathias answered. "Johanan will have two-fifths of my land, and I'll provide all the necessary tools and animals he'll need to farm it."

For a few moments Nashon hesitated; then, he slowly nodded. "Write it all out," Mattathias told Simon.

Everyone at the table uttered a sigh of relief, and then Nashon brought up the next point of contention by saying that he expected Johanan to live in his house. "I'll provide a room for him and my daughter," he said.

Mattathias vigorously shook his head. "His land is here," he told Nashon. "What sense would it make for him to walk from your village to Modin. It would be a waste of time. Besides, in these troubled times, a man must have his sons with him."

The two fathers immediately set about haranguing each other over the question of where Johanan and Sarah would live once they were married.

Each man cited precedents, both biblical and civil. The discussion became more and more heated. Tears started to flow from Sarah's eyes.

Miriam, though she didn't speak, moved away from the hearth. To indicate she agreed with Mattathias, she stood directly behind her husband.

Esther, not to be outdone by the groom's mother, settled her hand on Nashon's arm.

Simon did not know what he might suggest to solve the dilemma. Each of them had valid reasons for wanting the couple to live under their roof.

Nashon did not have a son, and he obviously hoped the marriage would provide him with something that God had not.

Mattathias, though he had five sons, would not surrender what God had so generously given to him.

Suddenly, Johanan said, "I'll bring my bride to my father's house, or there'll be no wedding."

Shocked at Johanan's intervention, the older men stopped arguing. They knew that the bridegroom, though present at the table during the negotiations, had no voice in them.

"My father," Johanan said, "has offered part of his house to me and my future bride. I accept. I'll have no other home. I'll dwell in my father's house. I'll give him a part of each day's labor. I owe him no less, for he's old now and needs my strength, as I once needed his."

Nashon looked at his daughter and, placing his large hand over her two smaller ones, he told her in a strangled voice, "You have found yourself a man. God grant he be as good a husband to you as he is a son to his father." Then, facing Mattathias, he said, "Your sons honor you; may our grandsons honor the two of us." Then he extended his hand across the table.

"It is time to drink and eat," Mattathias exclaimed. "It is time to be happy."

* * *

The weather turned back to winter again. The sky was filled with gray clouds. By late afternoon a mizzling rain had begun to fall.

Judah was busy examining the stone wall on the west side of the north field. Mattathias was doing the same thing on the crest of the hill above the olive grove. Wherever possible, Judah replaced a stone that had become dislodged. It was hard, sweaty work.

Since he had no love for the soil either, Judah had decided to give Johanan his share of the land as Simon had done. But Simon at least seemed to have some sort of a goal, whereas Judah had none. There was nothing in particular he wanted to do.

He bent down and picked up a long stone. Just as he was about to set it into place, he saw Dion, the Seleucid tax collector. Offering no word of greeting, he stared at the man.

Dion's thin lips twisted into a half smile. He was a frail man with crooked teeth, a bald head, and a lust for young men.

Judah set the stone into place in the wall.

"Are you Mattathias' son?" Dion asked, in an official sounding

voice.

"You know who I am," Judah answered curtly.

Dion did not answer. He drew his cloak more securely around him and studied the blonde giant. For a long time he had sensed that this

Jew was different from the others.

Judah set another stone into place.

"I've been watching you," Dion said.

Judah looked at him with disdain and began to walk along the wall, up toward where his father worked.

Dion followed him, remaining on the other side of the wall. He hated the Jews, not so much for their absurd belief in an unseen God, but rather because they were able to make a harsh, unyielding land yield bountiful crops. But the Jew in front of him was so beautiful that, given a reason, he could easily forget his origin.

Abruptly, Judah stopped.

"So you too want to talk?" Dion questioned.

"No."

"Then why do you stop?"

"To tell you not to follow me," Judah said.

Dion's eyes went to slits; his face became livid and his hand went to his sword.

"Draw it, Dion," Judah told him, hearing the blood pounding in his ears. "Draw it and you're a dead man." He hefted a good-size rock in his fight hand.

"You dare to threaten me," Dion sputtered. "You filthy Jew, you son of a whore . . ."

Judah hurled the rock. It crashed against the man's forehead and sent him reeling backwards.

Blood poured down Dion's face. He struggled to regain his feet and at the same time to draw his sword. "You'll die for this Jew," he shouted. "I'll kill you myself."

Judah threw another rock at Dion. It smashed across the bridge of his nose, breaking it. More blood streamed down his face. Realizing he must stop Dion from drawing his sword, Judah leaped over the wall and threw himself on the bloody man.

Dion was unable to overcome the force of the impact, and he went down. He struggled to push Judah off of him. But he was far too weak to move the giant. Then, suddenly he felt the Jew's hands close around his throat. Dion began to scream and thrash wildly about as he struggled to free himself.

Judah tightened his grip on the tax collector's throat.

"Let me live," Dion croaked, "let me live and I promise I'll take nothing from your father."

Judah pressed harder.

Dion beat against the Jew's chest with his fists, but his blows made no impression. Through the blood clouding his vision, he saw the face above him; it was an obdurate mask. The man's lips were not even drawn back in anger. But hate and rage burned deep in his blue eyes. In those depths, Dion saw no mercy, and in them he saw his own death.

Judah took a deep breath and, exerting all his energy, he snapped Dion's neck. The man uttered a cry of agony, and then his head fell limply to one side.

Judah reached under Dion's cloak, drew his short sword and standing up, he pushed the blade into the man's heart. Then he took several steps backward and looked down at the body of the tax collector.

It was the third time he had killed a man and felt no remorse. He was breathing somewhat harder than usual, but that was the sum total of his reaction.

Then he heard a soft sob; he turned and saw Mattathias. Gesturing toward Dion with the bloody sword, Judah commented, "He deserved no better."

Mattathias remained silent.

"I'll bury him under the wall," Judah said and pulling the sword out of the dead man's chest, he used it to hollow out a grave for Dion.

Mattathias lifted himself over the low wall and, with tears streaming down his face, he wordlessly helped his son conceal the body of the tax collector. He was doing what his son had done for him when he had himself killed a man. But now he was the one who wept, shedding his tears for the blood on the hands of his son, and for the blood on his own hands that Judah had seen so many, many years before.

When the task was done, and the wall made whole again, Judah buried the sword nearby. Then he went to his father and in a gentle voice, he said, "Come, Father, let us go home. We have done enough for today."

CHAPTER IX

On the morning of Johanan's marriage, Mattathias rose before anyone else in the household. He donned his phylacteries, faced south toward the Temple and softly intoned his prayers.

Ever since he had helped Judah bury Dion, Mattathias felt as if he were slowly withering. The days held no meaning for him, and the nights were filled with bloody visions. Everything had a dream-like quality. He would gladly sleep forever, if God would have it that way.

Finished with his prayers, Mattathias removed the phylacteries and, turning around, he saw Miriam watching him.

"I heard you stirring," she explained, "and I thought it would be a good idea to start the fire in the hearth early. I still have a great deal of cooking to do before the guests begin to arrive."

Mattathias nodded. He replaced the bag that held his phylacteries on the shelf opposite the hearth.

Miriam went to the shutters and opened them. Though the sun shone brightly and the sky was a lovely blue, there was still a chill in the air. "It's a beautiful day," she said. "A good omen for the marriage."

Mattathias agreed and sat down at the table.

"Nashon has sent several baskets of food and ..." Miriam began. "I know," Mattathias said, with a wave of his hand, "he's a very generous man."

"I thought you liked him," Miriam commented, busying herself at the hearth. She was very much aware of her husband's strange mood. Her intuition told her the source of his trouble lay closer to home. "Well, do you like him?" she pressed, realizing he would not answer unless she made him.

"Yes . . . yes . . . he's a good man . . . I never said he wasn't."

Miriam moved to the table and, resting her small hands on it, she said, "This isn't a day to go moping about or to be in a bad temper. Your first-born is to be married. You'll soon gain a daughter-in-law and, with the help of Yahweh, within the year you'll have a grandson."

He nodded.

"Then why are you so sad looking?" she questioned.

Mattathias stood up. "These are sad times and their sadness weighs heavily upon me." He went to her and gently turning her to him, he said, "But I'll cast aside my sadness today and rejoice in the happiness of the occasion." Then he did something he never did unless they were in bed. He bent down and pressed his lips to hers. "I have always loved you," he told her a few moments later.

Miriam was so surprised she could not speak. Tears filled her eyes and she pressed her face into his chest.

He ran his hand over the back of her head, and still holding her in his arms, he whispered, "I ache for my God and for my people."

"I know," she answered tenderly. "All know you walk with God." "I weep for Him," he said. "I weep for Him."

Miriam embraced her husband. Had they been much younger, she would have led him back to bed and would have soothed him the way a woman could soothe a man. But that time had long since passed. Now she could only hold him very tight and tell him everything would be all right, though she herself could not be at all sure that it would be.

"See, I'm much better already," Mattathias said, separating himself from his wife. He managed a smile and asked, "Is there anything I can do to help?"

"No. Take your walk, and be back here in time for your morning meal."

Mattathias put on his cloak and took his staff, then with a nod, he opened the door and walked out into the front yard.

Miriam watched him. In her fifty years of marriage, she had always thought Mattathias to be a strong man, perhaps the strongest man in all of Judea. But now she realized that during the past few months, his strength had waned considerably. She returned to the hearth and wondered if Mattathias would soon die.

"God forbid!" she exclaimed aloud. Pausing for a few moments, she cast her eyes downward and reverently asked Jehovah to take her first, and spare Mattathias a while longer. "He's a good and worthy man," she whispered.

"Who's a good and worthy man?" Judah asked, coming into the main room from the other part of the house. He walked to where the shelf was and took down his bag with the phylacteries.

"Say your prayers," his mother told him.

He chuckled and put the phylacteries on. When he was finished praying, he again asked his mother who was "a good and worthy man." "Your father," she answered.

Judah smiled briefly and replaced the bag on the shelf.

"I don't think he is well," she said and, facing her son, she found herself wondering, as she had so many times in the past, how she came to give birth to a blonde-haired, blue-eyed child.

"These are sad times," Judah answered.

"That is exactly what your father had said," she told him, surprised by the sameness of the answer. "Only, he had added that they weigh heavily on him."

"The people are sick from the sadness," Judah said. "Everyone feels it. It's always there. I even noticed the children in the village hardly laugh anymore." Then he went to the window. "But today looks fine," he told her. "Johanan should have a good marriage."

* * *

Soon everyone in the household was up and preparing for the ceremony and the feast that would follow.

Johanan was freshly bathed and anointed with a pleasant scented balm. When he was finally dressed in his new clothing, his brothers teased him about the time he would first know Sarah.

When the sun was past its high point in the sky for the day, Johanan, escorted by his brothers, his sister and his mother, went to meet his bride. He was very pale. His heartbeat quickened and his lips went dry. He whispered to Simon, "I should have drunk much more wine."

Overhearing the comment, Judah said, "Then you would sleep when you should be most awake, and your bride would have to wait." "Quiet!" Miriam ordered.

"Johanan wants wine to stiffen his courage when another part of him should be hard," Eleazar laughed.

"Enough, enough," Miriam told her sons. "Your comments only make him more nervous."

"He has lain with a woman before," Judah said. "The experience won't come as a surprise to him."

"By the living God," Johanan responded, "once this is all over, I'll box your ears!"

"That'll be an exciting event," Judah laughed.

Then they saw the bridal procession. It came up the twisting road toward the center of the village. Because of Mattathias' standing in the community, the bride was being brought to the groom's house.

"I can't see her," Johanan whispered.

"Who is 'her?'" Jonathan asked with a snicker. "Is that what you will call her tonight?"

"There she is," Miriam said, catching a glimpse of the purple silk wedding gown and garland of small yellow and blue flowers on her head. "She's behind the group of friends and relatives."

The bridal procession stopped and the way opened up for Sarah to walk toward Johanan. She came to him with her father on her right side and her mother on her left.

"She's lovely," Miriam whispered to her son.

Johanan nodded and, taking a deep breath, he walked alone toward his bride. When he was very close to her, he stopped.

Nashon said, "I have brought you my daughter to wed you this day."

"And I gratefully receive her to be my bride this day," Johanan answered, extending his hand to take hold of Sarah's.

As soon as the groom and bride had joined hands, the flutes, harps, and tambourines struck up a lively tune. Johanan's lips parted in a broad smile and, leaning toward Sarah, he asked if she was as frightened as he.

"More," she whispered. "Much more."

He patted her hand, and he led her toward the house. They walked slowly. Behind them trooped the entire village.

Because of the limited space, only the immediate members of each family attended the actual wedding service, while the rest of the guests crowded around the open windows and door.

For the occasion, Mattathias wore his white robes. His sadness seemed to fall away and his face was radiant with joy as he performed the ancient marriage rites. The words came from the time of Moses. He uttered them in a great dark voice that gave them deep religious meaning. He spoke to his son and his future daughter-in-law about their obligations to each other and to the rest of the people.

Then he read the last chapter of Proverbs.

When he was finished, his gray eyes went to Johanan. "Be a kind and generous husband, a loving father, and always honor God." Joining the hands of the groom and the bride, he asked God to make their union fruitful. Then he pronounced them husband and wife.

Johanan was handed a small hoop with a skin stretched over it. He laughed and drove his fist through it to signify he would do the same to his wife's maidenhead that very night, when he lay with her for the first time. He took Sarah in his arms and kissed her fully on the lips with such ardor that her face became flushed.

The guests waited until Johanan and Sarah were seated in the middle of the main table before the toasting began.

Mattathias took his place at the table with Miriam. Then came Nashon and his wife. Simon, Judah, Eleazar, and Jonathan occupied the other places.

Judah drank a great deal of wine, though not enough to rob him of his senses. He sat back and watched the people of the village enjoy themselves. Now and then, he even joined the dancing. But his thoughts strayed to Ismene. He longed for her.

"You look far away from here," Simon commented, glancing at Judah.

"Only a short distance in the past," Judah answered.

Simon gestured toward Johanan who was dancing with his fiends. "Be here for his sake," he told his brother.

Judah nodded and with a smile, he offered his brother a drink.

"Can you still drink?" Simon asked.

"Much, much more."

"Then pour, Brother," Simon responded.

Judah filled their cups and, just as he lifted his, the music abruptly stopped. The guests parted to make way for a raggedly dressed man and woman. The man carried a short sword under his cloak.

Judah slowly put his cup down. He stood up and called out "Glacon?"

The man stopped and looked at him. Then, shaking his head, he put his arm around the woman. "There isn't anywhere else for us to go," he said.

Judah vaulted over the table. He went to his friend. "My brother was married today," he explained. "This is his celebration."

"I'm sorry," Glacon told him. "The scent of the food—"

Mattathias suddenly got to his feet. In a tremulous voice he asked who the stranger was.

"His name is Glacon," Judah answered. "He's a friend ."

"And the woman?"

"Her name is Helen," Glacon told Judah, who repeated it to his father.

"He and the woman are welcome," Mattathias said. "Bid them stay, bid them stay. I've been waiting for him. God has been waiting for him."

Judah looked questioningly toward his father. But the old man avoided his eyes, and Judah would not dare to question him in front of the entire village. He turned back to Glacon and said, "You and the woman are welcome to Modin. Come eat and drink."

Glacon spoke to the woman in her native dialect, and tears filled her eyes. She answered Glacon and the former Seleucid officer said, "She's grateful for your kindness and hopes someday to be able to be as kind to you."

Judah suddenly realized that all of the guests were staring at the three of them. "An old friend of mine," he explained, circling Glacon's shoulder with his right arm. "And his woman," he told them putting his left.

"Even though you know what the consequences might be if I am discovered?"

"To your never being discovered," Judah toasted.

They touched the rim of their cups together, drank, laughed and drank again.

"Come," Judah said, "let's pay our score here and return home. I'm sure Helen is wondering where you are. By the way, Glacon, she's a beautiful woman."

"She is indeed, she is indeed," Glacon answered.

* * *

Sostrates now occupied the same rooms in the palace that Antiochus had. But they were far more Spartan than they had been when the King had used them. Not only had Antiochus taken many of the beautiful pieces of furniture and tapestries, but also Sostrates had burned many of those that had been left.

He was a man of plain tastes: a place to sleep, with a woman if possible, food to fill his stomach and wine to slake his thirst. He had little use for any man who was not a soldier or had not been a soldier. He had been in the army most of his life. By proving his skill in battle, he had risen from the ranks to his present position of Commander of the Jerusalem garrison.

Sostrates was a mixture of many different peoples, including on his mother's side, Jews. Because he considered the Jewish portion of his family to be less than all of the others, he hated Jews with the consuming passion of a man in love.

He did not believe it was possible for any Jew to renounce his faith and become a Greek. For this reason, he did not stand when Menelaus entered his workroom. Without looking up from the map spread out on the table in front of him, Sostrates said, "I have also sent for Tyropus and Dryas. They should be here shortly." He made no effort to offer the High Priest a place to sit. He ignored him and continued to study the map.

The High Priest did not move from where he was standing. He would not under any circumstances give Sostrates cause to look up from his map. Serving Antiochus, for all his whims, had been far easier than living under Sostrates' fist. Had Lysimachus lived, Menelaus was quite sure his relationship to the city's Commander would have been much different. Lysimachus would not have allowed Sostrates to insult him; he would have found a way to kill him. But, alone, Menelaus felt powerless to do anything, other than obey.

Abruptly, Sostrates left the table. He went to another one where there was an amphora of wine and several delicately wrought goblets of silver. He poured wine into one of them and, without drinking, he walked to the window. The late afternoon sun touched the roofs of the buildings in the city, and already most of the streets were drowned in shadows. He stood there a long time.

Menelaus looked at him.

He was tall and lean, with deep-set eyes and a hawk-like face. It was difficult to guess whether he was deep in thought, or, indeed, if he was thinking at all.

A soft knock at the door drew Sostrates' attention, and he called out, "Yes."

A soldier entered and announced the arrival of Tyropus and Dryas. "Let them enter," Sostrates ordered, and he returned to the table. He set the goblet down without drinking from it.

The two men entered the room. They acknowledged Menelaus' presence with a nod but greeted Sostrates effusively, while he, in turn, said nothing. He waited until they had run out of words; then he picked up the goblet, took several sips of wine from it and said, "I have had word from the King today. He is concerned about the slow progress we are making in his project to convert Jews from their God to ours."

Dryas, the priest to Zeus, took a small step forward and he said, "For the past week or two, I thought that it needed to be improved."

"Then why did you wait until now to mention it?" Sostrates demanded, setting the goblet down on the table again. "I rely on you to tell me what is happening." His dark brown eyes moved to Menelaus, and he asked insolently, "What have you to say about it, Jew?"

"Progress is being made," Menelaus answered in a voice choked with indignation.

Sostrates sipped more wine. "Interesting," he said. "Most interesting. Unless I have lost my hearing, I would say there is something of a contradiction between what I was told by Dryas and what I was told by the High Priest of the Jews. Am I right, Tyropus, in thinking that, or have I heard incorrectly?"

Before Tyropus could answer, Menelaus said, "The amount of progress depends on how we define it. Many, many Jews have accepted Zeus."

Sostrates nodded and, still looking at Tyropus, he told him, "I hope you are capable of speaking for yourself."

"I am. Progress has been made but only toward the South and East of the city. There are only so many men available for duty. And . . ." He hesitated.

"And what?" Sostrates questioned.

"I think it would be dangerous to send more than half our strength into the countryside at any one time."

"Dangerous?" Sostrates asked with disbelief. "Why should it be dangerous?"

"We have reason to believe that one of our tax collectors was recently murdered."

"When?"

"Several days ago."

Sostrates' face flushed with anger. He demanded to know why he was not told about it.

"Word only came to me this morning," Tyropus explained.

Sostrates drank more wine and looked at the three men over the rim of his goblet. None of them were good for anything. But the King had saddled him with them, and he could do nothing but carry them on his back. But he felt their weight, he felt it keenly.

"Suppose, Tyropus," the Commander said, setting the empty goblet down, "that you tell me exactly what happened and where it happened?"

"The tax collector was named Dion," Tyropus said and he went on to explain that after having left his station for an afternoon stroll, the tax collector had failed to return.

Sostrates repeated Dion's name several times and then he admitted he had not known the man.

"He had a predilection for young men," Tyropus said.

Sostrates uttered a sound of disgust: the way he could not abide Jews, he could not abide pederasty, though the Seleucids practiced it with great avidity. Even the King himself from time to time had taken a young man for a lover.

"Where was his territory?" Sostrates asked.

"In the area around the village of Modin and Lodi. There are many small hamlets in that area. But most of them are poor. The land is hilly and most of the farms are terraced."

Sostrates scanned the map on his desk and put the tip of the forefinger of his right hand between Modin and Lodi. The map gave no indication of the terrain. With his finger still on the map, he looked up and asked. "Our effort to convert the Jews has been restricted to the South and East of the city; is that right?"

"Yes," Tyropus answered.

"And from your remarks about Dion, you're suggesting he might have been murdered somewhere in the territory around Modin?"

"It's only an assumption."

"Probably an accurate one," Sostrates commented. "But the only way to test it will be to test the people there. I want an officer and a rank of men to go to the village of Modin and make Greeks out of the inhabitants."

"Why Modin?"

"It appears to be in the center of Dion's territory. If conversion takes place there, then we can be almost sure that the other villages around it will follow its example. Once the villages become Hellenized, we can then begin to look for Dion's murderer. Those that convert will be anxious to cooperate with us, and those that do not convert, we will punish according to the King's decrees."

"Within the next few days," Tyropus said, "Apelles and his men will be available."

"Excellent," Sostrates responded. "Apelles is a good officer. He will not act rashly, but if forced to act, he'll follow the letter of the law." He went to the small table and refilled his goblet; then he told Tyropus to give him a full report about Apelles' activities.

"I will write it myself," Tyropus answered.

Sostrates nodded, dismissed them and when they were gone, he called for a slave to light the oil lamps.

* * *

The morning sky was a bright blue. As the sun would climb higher, Judah knew, the color would become so intense it would be impossible for a man to look up without squinting or shielding his eyes. It was a good day to begin planting.

Judah had risen before the coming of first light. He had left his father's house to come to the place on the crest of the hill, just above the grove of olive trees, beyond the stone wall, where the huge boulders were.

He was more restless than usual. The spring of the year was for him a time of keen yearning for something beyond the life he knew at Modin, and even beyond his experiences in Jerusalem. This morning, the memory of Ismene was particularly strong. He tried many times to put her out of his mind, but he failed. Though he would have other women, he never would be able to forget what had happened to her because she had showed her love for him, a Jew!

Then Judah's eyes caught the flash of the sun on the crested helmet of a Seleucid soldier. Within moments, he saw two horsemen, one behind the other, riding at a gallop for Modin. An instant later, the sun flashed on the helmet of the second rider.

Judah started down from the hill, sure that if he or Glacon were in any danger, more than two lightly armed riders would have been sent. They were coming for something else. Perhaps to announce a new edict?

The two riders were covered with dust. The shorter of the two demanded to see the priest of the Jews.

Mattathias stepped forward and said, "I am the Priest here in Modin."

Judah saw his brothers. Two stood on either side of the old man. He caught Simon's eye and with a quick motion of his hand indicated he would remain off to one side, but close enough to strike the other rider with his staff, if the situation demanded it.

"You and your people will assemble here in the village square," the short man said, "at noon today, when Apelles, an officer in the army of Antiochus-Epiphanes, will bring Zeus to you and your people."

Then the taller rider said, "Everyone will be in the square, with the exception of the infirm and infants. You, Priest, will wear the robes of your office. Everyone else will wear clothing suited to the importance of the occasion."

Mattathias said nothing.

"Do you understand, Jew?" the same rider asked.

"He understands," Simon answered.

"And who are you," the short man asked, "that you can speak for him?"

"His son," Simon replied.

He glanced at his companion, nodded and demanded the horse be given water and oats, while they themselves would slake their thirst with wine. These requests were quickly met by Simon, who took the initiative and told Eleazar to bring the water for the horses, Johanan the oats, and Jonathan, the wine.

Judah moved slightly closer to his father. There was dark smoke in the old man's eyes. The vertical ridges that formed on his brow were hard with anger.

Judah took a deep breath; his heart was pounding so loud he could hear it. He was afraid his father might say something to infuriate the two soldiers. He moved closer to the old man.

"This is a peaceful village," the tall rider said, "and Apelles will come in peace. That he leaves in peace will be entirely up to you."

"We'll be here when he arrives," Mattathias replied. The tone of his voice was at once dark and rich. "You can be sure that we'll be here."

The two soldiers took several more gulps of wine, threw their clay cups to the ground, wheeled their mounts around and trotted out of the village.

Mattathias waited until the riders were out of sight before he said, "All of you will assemble as ordered."

Abraham, the blacksmith, called out, "They'll make Greeks out of you."

And Bozrah, the schoolmaster, said, "We'll be forced to bow, yea, to kiss the image of Zeus."

"We'll trust in our God," Mattathias' voice swelled up. "We'll trust in our God to save us." Without uttering another word, he turned and walked slowly back to the house. He was as tall as he ever was.

Judah immediately joined Simon. With a gesture toward the fallow fields, he said, "There'll be no plowing today."

Simon nodded.

"You know they'll bring a statue of Zeus and a swine to the village," Judah said, as they went toward the house.

"The statue, I am told," Simon commented, "looks very much like Antiochus."

Judah squinted thoughtfully. "Antiochus claims to be God . . . Manifest," he said.

They were joined by their other brothers, and all of them followed their father into the house.

Mattathias looked at the men around him. His eyes rested on

Glacon longer than on any of his sons. Then in a soft, but very firm voice, he said, "We're God's chosen people. He'll find a way to deliver us." The men chorused their praise of God and blessed His name. Mattathias left the table and asked Simon to accompany him. He explained to the others that he wanted to make sure the village elders were aware of what might be expected of them. "And," he added, "I want to have a fleet-footed youth posted along the roadway to alert us when Apelles approaches the village."

Judah beckoned Glacon to follow him, and when they were outside, he asked, "Do you know this Apelles?"

"Not so well that I am able to tell you anything important about him, except that he'll carry out his duty, no matter what the cost." Judah nodded; he had not expected a much different answer.

"But perhaps," Glacon said, "you might be able to answer a question of mine."

"I think I know what it is," Judah told him.

"Can you answer it?"

Judah shook his head. "My father," he told his friend quietly, "was never one to share his thoughts with others, especially not with me."

With a chuckle, Glacon asked, "Has anyone ever told you how similar the two of you are?"

"On the outside, perhaps?"

"No," Glacon said, "I mean the man he is and the man you are."

With a swift movement of his hand, Judah brushed the comment aside. Then he warned Glacon to have Helen keep her blonde hair covered. "We don't want to arouse Apelles' suspicions or anger him in any way."

"I can see the logic of avoiding suspicion," Glacon said.

"But not the anger; unless everyone in this village is prepared to accept Zeus for their god, you will indeed anger him."

Judah looked away; he did not know the answer.

Placing his hand on Judah's shoulder, Glacon said, "Whatever happens, I'll be with you." Then he walked away.

Judah squinted up into the intensely blue sky. From where the sun was, the morning was only half over. For everyone, the next few hours would seem like many long days. Judah prowled the village. He walked to Abraham's shed. The fire was out. He retraced his steps. From the inexorable shortening of his shadow, he knew that the sun would soon be at its highest point in the sky.

Then suddenly the boy posted on the road to warn of Apelles' approach came racing into the village. "He comes," the youth shouted, gasping for breath between words, "Apelles comes! The soldiers are coming! They're coming!" The people came slowly out of their houses and moved even more slowly to the small square. They were silent. All of them looked toward the road where already they could see not only the fine brown dust rising up from under the steady tramp of the soldiers' feet, but also the glint of the sun on the spoon-shaped heads of their long spears.

Judah joined his brothers, standing next to Eleazar.

"How many do you count?" Eleazar asked.

"Sixteen," Judah answered.

"One rank," Simon said.

Mattathias came out of the house. A pathway opened for him. He was dressed in the white robes of his office, and in his hand he held his staff. When he stood in front of his people, he said, "Be calm. God will deliver us."

He told his people to arrange themselves into an open-sided square, thereby forming the Hebrew letter *het*. "It is our way," he said, almost gently, "of reminding ourselves and telling them that we are Jews."

Even before his father had given an explanation, Simon understood its significance. It was an act or defiance that could imperil the entire village. He whispered as much to Judah.

"I'm sure he knows it," Judah answered.

"But why then . . ."

"Our visitors have arrived," Judah said, tilting his staff toward the beginning of the village.

The Seleucid troops marched into the town. Apelles was in a litter. He was a broad-boned, corpulent man, with heavy jowls and a thick, bull-like neck. Wet with sweat, he looked uncomfortable in his battle dress. He wore a short sword, but his escort was armed with the usual long spear and sword.

Several of the soldiers carried an altar with a statue of Zeus on it and another held a small swine under his arm.

Apelles signaled his bearers to ground the litter. Then he pulled himself up. He was much larger when he stood erect than he appeared to be in the litter. Without even looking at the Jews, he ordered the altar to be placed in the open end of the square and the swine be made ready for the sacrifice. Then his eyes rested on the man who was his real adversary: the old Priest in the white robes. His spies had provided him with the old man's name. Apelles waited for him to be the first to speak.

Mattathias said nothing. He knew what would be asked of him. The same ceremony had taken place in other villages and towns throughout Judea. And perhaps, even now, the same thing was happening in some other village.

Apelles realized for the first time that the old Priest would stand there for the rest of the day and into the night without uttering a word. He was anxious to bend these Jews to the will of his King and be gone. He cleared his throat and in a harsh voice, he said, "I am here as a royal emissary, to see that the commands of Antiochus-Epiphanes are carried out. The villagers will be initiated into the worship of the god Zeus. This will be accomplished by a public sacrifice of the swine, the animal sacred to the god Zeus and then by each of the villagers tasting of its flesh. This is by order of the King and it will be followed."

None of the Jews moved; all of them realized that to defy the order of the King would mean their death.

Apelles looked at Mattathias, and he said, "If you come forward, the others will follow. I promise you and your family rich rewards. I ask you to step forward."

Mattathias remained motionless; he knew that once he moved toward the altar, everything would be lost. His sons would become Greeks. His people would become Greeks, and his God would be forsaken by the very people He had chosen. The Covenant would be broken between them. He could not do that. He would not do that!

"I want an answer, Mattathias," Apelles shouted. "I want an answer."

Mattathias said calmly, "Though all the nations within the King's dominions obey him and forsake their ancestral worship, though they have chosen to submit to his commands, yet I and my sons and my brothers will follow the Covenant of our fathers. Heaven forbid that we should ever abandon the Law and its statutes. We will not obey the command of the King, nor will we deviate one step from our forms of worship."

The Jews took several steps back, leaving their Priest and his sons standing in front of the rest of them.

Apelles unsheathed his sword. His face was flushed. He glanced back at his men and with a slight movement ordered them forward to his side; they immediately formed four ranks of four men.

Judah's eyes moved quickly over the people. Then he saw Jehubabel, the village miller, push his way forward into the open space. Jew and Seleucid alike watched him.

The flush left Apelles' face; at least there was one sane man in the village.

Jehubabel stepped up to the altar. He was thin, a wily man with a small well-trimmed beard. He said, "I will make the sacrifice."

"Your name," Apelles asked.

"Call him apostate!" Mattathias shouted.

"Silence!" roared the Seleucid commander, wheeling to glare at the old Priest.

"My name is Jehubabel," the man at the altar said.

"You and yours will be richly rewarded," Apelles told him, and he ordered the swine to be prepared for sacrifice.

The Jews of Modin and the Seleucid soldiers watched what was happening at the altar.

Apelles walked to where Jehubabel stood and, handing him the knife, he said, "You are wiser by far than the rest of the people here."

As Jehubabel reached for the knife, Mattathias rushed toward the man. He wrested the knife from Jehubabel's hands and plunged it into his heart. Then he whirled and drove the blade to the hilt into Apelles' stomach.

The women began to scream and, too terrified to move, the children wept.

The soldiers, too, were stunned and remained immobile. They had not expected anything to happen.

"The others!" Judah shouted. He ran toward the tight formation of troops and jammed the end of his staff into the right eye of a red-faced soldier.

The man howled with pain. Gore ran down his face. He thrust at his assailant, but the pain caused him to miss his mark.

Judah ripped the spear from the wounded man's hand and drove it into his neck. A fountain of blood gushed forth.

Eleazar bounded forward with Judah. He threw his knee into the groin of a thin soldier and when the man doubled over, he smashed him across the bridge of his nose with his fist.

With blood pouring from his nose, the man tried to crawl away, but Eleazar grabbed hold of the stricken man's sword and gutted him with it.

Jonathan moved too and with a huge rock, he smashed the forehead of a grizzled veteran.

Simon dashed to protect his father and, picking up Apelles' sword, he severed the head of the Seleucid commander.

In the first fury of the assault, half the formation lay dead or was dying. The market square was filled with the terrible shouts of men fighting for their lives.

Judah took hold of a dead man's sword; then, plunging into the Seleucid ranks, he scattered the rest of the troops. None of them could withstand his vicious attack. Judah was filled with a strange, frightening sense of exhilaration. Men fled in terror from his terrible slashing strokes. He gutted men, twisting his sword in their bloody wounds to pull out their entrails; he clove men in two and hacked at his opponents until there was nothing but a red mist in front of his eyes. His sword dripped with blood and his arms were covered with it. But in the frenzy of the slaughter, Judah realized he had found what he had been looking for, what he could do better than anyone else, what perhaps his father, in his deep wisdom, had always known.

"Do not let the rest of them re-form," Glacon shouted, as he too grabbed a weapon and began slashing at what remained of Apelles' guard.

The other men from the village joined in. Some fought bare handed, bringing their prey down by leaping on them.

Several of the soldiers tried to flee. But the Jews, having drawn blood, pursued them.

Judah and Glacon fought side by side. And over and over they shouted, "Do not let them re-form."

Then it was over! Within a matter of minutes the entire Seleucid force lay dead, either in the square, or a short distance from it.

The men who had fought and won gathered together.

Several were wounded but none seriously. They were wet with sweat and stained with blood. Many felt as if their legs would without warning give out from under them.

They looked at each other, hesitantly at first, but then with big, broad smiles. And finally they began to laugh and slap each other on the back. Their laughter became louder and louder.

"We beat them," Eleazar shouted above guffaws. "By the living God Jehovah, we beat them!"

His words were repeated over and over again.

Suddenly Mattathias pushed over the statue of Zeus, and he cried out, "Hear, oh Israel, the Lord is our God, the Lord is one!" Then, walking toward his bloodstained sons, he thundered, "And a mighty army has been raised up. A mighty man has come to deliver us. The prophecy has been fulfilled."

CHAPTER X

The killing of Apelles and his soldiers had taken only a few minutes to accomplish. The men from Modin experienced the intoxicating exhilaration that came from having bested their enemy. They laughed. They embraced one another and with pride they pointed to the bodies of the Seleucid soldiers they had slain.

The village square was full of a joyful noisiness. The frightened screams of the women and fearful whimpering of the children changed into tumultuous shouts of triumph. Every man, woman and child became caught up in the pleasure of the victory.

But then, almost imperceptibly at first, the happy boisterousness diminished. One by one, the men who had struck down the soldiers of the King stopped laughing, stopped speaking altogether. After a while, an awful silence settled over the people of Modin.

Their eyes sought out Mattathias and they drew away from him. Their eyes found Judah and they drew away from him, too. One by one they looked at the other sons of their Priest and drew back from each of them. They even drew away from Glacon.

In the warmth of the afternoon sun, the people trembled with fear.

Every man and woman harbored his or her own terrible visions of what Sostrates would do to them for what they had done.

Then, Ethan, a man whose small farm of thin, rocky soil gave a poor yield, pointed a finger at Mattathias. "Tell us now," he shouted, "now that you've led us to do this bloody work, what do we do?"

Because he was still trembling with ecstasy, Mattathias could not answer.

Another villager called out, "We can't hide what we've done. Sooner or later more soldiers will come looking for those we've slain."

A third man shouted, "How many of us will suffer because of what you have started here today?"

The shouts and cries against Mattathias became louder and louder.

"You're to blame," some of the people called. "You and your sons." With the bloody sword he held, Judah motioned to his brothers.

Obedient to his silent command, they gathered in front of their father. Glacon joined them and took his place next to Judah.

"Let's deliver them to Sostrates," a man shouted, "and then throw ourselves on his mercy."

"The first man who moves toward us," Judah answered, "will die."

"So will the second man," Eleazar added in a loud, angry voice. "They're the guilty ones," the same man cried. "And we will suffer because of them!"

"We must go to Sostrates and beg his forgiveness," another man shouted.

Mattathias mounted the platform where the statue of Zeus had stood.

The shouting instantly ceased.

Mattathias pulled himself up on his staff. He said nothing, but his gray eyes moved restlessly over the people and over the space that separated them from himself, his sons, and Glacon. "It was either Zeus or what we have done," Mattathias told them, his voice booming out in the square. "It was either breaking the Covenant, or killing those who would make us break it."

"But what will we do now?" one of the men called out.

"We'll leave here," Mattathias answered almost gently, as though he had been thinking about it for a long time and could not understand why such a question should be asked.

More than one man shouted, "This our land, our homes. Where would we go? What will happen to us?"

Mattathias would not raise his voice against the storm of outcries. He waited until they fell quiet of their own accord; then he said, "We've done Yahweh's work here today; we've begun to carry out the prophecy that will eventually bring Antiochus down. We're His chosen people and now we must take arms against His enemy."

"Fight the Seleucids?" a villager asked.

"Continue to do what we have done here today," Mattathias said.

"But how? How can we do it?" the same man called out.

"First, we must leave here," Mattathias said. "We must go where the Seleucids won't be able to follow us. From there, we'll do what must be done. But, if we stay here, we'll perish. Those of you who have cried out against me and my sons will find the Seleucids no less harsh with you than they would have been with us. But, if we stay together, if we remain strong in our determination to be Jews, then we'll gather other Jews to us, even as one stream gathers other streams to become a river."

"You're asking us to rebel?" a man asked loudly.

Gesturing toward the bodies in the square, Mattathias said, "There's proof that we have already done it. We can't bring those soldiers back to life. We fought them and won a great victory; we'll fight many more times and win still greater victories. But we must leave here; we must go, like our forefathers did, into the wilderness. For us the wilderness is the Gophna Hills."

Another hubbub erupted. The Gophna Hills was a forbidding place of rocky gorges, a barren place with little water during the summer and sudden wild torrents during the winter. It was a place of lizards and small creatures, of vultures and scorpions. The people knew it was a place of death, and they were afraid of it.

This time, Mattathias raised his voice above all of theirs and demanded silence. When it came, he again let his gray eyes move over the people. In the upturned faces he saw the reflection of their fear. It twisted inside of them like some living thing. He wondered if they could see the same fear in him, because it was there, causing his heart to race and his old legs to feel as though they would dissolve to nothing.

He looked down at his sons and at Glacon. They too had their faces turned toward him, waiting to hear what he would say next.

He focused his attention back to the people. He waited, letting the words run through his thoughts before he spoke them. When he was absolutely sure of what he wanted to say and what his purpose was, Mattathias slowly raised his staff.

In a thunderous voice, he said, "We'll not let our enemies kill us. We'll not be forced to end the Covenant between ourselves and Yahweh. We will fight!" He paused again and sucked air into his lungs, and after several deep breaths, he challenged, "Those who'll fight for the Law and the Covenant, let them follow me!" And with a nimbleness uncommon for a man of his years, Mattathias leaped down from the platform and started toward the people.

The square was wrapped in silence, and then Judah, sensing the intensity of the movement, lifted his bloody sword and shouted, "For the Law and the Covenant, follow me!"

In an instant, that same cry of defiance came from the lips of every man and woman in the square. Mattathias moved through the throng of the people, while they eagerly reached out to touch their Priest.

"Go to your homes," he told them, "and prepare for the journey; we must leave before nightfall."

Slowly the gathering of the villagers dissipated, and Mattathias turned toward his own house.

Judah lowered his sword and dropped back to walk alongside of Simon. "Do you know what prophecy the old man spoke about?" he asked.

"No."

"I didn't expect something like this to happen," Judah said. "He was more magnificent than I ever remember him being."

"Judah," Simon whispered, "he was magnificent, but it was you who finally brought the people to him. I don't know how you did it, but you did."

Mattathias looked back at them and smiled.

"He appears to be happier now," Simon commented, "happier than I've seen him in months."

"Perhaps he knows something that we don't," Judah suggested. "Perhaps, or perhaps he just thinks he knows."

Judah nodded, and he followed his brother into the house.

* * *

Preparations that ordinarily would take several days had to be accomplished in a matter of hours. Each household gathered food, water, clothing and many other articles that would be required for their journey into the wilderness of the Gophna Hills.

Judah and his brothers removed the weapons and the armor from the bodies of the Seleucid soldiers, took what they needed to arm themselves and held the rest of the weapons to distribute to the fathers and sons of their relatives.

Simon returned before his other brothers and drew up a list of all the people who would take part in the march. When he was finished, he waited for Judah and called his attention to the fact that Jehubabel had two sons, Nachim and Boaza. "They're old enough to fight," Simon said.

"And to hate," Judah responded.

"What do we do?"

"What we must do," Judah answered, "to protect the others." Simon nodded. In a low voice, he said, "Nachim, the elder, is interested in our sister, or at least seems to be."

Judah shrugged.

"And their mother . . ."

"She too must die," Judah told him.

Simon was silent. He had always known Judah was more severe than most men, but until now he had never divined the extent of his brother's relentlessness. Perhaps at some future time he would learn its cause, but now he realized that in the days ahead, it would become the force that would bind the Jews together. Their father was much too old to do the things only a young man could do.

"I'll be merciful with them," Judah finally said.

"What if they decide to fight?"

"Glacon will be with me," Judah answered.

"When the people discover they aren't with us," Simon asked, "what will we tell them?"

"The truth," Judah answered without hesitation. "If we don't tell them the truth, they won't trust, and if they don't trust us, they'll turn on us." He shook his head. "You and I know what took place here today is the most important event in our lives, and we have a great deal to discuss.

But for now, our only task is to move all of the people to the safety of the wilderness as soon as possible."

"Will you take command, Judah?"

"Father is the Priest here."

For several moments, Simon looked at his brother without speaking. Then he said quietly, 'There isn't anyone else."

"You, yourself," Judah responded quickly. He had never been one to seek out responsibility for others.

"I'll help you, but you must command," Simon told him.

"And what about our father?"

"He'd lead," Simon replied. "But he's too old to command, and our brothers are too young."

"There is Johanan."

Simon shook his head.

"He is the eldest," Judah said. "It's his right."

Again Simon shook his head.

"But why not? He's well liked by everyone."

"He has a wife," Simon responded, "who even now is weeping about what they must give up. He'll fight as bravely as the next man when the time comes, but he is only a fanner and not a leader of men."

Judah did not respond. He had never thought about his brothers in any other way than that they were his brothers. His preference for

Simon had always been accepted by the family, even as had Eleazar's partiality for him.

"Things have happened so quickly," Simon said. "I have not yet had time to think everything through. But I will, and when I have, we'll sit down and lay our plans. Believe me, my brother, what we are about to do will have more meaning than any one of us can imagine. But what has happened and what will happen is Yahweh's will, of that I am sure."

"I don't think about Yahweh's will," Judah replied and, flourishing his bloodstained sword, he added in a low voice, "But I will command."

"We'll talk about many things in the days ahead," Simon said, extending his hand to his brother.

Judah clasped it, nodded and said, "I trust you, Simon, more than I trust myself." Then he left and went looking for Glacon.

Glacon agreed Jehubabel's family presented a threat to the rest of the villagers. "His sons have taken his body," he said.

Judah made no reply and side-by-side the two men walked toward the far end of the village.

"We're being followed," Glacon said.

"I had no doubt we would be," Judah responded. Regardless of its necessity, he did not look forward to what he was about to do. He had known the miller all of his life, and when he had been a small boy, he, like all of the other children in the village, had played at the mill.

Jehubabel was one of the wealthiest men in Modin. His house was large and most of it was made of stone and it was roofed over with cedar. Next to it was his mill and olive presses. These were housed in structures of dried mud.

Judah entered the house without knocking on the door. Glacon immediately followed him. The light in the main room came from the late afternoon sun that streamed through the open window.

Jehubabel's body lay on the table. There was blood on the floor and his clothing was stained red. His eyes were still open and there was a strange expression of surprise on his face.

"We were just about to wash him," Nachim, the elder said. He was a good-looking young man with the same fine features as his father. Boaza stood close to his mother. He was sullenly silent.

Judah looked at Rodah, Jehubabel's wife. She was younger than Judah's mother by several years. Her eyes were red from weeping. She had already put on the black gown of a widow. Her brown hair was disheveled.

"My sons," she told him, "said either you or one of your brothers would come to kill us. But I said you would let us live."

Judah glanced at Glacon and moved his eyes to Jehubabel's sons. There was more hate expressed in the countenance of the younger one than in the elder. Perhaps Nachim was, indeed, interested in Rebecca? He looked at Rodah again and pursed his lips. He did not expect to be confronted in this manner and he was unprepared for it. To feel the way he had when he had killed the Seleucids, or even the rage he had felt when he had killed Dion, had been something altogether different from the way he now felt about killing these people.

"Will you let us live," Rodah asked, "or will you punish us because of my husband's fear? Oh, yes, that was why he offered to sacrifice for Zeus. He was afraid of what the Seleucids would do if someone did not step forward. Jehubabel was a good man. He only wanted to prevent trouble."

Judah cleared his throat and he lied, "You were right, Rodah. We came here only to warn you and your sons not to be as foolish as your husband. Gather your belongings together and join us."

"Praise God," she exclaimed and threw herself at Judah's feet. "We'll join you," she wept, "with willing hearts and helpful hands."

Judah raised the woman to her feet. "Be as quick as you can," he said, "we must leave shortly."

She nodded.

Judah motioned to Glacon to leave and then he turned toward the door. He had almost reached it when suddenly Rodah uttered a piercing shriek. Judah leaped forward and whirled around with his sword up. The point of the blade went into Rodah's right breast.

She screamed obscenities at him and still tried to slash him with the knife she held in her hand.

The next instant, Glacon was back in the house. He ran his sword into Boaza's chest, killing him instantly.

Judah shook Rodah off his weapon and thrust it deep into the stomach of Jehubabel's oldest son. Then he went back and killed Rodah. When it was over, he was breathing hard, and he said to his friend, "I should have immediately done what I had come to do."

"Yes," Glacon answered, "you should have."

Judah nodded and, stepping out of the house, he confronted the men who had followed him. Fear was deeply incised on all of their faces. "They're dead," he said.

The men looked questioningly at each other.

"Take what food you find in the house and anything else that we will be able to use," he told them.

"What about the animals?" one of the men asked.

"Take them," Judah answered and, with Glacon at his side, he walked past the men. That they were so obviously afraid of him deeply saddened him.

* * *

The people of Modin assembled in the square, where the bodies of the Seleucid soldiers were already beginning to stink. The women wept and there were tears in the eyes of some of the men.

Once more, Mattathias stood on the small platform and he told the people, "We must move all the rest of the day and well into the night. It is important we put as much distance between this village and ourselves as possible."

"Do you think the Seleucids will follow us?" one of the men questioned.

"God will protect us," Mattathias answered, and then he sought Johanan to help him down. With his staff in his hand, he walked toward the end of the square that led to his land, beyond which the dark masses of the Gophna Hills were always visible.

Again and again, Judah, his brothers, Glacon, and Joseph urged the people to hurry, to move closely, one behind the other. The more difficult the terrain became, the more articles the people discarded, and soon their way was marked with pots, pans, clothing and dozens of other superfluous items. The line quickly became extended a full ten stadia and they had not yet begun the steep ascent into the gorges of the Gophna Hills.

Whenever Judah passed Sarah she was weeping, and almost always Johanan was at her side, trying to comfort her. Finally he realized his oldest brother had not for some time bothered to walk the line of march. He fell in alongside of him and said, "You're needed elsewhere more than here, Johanan."

"She's afraid she will never see her parents again," Judah's brother told him. "I tried to tell her that she will, that all of this is temporary. You tell her, Judah. Maybe, she'll find comfort in your words."

"I can't offer her comfort," he said, "other than to tell her as our father has already told all of us, there isn't any other way for us. We're doing the only thing we can do. Now, Johanan, go and join the others."

"Are you asking me, Judah?"

"No, I'm ordering you to go."

"So you have taken command, even though our father still lives?" "Yes," Judah answered without hesitating. "I've taken command." "But you're the oldest, Johanan," Sarah said, aware of what the two brothers were talking about.

"Then you and Simon have settled the matter between yourselves," Johanan questioned, "without consulting the rest of us?"

"We have the Seleucids to fight," Judah responded, "and not each other. Now go and join your other brothers."

There was an unfamiliar authority in Judah's voice that made Johanan nod, turn, and walk back toward the end of the line of march.

When his brother was out of earshot, Judah told Sarah, "I've taken nothing that belongs to Johanan; don't make trouble between us. I've always loved him and still do."

Without saying more to his sister-in-law, he moved forward to where his father and Simon walked. He did not speak to either of them of his conversation with Johanan, but throughout the day it was very much in his thoughts.

At sunset, the western sky was ablaze with fiery red clouds that stretched across its whole length from north to south. The people whispered to one another that it was a bad omen, that it portended disaster for all of them.

The sky darkened. The red clouds soon turned to mauve and the evening star came up in the East. Within an incredibly short time the sky became black and full of stars.

Mattathias continued to walk, though his pace was now much slower than it had been, and he leaned more and more on his staff.

Even Judah was beginning to feel weary, but as long as his father kept moving, so would he and so would the rest of the people.

With the darkness, came the cold. It was colder in the hills than it was in the village. The barren land around them quickly gave up what heat it had built up during the day.

Then suddenly, a low agonized moan passed along the line like the sign of an autumn wind over a field of grain. Judah turned.

In the distance he saw the flickering red glow of fire. The Seleucids had come to Modin, found their troops had been killed and had put the village to the torch.

Now, men and women alike stopped to look at red blotches in the darkness that had been their homes. They wept openly. Judah felt his throat tighten and was unable to speak.

Only Mattathias could find his voice, and he said, "We must not stop; we must keep going until midnight. By then we'll be far enough away to pause for a few short hours."

They climbed, higher and higher into the rocky defiles of the hills. When they finally stopped, all of them were exhausted, cold and hungry.

Judah and Glacon moved among the people. "Don't light a fire," they told them. "Eat whatever you have and then sleep. Tomorrow will be a hard day."

Judah assigned many men to keep watch over the sleeping camp. With Glacon's aid, he placed them on the high places around the long twisting encampment. Then, he and Glacon returned to where the head of the column was. Each of them stretched out on the ground, Glacon next to Helen, and Judah, alone.

CHAPTER XI

The people were awake long before the sun came up. The men put on their phylacteries and Mattathias led them in their morning prayers.

As soon as their obligation to God was completed, no time was wasted. They began to move at once. Everyone ate on the march and drank a small amount of water.

The sky soon began to grow light. The stars faded. But in the narrow, twisting gorges through which Mattathias led them, the dark shadows lingered until the sun was well up in the morning sky. Then the heat began. The sides of the passes shimmered in the blinding light. More things were discarded by the marchers. Many of the old fell in their tracks and were carried by the younger and stronger men. Every so often, the people would scramble to the top of a sunbaked hill and looked back toward Modin. The blue sky was stained with dark gray smoke. With tears and sobs, they turned away and continued their march.

By midday, Mattathias called a halt and the people dropped to the hard ground where they stood. "Take only a mouthful of water," he told them. "Take only a mouthful. What we have must last us until we arrive at the place where there will be enough water for everyone."

Judah stretched out. He closed his eyes, but the bright glare of the sun penetrated them. He could hear his brothers stirring next to him. His mother whispered something. The words themselves were unintelligible. But his sister's answer was very clear.

"He didn't have to kill Nachim," Rebecca wept. "He didn't have to do that, Mama. I hate him. I'll always hate him for killing Nachim. As God is my judge, I'll always hate him."

And Judah's mother again spoke in a voice too low for him to hear. He cracked open his eyelids and looked in the direction of the voices. His mother was holding his weeping sister in her aims.

Judah never had much to do with his sister. In his eyes, she had always been a little girl. It was impossible for him to conceive of her as anything else. That she could have felt for Nachim the passion a woman might feel for a man seemed unbelievable, yet there she was in her mother's arms weeping for the young man. It struck him then that Ismene might have been, at the very most two, perhaps three, years older than Rebecca. With a sigh, Judah closed his eyes.

Mattathias did not let his followers rest too long. He did not want them dozing off and then, still heavy with sleep, to begin the trek again. It would be much easier for them if they rested for but a short time, and then continued to push into the wilderness.

All through the day, the black shadows of the vultures sailed slowly over them. The people looked up at those silent birds of death and whispered to each other that they would probably die there in the wilderness and be left for the birds to eat.

Judah moved up to where his father was and asked, "How much farther to the water, Mattathias?" Since the day they had together buried Dion, he had taken to calling his father by his name. Though none of the other members of the family would dare do the same thing, Mattathias tolerated it from Judah. There was a strange equality between them that Mattathias did not allow with any of his other sons, even with Simon.

"We've only to cross those hills," Mattathias answered, making with his staff a vague gesture that lacked a specific direction.

Judah glanced back at the ragged line of people following them. They did not look as if they could endure more than a day or two at the very most.

"Point to where the water is," Judah demanded. Up until a few moments before, he had no doubt Mattathias knew exactly where he was going. But Judah was no longer sure of that.

"It's there," Mattathias answered him. "God will guide us to it." "Do you know where it is?"

Wild-eyed, Mattathias faced him and with his staff he pointed to the darkening path in front of them. In a low voice, he said, "Yea, though I walk through the valley of the shadow of death, I will fear no evil, for Thou art with me; Thy rod and Thy staff they comfort me."

Judah's heart began to race. His face flushed with anger. He did not know what to answer. Surely by now, the Seleucid soldiers were scouring the hills near Modin for them, while in front of them lay slow death from hunger, thirst and from the heat.

"Yahweh will be with us," Mattathias said.

Judah nodded and then, raising his blackened staff, he called a halt to the day's march. Mattathias objected.

"We'll stop here for tonight," Judah answered sternly.

"Why are we halting?" Johanan questioned, immediately coming up to the head of the column.

Silently, Mattathias pointed to Judah.

131

"Call your other brothers," Judah told his oldest brother. Johanan hesitated.

"Call them!" Judah ordered.

Johanan nodded and hurried toward the rear of the column, while Judah told his father to go among the people and tell them the day's march has come to an end, that they might light small fires but only to warm themselves.

Mattathias objected to the fires, claiming the Seleucids might be close behind and would be able to see the flickering light of the fires.

"They need the fires to warm and reassure themselves," Judah said. "They don't have the vision of Yahweh that you do."

"And your vision of Him is less than anyone else's," Mattathias responded hotly.

"Go speak to the people, Mattathias," Judah answered, turning his back toward the old man, "they're waiting to hear your words." His father did not answer.

When the sound of the old man's footfalls ceased altogether, Judah turned around and waited for his brothers. Eleazar came first, and he sent him for Glacon and Joseph.

Finally, when they were all assembled, Judah drew them some distance away from the head of the column, where Mattathias sat hunched up close to Miriam and Rebecca. Coming directly to the issue, Judah said, "We're lost; Mattathias doesn't know where the water is."

For a few moments, they were too stunned to speak.

But then Simon asked, "Can we find it on our own?"

"The Gophna Hills . . ." Eleazar began, shook his head and fell silent.

"We can't turn back," Glacon commented. "If we do, we'll be taken by Sostrates' troops. I can assure you, they will deal harshly with every man, woman and child."

Judah and the others nodded.

"Where did he think he was going?" Joseph asked.

"To some place he thought he remembered," Judah answered, glancing at Simon.

"He had mentioned it to me," Simon said, picking up Judah's lie. "He said it was somewhere here in the Gophna Hills."

"Tomorrow we will continue the march as we have today," Judah said. "But the following day, we'll send out groups of men to look for the water."

"And what if they don't find it?" Johanan asked.

"We'll look again the next day, and, if need be, every day after that until we do find it."

Johanan motioned back toward where the people were. Already dozens of small fires flickered in the gathering twilight. "In not too many days," he said harshly, "you won't have to bother about looking for water. There won't be anyone left to drink it."

"Maybe one of us can strike a rock with his staff," Judah growled, "and like Moses have water pour forth."

"The rest of you," Simon said, "go back to the others. If they see all of us here for any length of time, they'll begin to worry. Sooner or later, one of them will chance upon the fact that we're lost."

The men returned to the column, leaving Simon and Judah alone. It was Judah who spoke first, and he said, "I really thought Mattathias knew where he was. It's not going to be easy to find water here. Johanan might well be tight."

"We'll find the water," Simon told him. "Somehow, we'll find it. Yahweh will help us."

Judah looked blankly at his brother and said, "I haven't had any indication that God has ever . . ."

"We'll speak about that another time," Simon said. "Now, I want you to think about what I have to say."

"I'm listening."

"This is more than what you see here," Simon told him, pointing to the people of Modin. "Father was right when he said a mighty army had been raised up. We're the beginning of that army. We must begin to form it so that a new Judea can come into being, a Nation of Israel can come into being. Judah, we can gain control of all of Judea. Yahweh has put that possibility within our grasp, and we must take it. Now, we must run for our lives, so that later we will fight the Seleucids."

"Jews, warriors?"

"They once were," Simon said. "Why not again?"

With a snort of disdain, Judah asked, "With the exception of perhaps twenty men, have you taken a good look at the rest of your warriors?"

"They'll harden," Simon answered. "It won't be easy to do, Judah. But I'm sure it can be done. Think about it. Even if we find water, we can't stay in this wilderness for the rest of our lives. We must do something to preserve our God, so the children of these people and people like them all over Judea will be able to worship the one and only God, the God that made the covenant with Abraham, the God that came to Moses and gave him the laws by which we live." He paused and in a much lower voice, he said, "We must keep the Covenant and the laws, Judah; that is truly the only thing the

Jews ever had, or ever wanted. Our father knew this when he slew Jehubabel and Apelles. If ever I saw a man moved by God's wrath, it was our father at that moment."

Judah glanced toward his father. A small fire now blazed in front of the old man. Its flickering light cast a reddish yellow glow over his face. "If God has a face at all," Judah commented, "it must look something like Mattathias."

Simon chuckled and said, "More than likely all our faces are in His."

Judah scowled, stood up. "I have something to speak to Rebecca about."

The two brothers walked toward where their family was.

Judah made it a point to settle down next to his sister. She started to move away.

"Stay!" he ordered.

"I'm not your servant," she answered angrily.

"You'll listen," he said, "then if you still want to move away from me, you may."

Rebecca did not move.

"I went there intent to kill all of them," Judah explained. "But when I saw them and listened to Rodah's pleading, I changed my mind. I said I came to warn them and I told them to hurry and join the rest of us. When I turned to leave, Rodah struck at me. She tried to kill me with a knife she had hidden in her girdle. I had no choice, Rebecca; after that, all of them had to be killed."

"I would have been his wife," Rebecca wept.

Judah made an open gesture with his hands.

"I was in love with him," she sobbed softly. "And he was in love with me."

"I didn't mean to hurt you," he said, reaching for her.

She hastily drew away and, sobbing, she told him, "Never touch me, Judah; never come near me. You'll die by the sword, Judah. You'll die by the sword, Judah."

Shaken, Judah stood up and hurriedly walked away from his family. Eleazar came after him and said, "Judah, she didn't mean it; she was hysterical. Come back. Come back."

Judah waved him away. "Let me be, Brother, let me be." To stifle his own sobs, he jammed his fist into his mouth.

* * *

Shortly after the Morning Prayer, the people began the trek again. The morning of the second day's march was even more exhausting than the previous day. The heat seemed to be more intense. The very air they breathed scorched their lungs. And always, overhead, the dark birds of death circled around and around, casting their dreaded shadows on the struggling people below.

Once the column began to move, Judah took his position close to its head, from where he could watch his father.

The old man never faltered. He led them from one defile into another.

Judah quickened his pace and came alongside of his father. Mattathias did not look at him, but he knew it was Judah. "You and Rebecca had words last night. She did not mean what she said."

"She knew well enough what she said," Judah answered, almost angrily.

With his free hand, Mattathias waved his son's reply aside. "She is young and foolish. Be generous and give her time to mature," he told him.

"None of us," Judah responded, "has that time any longer. The children are no longer children. The women are no longer just women. We are all soldiers."

Mattathias looked at his son.

Judah could see the fire in his father's eyes; not the black smoke of anger that so frequently in the past rose behind the gray circles, but a light, a sharp, hard light that shone deep inside of them.

The old man nodded and looked away.

Judah did not understand the nature of the light he saw in his father's eyes. It could have been put there by God, or it could mean the old man was mad. More than once, Judah had seen that same burning light in the eyes of madmen on streets of Jerusalem. In the past, many of the sages claimed the mad were God's special people. Even the Greeks had similar thoughts about them.

Again he questioned his father about where they would find water.

"Yahweh will provide," the old man answered. "We have shown our love for Him, and by the Covenant that binds us to Him, He will not let us go thirsty."

Judah said nothing. He dropped back to where he previously had been in the line of march. His father was afflicted with God. That too, could be a form of madness, especially when it blinded the victim to reality.

Sometime before the sun reached its highest point in the sky,

Mattathias led his followers into a broad valley, where the ground beneath their feet was a yellowish white rock.

The sun made the land in front of them move as though it were nothing more substantial than windblown water.

The old man lifted his staff and, pointing to the far side of the valley, he shouted, "We must go there. We must go there!"

A low moan arose from the people.

Mattathias still held his staff aloft and started across the valley.

"Let us rest," several of the men called out, "let us rest!" Mattathias paid them no heed.

In the afternoon they rested in the valley. The sun robbed them of their strength. When Mattathias called for them to continue, many would not, and some could not stand.

Judah, his brothers, Glacon and Joseph went to those who would not stand and pulled them to their feet. By entreaty and by threat, they finally forced them into their places in the column.

The pace was very slow.

The afternoon became an agony for everyone. Then suddenly, Judah saw the horsemen; three were on the right. He looked toward his left. Three were there, too. They were no more than black specks in the distance, but from the sudden spurts of movement, he knew they were mounted.

Immediately, he dropped back to where Glacon was. "Seleucids?" he asked, pointing to the riders.

"Slave traders, I'd guess," Glacon answered.

"I only saw them a short while ago."

"They'll try to take some of us," Glacon commented. "Better arm as many as you can. The horses we have will be no good against them."

"Are you certain they'll attack?" Judah questioned.

"We're money to them," Glacon answered, "nothing more."

"They're moving closer," Judah told his friend.

"Yes, I see. They'll try to capture as many of us as possible before we reach the other side of the valley."

"How long do you think they've been following us?" Judah asked. "Probably since last night when we lit our fires," Glacon said.

"But they had to wait until we were in the open country before they could move against us."

Judah gestured toward his father and said, "Mattathias didn't want us to light fires last night."

"He was right," Glacon commented.

"Yes," Judah answered, "my father was right. And because I was wrong, we'll have to fight, to pay in blood for my mistake."

"The people needed warmth and you gave it to them."

"They'd have been better off to have endured the cold last night, if by doing that they'd have avoided the slavers today."

"Hindsight," Glacon responded.

Judah nodded. With Glacon at his side, he went about the task of distributing the remaining weapons taken from the bodies of the Seleucid soldiers.

The people quickly realized the danger, and even those who were aimed began to bewail their circumstances. They cried out that it would have been better to obey Apelles than to become slaves. Arguments broke out. Friend turned on friend, each accusing the other of having been responsible for his woe.

Mattathias looked at his people and with tears in his eyes, he cried out, "Fear not, we are a mighty army. Our victory has been foretold."

"Go to him," Judah told Eleazar, "and bring him here to me." Then raising his blackened staff, he shouted, "We'll fight those slavers as we fought the Seleucids. They want to take us captive but . . ." He paused, hoping to think of something to give them courage.

The people gathered around Judah. Mattathias came close to his son.

"Tell them, Father," Judah said, "how we'll fight because we want their horses. Tell them how we've come to this valley to lure them to us." Mattathias blinked.

"Let them hear those words from your lips," Judah urgently told his father. And Mattathias shouted, "We've come here to be free. We've come here to capture their horses and not to be captives of those who ride them. We're more than what we were, my children. We're a free people willing to fight for God and His Law!"

The people responded with shouts of approval. When the noise diminished, Judah told them to form themselves into a circle and to move toward the distant mountains in that shape.

"Tell them," Glacon whispered, "that the aimed men will ring that circle."

Judah repeated what his friend said and he added, "No matter what happens, you must keep moving. We can't stop to pick up our wounded. The women will arm themselves with rocks and when the slavers come close enough to the circle they'll throw the rocks at them. Remember, we must have those horses."

The circle was formed. The armed men quickly dispersed themselves around its circumference.

"When the slavers come," Judah called out, "you must keep together. Always together!"

"We will, Judah," many of the people answered. "We'll do everything you ask."

There was no hesitation in the pace of the people now. Despite the intensity of the heat, they moved swiftly, almost at a run.

"Keep together," Judah shouted again and again. His throat was dry; his lips were parched and his chest felt as if it were filled with fire.

The slavers came in very close. They were garbed in flowing black robes and the chains they carried with them jangled ominously. The horses were swift, and the riders were expert.

The slavers made several passes at the moving circle of people, but did not come within striking distance of them. At the last instant, they either forced their mounts to halt, rear up and then turn to gallop off, or they just veered off. The valley reverberated with the pounding of the horse's hoofs and their high, shrill neighing whenever they reared up and beat the air with their forefeet.

Judah soon realized the people would not be able to continue to run much longer; he must find another way to either drive off the slavers or kill them.

He ran to Glacon and said, "Three or four of us might be able to bring one of them down."

"If I can get close enough," Glacon said, "I'd be able to use a spear."

"They cannot keep running like this," Judah told him, gesturing to the people.

"Neither can we," Glacon answered.

Judah shouted for the people to halt. Then he summoned Simon and Johanan. But before he could tell them his plan, the six horsemen came thundering down on the circle of people.

With swords drawn, the slavers swept down on their prey. "Fight them!" Judah shouted.

Glacon took his spear. He sent it hurtling toward an on-coming rider.

The spearhead caught the man in the shoulder and knocked him from his mount. But the horse continued to rush toward the people, scattering them before him. Several fell beneath the animals before one of the men managed to bring him to a halt.

Eleazar rushed out to the fallen slaver and dug his sword into the man's chest.

The other riders swung wide. They re-formed on the opposite side of the people. Within moments they came rushing back.

Many of the men tried to throw spears with the deadly accuracy that Glacon had shown, but none of them possessed the skill. The spears fell far short of their target.

The raiders rushed in and cut two men down, leaving them in a swiftly spreading pool of blood before swinging away.

The people screamed in terror. The members of families clung to one another and prayed for God to help them.

Jonathan and Eleazar ran to Judah and told him they had a way to stop the slavers from killing any more men.

"Then use it," Judah answered. "Use it as quickly as possible." The riders came galloping back toward the circle of people. Their swords flashed in the brilliant sunlight as they waved them over their heads. The five marauders rushed toward them; two in the lead and three following.

Suddenly Jonathan and Eleazar broke from the circle. Keeping close together they ran toward the on-rushing riders, "Come back," Judah shouted, "come back!"

His brothers continued to run toward the riders.

Judah saw that between them they carried a coil of stout rope. He knew their plan. "After them," he cried, "after them!"

Jonathan and Eleazar separated, drawing between them the length of rope. They were so close to the riders and their action was so swift, the raiders could not swerve away.

The first two riders screamed and went down over the heads of their mourns, the following three riders were able to bring their animals to a rearing halt, but they were not able to escape the scythe-like action of the rope, as Eleazar and Jonathan pulled it across them.

Judah and the other men ran to the fray.

The slavers tried to scramble to their feet.

Judah rushed down on a slaver with large, pig-like eyes. Before the men could stand, Judah slashed his neck, severing most of it, but not taking the head off. Blood surged over the blade of Judah's sword.

Glacon killed another slaver by running him through.

Simon speared one through the groin. Then he finished him with a sword.

The rest were put to death by the other men.

Two of the horses had broken their legs and were killed before the men returned to the people, whose shouts of joy were even louder than their screams of terror.

Wet with sweat and stained with fresh blood, Judah and his brothers made their way toward where their father stood.

The old man looked at them, nodded approvingly and asked Judah, "How many horses did we capture?"

"Four," he answered, between gasps of air.

"And how many of us did they capture?"

"None."

"God is with us," Mattathias said and, raising his staff, he called to his people to follow him.

Neither Judah nor any of his other sons told him about the people who had been killed.

And much later, when they were close to the hills they had seen earlier from the other side of the valley, Judah called Johanan and said, "Tomorrow morning, you and Joseph will take the horses and look for water."

Johanan nodded, turned, took several steps, and stopped.

He hesitated and then, facing Judah, he said, "I couldn't have done what you did this afternoon. Without you here, none of us would have had the courage to fight. I spoke to Simon; he told me about the horses. Judah, I am sorry . . ."

"We are brothers," Judah said.

"My hand," Johanan offered, "and my love."

Judah took his hand in his own and said, "And my love, Johanan, my love, too." Then they embraced one another.

CHAPTER XII

The night came cold with a black sky resplendent with stars. Judah did not allow the people to build any fires. Wrapped in their cloaks, they huddled together, not only for warmth but also to diminish the desperate feeling of fear that came to them with the darkness.

There was no movement in the encampment and very little talking. Most of the people stretched out on the hard ground and almost immediately dropped into the welcome abyss of sleep.

Judah sat with his legs drawn up, his cloak wrapped tightly around him and his eyes looking out over the sleeping people. Now and then one would cry out, or moan in anguish, but most slept deeply. He nodded, crossed his arms over his knees and lowered his head.

The conversation he had with Simon the previous evening came back to Judah. He did not really understand Simon. He did not have his brother's vision of the future, the distant future. To him, the future was related to the coming of the sun and to the desperate need for water. If he were to look beyond that, Judah could only see the desperate struggle that would enable them to survive; a struggle that would have to be constantly waged between them and the wilderness, and between them and the Seleucids, who sooner or later would come to slaughter them.

He heard someone stirring. He lifted his head to see who it was. Mattathias had gotten up to urinate. When he was finished, he looked around the encampment and then at the sky.

"Let them sleep," Judah called softly to his father.

"It would be best to start early," the old man said, leaning on his staff.

"We'll not journey today," Judah responded.

Mattathias remained silent. In a disturbing dream just before he had awakened, a faceless man had come to him and had taken his staff and the white robes of his office, and had left him standing naked in the wilderness. That the man in his dream should turn out to be Judah did not in the least surprise him. The blood that bound them as father and son was weaker by far than what each knew about the other.

Despite the fact he had once killed a man in a blind rage, Mattathias had come to walk with God and felt His divine presence, even as he stood before his son, who, though a multitude would follow him, would always walk alone.

"Johanan and Joseph will look for water," Judah explained, "while the people rest."

"Are you sure . . ."

"I'm sure it must be done that way," Judah said.

Mattathias nodded. For a few moments, he said nothing. Then he asked, "Am I to hold no authority over my people?"

"You're their Priest," Judah replied, "their leader."

"Any man could walk at the head of the column," Mattathias commented. "As for being their Priest, you seem to have partially taken that office to yourself."

Judah vigorously shook his head.

"If I only lead," the old man told him, "but don't command, the one who does command has taken from me the most important part of my office."

"It must be that way, Mattathias," Judah said.

"It isn't easy to give up what I've held so many years."

Judah nodded.

"Will you speak through me," the old man questioned, "or will you speak directly to the people?"

"Whenever possible and wherever I can, I'll speak through you."

Mattathias turned away from his son. In a barely audible voice, he said, "I'll let the people sleep." Then with his shoulders back, he returned to where he had slept and, stretching out on the ground, he wrapped his heavy woolen cloak around him to keep the cold away from his trembling body.

Judah walked quietly toward the edge of the encampment and joined the men who were guarding it. The dawn was already beginning to creep up the eastern portion of the sky, annihilating countless numbers of stars in its gray wake. Judah watched the transformation from night to day and derived from it a sense of determination to see the people safely through another day. He would let Simon see into the distant future; for him the present was all-important, his only reality.

* * *

Johanan sat with greater ease on the roan than Joseph did on the piebald. The two horses were magnificent animals, with long, flowing manes and bright, intelligent eyes.

Their instructions from Judah had been to always ride together, to move in a straight line, marking their way at intervals with small piles of stones set alternately against the sides of the defiles through which they would pass. If by midday they had not found water, they were to swing to the right and continue in that direction until just enough of the day would be left to allow them to find their way back to the encampment.

Johanan was not much of a talker. The words he spoke to Joseph were limited to brief comments about where along the way to set the various piles of stones.

Joseph did not enjoy his cousin's silence. By nature, talkative and often boisterous, he found the silence oppressive, even more so than the intense heat.

Johanan was weary and greatly troubled by everything that had happened in the last few days. In one fell swoop, he had lost his land and, like the rest of the villagers, was probably being hunted by Seleucid soldiers. But he was even the more troubled by his relationship with Sarah.

In the short time she had been his wife, he discovered a side of her nature that he would never have guessed existed. She was grasping and envious of practically everyone and everything. Last night when he tried to make love to her, she pushed him away saying, "You gave away your birthright." When he asked her to explain, she would not.

"Your whole family must be very proud of Judah," Joseph commented.

Johanan looked at his cousin.

The young man nodded. "I am proud too, even though I am distantly related."

With a swift movement of his arm, Johanan wiped the sweat from his forehead.

"Judah," Joseph said, "is the bravest man I ever saw. The people say that he has the strength of ten men."

"We will ride a bit further," Johanan told his cousin, "before we swing around to the right."

Joseph nodded. He kept silent for a while, measuring Johanan's actions and then he commented, "But the people fear him. Well, fear isn't exactly the right word. What I mean is that they don't trust him. No, that isn't right either. What I'm really trying to say is that his reputation from the past doesn't sit well with them in the present."

Johanan glanced at his cousin but did not speak. Some of what the young man said he had already heard from Sarah.

"Some of your own friends," Joseph said, "claimed he needlessly slew Jehubabel's family, that if Glacon hadn't been there with Judah, it wouldn't have happened."

"People talk about things they don't know!" Johanan answered sharply.

"No matter what they say," his cousin answered, "I'd still like to be as good a fighter as Judah. He's afraid of no man and every man is afraid of him. Some day, I hope he'll let me lead men."

Johanan frowned, and he looked questioningly at his cousin.

"Your own father, Johanan, has said it many times, 'a mighty army has been raised up' and I want to be one of the leaders in that army. I want to lead it to victory for God and for His people."

Johanan looked away. He was a farmer. They were all farmers in the village of Modin, even the craftsmen were farmers, owning a plot of land on which they raised practically all the food for their own needs. Farmers were not soldiers.

Ruffled by a gentle breeze and his gray eyes full of fire, no one watching him then could doubt that God stood next to their Priest as he spoke to them. "We've done," he said, "what Jews haven't done since the days of Moses. We've come out of a place of oppression. We've smote those who'd have bent us to their will. But it was His will that prevailed."

Mattathias' words to the people were more than just the words of a man. He had, like Moses, led them through a terrible wilderness to keep them safe, to keep them from committing apostasy. Now they loved him for what he had done for them.

After a pause, he said, "We will prevail. It was His will that has brought us here and it will be His will that, until time is no more, will guide us and those who follow us. Yahweh has seen fit to make us His defenders, to test us and by testing us, to renew His love for us and our love for Him. Long, long ago, He said, 'Thou shalt have no other gods before Me.'"

"That was what he said to our forefathers and that is what He has said to us. If we don't hold to the Covenant between us, or the laws He gave us, then we aren't His people and He'll leave us to the abominations of paganism. He'll turn away from us, and our lives will be full of woe. What we've done and what we'll do, is to keep Him with us for the rest of our days and teach our children to do the same, so that they'll teach their children. The Covenant between the Jews and God a thousand years from now, two or three thousand years from now, will be the same as it is between ourselves and Him. They'll follow His laws even as we follow them. He'll triumph over Zeus and over all of the other false gods because of what we've done and what we will yet do to keep all that He has given to us."

For several moments everyone was silent, and then as if they were one voice, the people shouted, "Hear, oh Israel, the Lord is our God, the Lord is one."

Many of the men rushed forward to Mattathias and, placing him on their shoulders, they paraded the old man along the shore of the lake, singing songs of praise.

Judah stood with his mother and watched the joyous procession. He was pleased that the people were honoring his father. Mattathias' faith was as beautiful and as alive as he was. He said as much to his mother.

"But it was you who . . ." she began.

Judah waved her silent and shaking his head, he told her, "It's his time, Mother; let him have it."

"You love him that much?" she questioned, gently touching her son's arm.

"I' in his son," Judah answered, patting her hand. Then looking past his mother to where Rebecca stood, he asked, "How is she?" "With God's help," his mother answered, "she'll soon forget." Judah looked down and said, "I'd speak to her if I thought she'd listen. But I don't think she would."

"Give her more time," Miriam said. "She'll understand Yahweh's hand was with yours when you . . ."

She could not bring herself to mention Nachim's name. Better than anyone in the family, she knew what her daughter's feelings toward the young man had been. But she also knew Judah was forced to slay him.

Judah suddenly caught sight of Glacon and Helen. They were walking hand-in-hand close to the edge of the water

"I must speak to Glacon," he told his mother. He did not wish to continue the conversation about his sister any longer. If Rebecca wanted to hold him responsible for what had happened for the rest of her life, she could. He would try to talk with her once more, but if that failed, he would not try again.

"He's a good man," his mother said, referring to Glacon.

"Very good," Judah answered.

"And she's a beautiful woman."

Judah nodded and told his mother he would return shortly; then he hurried to Glacon and Helen.

Speaking first to Helen, Judah told her what his mother had just said about her.

She laughed and said, "Her own daughter is as beautiful as any woman could hope to be."

With a nod, Judah acknowledged the compliment for his sister and then, looking at Glacon, he said, "We must find out more about this place."

"Make a reconnaissance," Glacon corrected.

Judah repeated the phrase and then he said, "I've much to learn, friend."

"You will," Glacon assured him. "You'll learn from me, and then you'll turn around and teach me."

"We don't have the time," Judah said. "Later this afternoon, you and I will make a reconnaissance of the entire lake. We'll go on horse."

"As you wish, Judah," Glacon answered.

"I'll find you when I'm ready," Judah told him. Then to Helen, he said, "I'm happy Glacon brought you to us. I think my mother would be willing to teach you our ways, if you'd be willing to learn."

Helen looked at Glacon. Her blue eyes were wide and beseeching.

"How could any man refuse that expression?" Glacon laughed and he gave his assent with a nod.

"Have you seen the slaves Johanan and Joseph have freed?" Judah asked.

"Some are with your people celebrating your father, and three are up there on the bank, just to the left of the gorge's mouth."

Judah saw them, a woman and an old man. "How many able-bodied men?" he questioned.

"Six."

"The rest?"

"Three women, one carrying a child in her belly and the other two no older than your sister."

Judah looked toward the throng of joyous people. The men were still carrying Mattathias on their shoulders, and he was laughing.

Judah turned his attention back to the woman and the old man. Without saying anything more to either of them, he left Glacon and Helen. Slowly, he made his way up the slope of the bank to where three people sat huddled together.

Becoming aware that the tumult behind him had ceased, Judah paused and looked back. His father was no longer being carried, and many of the people had clustered together in family groups. Some began to gather firewood.

Judah cupped his hands, and from where he was, he shouted down to them, "There'll be no fires!" He repeated it several times, and his words like those of his father's echoed and re-echoed across the lake.

"Why not, Judah?" one of the men challenged. "We need hot food."

"There'll be no fires!" he shouted again.

Several of the villagers started up the slope of the hill. One of them called out, "We've come all the way. Now we need food and rest."

"What if the smoke should be seen?" Judah spoke back at them.

"But we are safe here," a second man shouted.

"We are safe as long as no one else knows we are here," Judah answered. "Go pick fruits and berries and eat them."

"When will we be safe?" the first man asked.

"Safe? Perhaps never," Judah answered. "But safe enough to light a fire soon, I hope, very soon."

None of them answered and they retreated down the slope.

Judah turned his back on the people and steadily made his way up to the mouth of the gorge. The slope was very steep. Several times, he was forced to use his blackened staff to help him climb. Almost there, he paused, wiped the perspiration from his brow and looked up at the woman.

She was olive-skinned. Her eyes were amber and her brown hair was long, but badly tangled. Her breasts were practically bare. She was slender but her hips were wide.

As for the old man, he sat with his eyes closed, but his build was the male counterpart of the woman's. He was narrow-boned and slender. His hair was brown like hers, though it was flecked with gray.

It took Judah a few moments to realize the man was moaning softly to himself.

"He will not live out the night," the woman said. She spoke Koine, rather than Hebrew or Greek.

Judah nodded and asked what the relationship between them was. "He is my father," she said.

"How did you fall into the hands of the slavers?" he asked.

She pointed to the southwest. "We were sold to them by the Seleucid soldiers at Ashkelon," she explained. "We are

Jews. My father was a merchant. Then a few days ago . . ."
She bit her lip to stifle her sobs.

"Where were they taking you?" Judah questioned.

Unable to speak, the woman shook her head.

He looked at her father and asked what had happened to
him.

"They beat him," she murmured. "They beat him, and
then they made him watch while they ..." She closed her
eyes and forced herself to speak. "They made him watch
while they raped me. When it was all over, they blinded him.
I think they had meant to leave him here to die."

"Your name?" Judah asked.

"Shulamith," the woman said.

"And his name?" Judah asked, pointing to her father.

"Imlah."

"Take my staff," Judah told her, "and I will carry your
father down to my family."

"And your name?" Shulamith asked, as she took the
staff from him.

"Judah," he told her, lifting Imlah into his arms. "I am
Judah, son of Mattathias, the Priest of Modin.

"But you are their leader," she said, following alongside
of him.

"My father is their leader," Judah answered. But after a
moment, he added in a lower voice, "but I command." He
glanced at her to see if she understood, but she was too intent
on caring for her father to be interested in what he had said.
She moved gracefully and he could not help but notice the
way her buttocks curved against the cloth of her dress.

When the slope became gentler, she asked, "Why have
all of your people come to this place?"

"It's a long story," he said. "But you heard my father. We would not bow to Antiochus and accept Zeus as our God."

"We did," she responded in a low voice. "But it didn't stop the Seleucid soldiers from killing my mother and taking us into slavery."

Judah stopped. In a hard voice, he said, "Say nothing about that to anyone here, not ever. Do you understand? Never tell anyone that you became Greeks."

Her brown eyes went wide with fear.

"We're Jews," he said. "We've fought for our God and have shed blood for Him."

She shuddered.

"You're Jews, that's all anyone has to know," Judah said.

Shulamith nodded, and in a whisper, she asked, "Are you filled with disgust . . ."

"I don't walk with Yahweh," Judah said. "I serve Him, but we're strangers to each other."

Without speaking, they continued down the slope. When they reached the place where Mattathias sat, Judah set Imlah down on the ground. He explained to his father who the man was and how his daughter and son were bought from the Seleucid soldiers by the slavers. He told his father he was leaving the three newcomers in his care while he and Glacon would spend the rest of the afternoon making a reconnaissance of the entire lake.

Joseph immediately asked to be taken along.

"No," Judah said. "Glacon and I will go alone."

"But what if you should run into trouble," Joseph argued, "would the two of you be able to fight your way out?"

"If we couldn't," Judah answered, "then we'd be killed."

"God forbid!" his mother exclaimed.

"Shulamith," Judah said, "my family will give you whatever you need."

She thanked him.

"I'll be back sometime after nightfall," Judah told them. Then, looking at Simon, he said, "Remember, no fires."

"Yes, Judah," Simon replied. "We'll carry out your order."

Judah turned and went to find Glacon.

* * *

To Judah, Glacon and the gray stallion he rode looked as if they were one entity, fused together by the expertise of the rider and the uncanny acknowledgment of that skill by the animal.

"This is a good mount," Glacon said, patting the neck of the animal. "But so are all of the other horses we took from the slavers."

"Horse flesh or human flesh," Judah commented harshly, "is all the same to them. Given an ability to judge one, I imagine the same ability develops to judge the other. From what I know of them, they think more of a good horse than they do of human beings, unless it happens to be a beautiful woman, and they either use her for their own pleasure or sell her to someone else."

The angry tone in Judah's voice warned Glacon not to pursue the subject. Most Jews, he had come to learn, hated the whole institution of slavery. Long ago they had written a provision into their laws requiring the owner of a slave to set him free after a seven-year period of servitude. No other people, as far as he knew, had a similar law. Except among the Jews, a slave lived and died as property of his master.

"You know," Judah said, looking at his friend, "my father had no idea where he was going."

"Perhaps he really did know."

"I think you'd agree with my father," Judah laughed, "if he told you he was God."

"He has been more than generous to me," Glacon answered, "even though I often have the feeling when he looks at me that he doesn't really see me, but sees someone else."

Judah nodded, remembering a similar conversation that he had with Glacon just before Apelles came to Modin. "He is an old man," Judah commented, "and the events of these times go hard with him. He remembers better days, and sometimes, I think, those recollections become his reality. Old people are that way."

"It's something more with your father," Glacon said. "Something he sees that no one else can. Perhaps it's your God, or some manifestation of Him?"

Judah cocked his head to one side. Though he knew his father walked with God, he had never thought of him as being one of the few chosen, out of the many, to speak for God.

"He's a good man," Glacon commented.

"Better by far than I'll ever be," Judah answered.

Glacon took time to weigh the meaning of his words before he said, "I once told you, my friend, you're more like your father than you realize, and you tried to deny it. But these last few days have strengthened that impression, not lessened it. Yet, I sense a barrier between the two of you, some invisible wall that neither one of you has the strength or even the desire to pull down."

"We know each other too well," Judah replied with a forced smile.

"Then you don't love him?" Glacon questioned with a frown of indignation, for he had grown to love Mattathias.

"I love him," Judah said, "as I know he loves me. But sometimes between father and son love isn't enough to bring them together. The very best that either of us can manage is what we now are to each other."

"But at Modin and on the march here, you held the people to his standards."

"He's my father," Judah responded.

"Is that your only answer?"

"Yes, it is."

"But you and all of the people here are in revolt against Antiochus! Is this the right moment to push your father aside?" Glacon exclaimed, stunned by the simplicity of Judah's answer.

"I will lead them."

"Why?"

Judah smiled wryly, and he said, "Because I can do it better than anyone else, and because I sometimes think my father made it happen this way."

"And what about your God and His laws?"

"I'll fight to preserve them."

"But do you believe in them?" Glacon pressed.

"Yes, but not the same way my father and so many of my people do. I told you once, I was born a Jew and therefore I am one."

"You could have changed that," Glacon said. "Many of your people have."

Judah shook his head. "From the eighth day of my life," he said, "I was bound to my father's God and can never deny that bond."

"I understand that," Glacon told him. "But I don't understand your relationship to your God."

"There isn't any," Judah replied softly. "I've never felt His presence as my father and brothers have."

"I can't believe that."

With a nod Judah said, "It's true, Glacon, I wouldn't say it if it weren't true."

After a pause, Glacon asked, "Is that what stands between you and your father?"

Judah shrugged.

They had circled the entire shoreline of the lake. The bank opposite the opening to the gorge was flat for five or six stadia, then the cliffs rose precipitously to a high escarpment.

On the southern shore of the lake there were thick growths of reeds, while on the northern end there were many different kinds of bushes. The soil was good only on the eastern side, where the people were already camped. The lake was really the bottom of a bowl, fed by underground springs. The only opening to it was the gorge through which Mattathias had led their people.

"We won't be able to grow enough food for all of us here," Judah said, as they rode up the slope on the eastern side of the lake. "Vegetables and a few goats and chickens would be the best that could be gotten out of the land."

"It won't be easy to keep the people content with such a meager diet," Glacon commented.

"It'll be impossible," Judah said, looking down from the ridge to where the people were. He searched among them for his own family, and when he finally saw them, he sought out Shulamith. A sudden warmth sprung into his groin, the way it once had when he had been with Ismene after not having seen her for a long time. He had not felt anything like that for a woman since the night that Ismene had been killed. To change the direction of his own thoughts, Judah commented on the ruggedness of the terrain surrounding the lake.

"It can easily be defended," Glacon told him. "Men on the ridges here would be able to see in every direction."

"We'll have to post guards," Judah said.

"But if we're ever trapped here," Glacon explained, "the only way would be to climb the cliffs . . . on the far side, where they're steepest."

"Do you think this might serve as our base?" Judah questioned. "Yes, a very good one."

They moved along the top of the cliffs, and by the time they had reached the eastern side, the sun was very low in the sky. The numbing coldness took hold of them.

"It'll be somewhat warmer," Glacon said, "once we are back at the lake."

Wrapping his cloak around himself, Judah asked, "Do you think you could train the men to fight?"

"If they're willing to learn."

"There isn't any other choice," Judah replied, "if they want to live. From here, we must take our first steps. Over the centuries we've somehow lost the will to fight and now, if we're to survive, we must regain it."

"I can only teach them *how* to kill," Glacon said. "Everything else must come from them."

"For all of us and for those of us who will follow," Judah said, "I hope it does, because if these men lack the will to fight, everything will end here. The Jews will cease to exist and God will cease to exist."

Before they reached the camp, darkness settled over the land. They dismounted and slowly led their horses down the steep slope.

When Judah finally rejoined his family, he found Shulamith crying over the cold body of her father, while Simon tried to comfort her.

* * *

In the weeks that followed their arrival at the lake, Glacon trained every able-bodied man to use a spear, a short sword, a knife, rocks, clubs and, if no other weapon was available, their hands. Judah and all his brothers were Glacon's students, too. But Judah soon proved himself even more skilled than Glacon.

At night, after the evening meal of dates and nuts, Glacon told them over and over again, "The strength of the Seleucid army is in its phalanx of two hundred and fifty-six men, which consists of sixteen men in sixteen ranks. When a phalanx is committed to action, the first five ranks hold their spears horizontally and the remaining eleven hold their spears vertically until they come into action.

"The phalanx," he said, "could move into a V formation, or wheel to the left or right at the command of its officers. They are protected on their flanks by light cavalry units armed with swords and lances. Slingers and archers often precede them. They fight best in flat open country. They are more of a fighting machine than anything else in the world. There are four phalanxes to a large unit called a chiliad and usually there are two of these for any moderate engagement. On the march, the front of sixteen is usually reduced to four."

Every night, Glacon would carefully explain the various actions in which he had taken part. Every detail was important, and he always made a point of first asking the men what they would have done in a particular combat situation before describing what really had happened.

Lying awake after having listened to Glacon, Judah pondered his situation. At his disposal he had a hundred men, less than one half of the size of a Seleucid phalanx. Though Glacon had trained them well, they would be no match for the discipline and precision of the troops in a phalanx. But he knew that, sooner or later, he would have to make a move, if for no other reason than to bring meat and flour to the people and, almost as important, to test his men in battle. They were growing restless and desperately needed to prove themselves.

Late one afternoon, when Glacon had just finished showing them again how to use a short sword, Simon beckoned to Judah. "Do you have time to walk along the shore of the lake for a while?"

Judah nodded and fell in alongside of his brother. Everything was in leaf and it was pleasantly warm. There was even the sound of bees in the air.

When they were some distance from the camp, Simon said, "Judah, it is time to strike, or the weapon will become blunted."

"We'll fight, Simon, and we'll win. I don't want to have one of my men killed because I made the mistake of thinking that the sum total of my force is more than it is. If we have an army and fight Seleucids as they'd like us to fight them, then, my brother, we'll be defeated, and all that we've done and all that we hope we can do, will be lost. We must fight them on our own terms, in our own way."

Simon nodded. Immediately, he knew his brother probably had been thinking about the matter in greater detail than even he had.

"I once told you," Judah said, "that I don't have your vision of what might come from all of this. That's still true. I don't know, as you claim to, that our father is considered by the people to be the High Priest and that each of us is heir to that throne. I leave that to you, Simon. You're far more learned than the rest of us and, therefore, in matters of policy and religion, you can guide us. But don't tell me what to do when it comes to fighting. Suggest, and I'll listen. But don't tell me!"

For several moments they looked at each other without speaking. Then Simon lowered his eyes and said, "I'm sorry, Judah. I was foolish not to have understood that you, more than anyone else, would be aware of what had to be done."

"Glacon, too," Judah said, "has been thinking about it."

Simon raised his eyes to meet his brother's and he asked, "Are you angry with me?"

"Annoyed, but not angry, Simon," Judah responded. "More than anyone in this world I trust you."

"I will not fail you."

With his arm, Judah circled his brother's shoulder and as they moved back to the camp, he asked Simon about Shulamith.

"She is courteous to me," Simon told him. "But nothing more. Why do you ask?"

"I've seen you sit near her many, many times since she came here."

"If you have any interest in her Judah, I will…"

"No," Judah responded, "I've neither the time nor the patience to pay court to a woman."

"But if you had?" Simon questioned.

Judah pursed his lips pensively and he said, "She'd be better off with someone like you than someone like myself."

"She mightn't think so," Simon told him.

Judah laughed and said, "That would be because she doesn't know me."

Without telling anyone, Judah left the camp before the first light of day grayed the eastern sky. He took only his water bottle, a small quantity of dried fruits and the blackened staff that had once belonged to the old priest, Eleazar.

He moved through the gorges around the encampment and, by nightfall, he returned to the campsite, satisfied that none of the twisting defiles provided a direct route to it.

He sat by the fire and explained to Glacon, "A man would have to know where this place was, unless he stumbled upon it by accident, as Johanan and Joseph had, or if he were able to follow someone here."

"Then you think we're safe here?"

Judah nodded and in a somber voice, he said, "Should I fail to return, stay with my people. Help them survive. For counsel, go to Simon, and for strong, willing hands to aid your own, seek Jonathan and Eleazar."

Glacon was keenly aware that Judah had not mentioned Johanan.

"If some of the men dispute your authority," Judah told him, "deal with them fairly, but don't let them decide what you must do."

"Yes, my friend."

"And as for my brother, Johanan," Judah said with a sigh, "burden him as little as possible; my sister-in-law is already a heavy burden for him."

"I'd go with you, if you'd have me."

Judah shook his head. "You're more valuable to them now," he told Glacon; "than I am. From you they learn how to fight in order to survive." Then grasping his friend's hand, he added, "Speak to no one about what I said. If I don't come back, after the solstice, then go to Simon and relate what I have told to you."

"Will you speak to him before you go?"

"He'll know by what you tell him that what you say is the truth. It's better that neither he, nor for that matter anyone else, know. I'll continue to leave the camp as I did this morning, then one day I won't return."

"They will panic," Glacon responded, "or, worse still, they might flee from here. It'd be better if you left me with some sort of explanation. They might even think you had deserted them."

Judah ran his hand over his beard and thought about what his friend had said. "Then tell them," he replied, "that I've gone into the wilderness."

"For what purpose?"

With a smile, Judah said, "They're Jews; they will fit the purpose to the action. It'll give them something to think about."

"Guard yourself," Glacon cautioned.

"If I don't," Judah smiled, "no one else will." Then he stood up and went to where he slept.

He lay with his hands behind his head and looked up. The moon was very bright, but not yet full. A few clouds in the south looked like puffs of silver. All around him the night was filled with familiar noises. The rustling sound made by the breeze as it moved through among the leaves and reeds. The croaking of the frogs. The sighs of the people as they slept, and even their whimpers.

Judah's conversation with Glacon made him keenly aware of his own mortality. It was then that he realized how much he loved life and, from now on, how close he must walk with death. The magnitude of such a thought before going to sleep was enough to keep him awake.

Then remembering his sister's malediction, Judah sat up and looked toward where she slept. There was nothing between them, no conversation, not even a meeting of eyes. She had become more and more withdrawn from everyone. He did not know how to deal with her. His second attempt to speak to her had not come to pass. He could not bring himself to do it. Perhaps in time, he would or she might by some miracle come to understand that he had not wanted to kill Nachim. But he doubted that either one of the two possibilities would ever happen.

Hunching his shoulders in resignation, Judah was about to stretch out again when he realized Shulamith was practically standing in front of him. He had been so deep in thought about his sister he had not seen the woman approach.

He started to stand but she motioned him not to.

Sitting down next to him, she said, "I wasn't able to sleep, either." After what she had experienced, he could understand why she could not sleep, "In time, it will be easier," he told her.

"Hold me Judah," she said in a low voice. "Hold me . . . the way no other man can hold a woman."

"My brother..." he started to say, remembering Simon's interest in her.

"I've come to *you,*" she told him, revealing her nakedness. Judah took her into his aims.

"Love me," Shulamith whispered, as she opened herself to him. His hand glided over the kinky thatch of her pubis and gently stroked the moist lips of her sex.

"Judah," she said, "I couldn't wait for you to come to me."

He kissed her deeply, enjoying the taste of her mouth. Then, very slowly, he entered her.

She moaned softly and moved against him.

Judah spread his hands over her breasts.

Shulamith looked up at him and with a smile on her lips, she said, "I knew it would come to this from the first time I saw you."

"I think I knew it, too," he told her, quickening his thrust. For the first time in months, Judah again experienced the pleasure of sleeping with a woman. Though he shared no more than his body with her, it was enough to satisfy both of them.

Some days later, when he rose to leave the camp before first light, as he had on previous mornings, Shulamith awoke and asked, "Will you return tonight?" Before he could answer, she said, "I dreamt you were lost."

He moved his hand over her breasts, enjoying their warm pliantness and the way her nipples hardened when he stroked them. "It was only a dream," he said.

"I don't think you will return," she responded, holding his hand hard against her breast.

"Go back to sleep," he told her.

"Have I been good for you?" Shulamith questioned.

"Yes."

She kissed the back of his hand.

Before Judah left, he bent close to her and whispered, "It was good to be inside of you." A short while later, he walked out of the Gophna Hills and circuitously returned to Modin.

Nothing remained of it. All the dwellings had been gutted by fire. Here and there a large rat darted from one protective place to another. In the burnt-out shell of his father's house, Judah changed clothing. Taking off the traditional vestments worn by Jews, he put on the dress of a Seleucid.

For several weeks, Judah moved around the countryside, ranging as far north as Samaria, west to Joppa on the coast and then to Jerusalem itself. He carefully noted every pass leading to Jerusalem from every direction. He frequented taverns and inns to learn what the people and the soldiers thought had happened to Modin. No one really knew. One rumor blamed the death of Apelles and his men on the plague. Another account blamed a band of nomads, who came out of the wilderness, killed Apelles and his men and then took the Jews captive. Only once, in a small tavern in Jerusalem, where Judah was chinking wine with a middle-aged Seleucid soldier, did the explanation come anywhere near the truth. The seasoned campaigner said, "I think the Jews did it. I was with the patrol that went into the village. Bodies everywhere. We followed the Jews into the Gophna Hills for a while, even came across things they discarded. But it did not make sense to continue the chase. Most of them had either died after a few days from thirst or were taken by slavers. Those hills are a terrible place, a terrible place to have to go."

Judah agreed and laughingly told his drinking companion he had no intentions of ever going near that dreadful place.

Judah was careful to avoid the taverns where he might be recognized. But, even with this precaution, he came face to face with Amran, Eleazar's son-in-law, who like himself was dressed in Seleucid clothing and looked exceedingly more prosperous than he had in the past.

Amran called out to him, but Judah turned the other way and quickened the pace. Amran came running after him, calling out his name. Judah stopped and turned to confront his pursuer.

"You are Judah?" Amran whispered, looking questioningly at him and at the blackened staff.

Judah shook his head.

"You must be," Amran insisted. "Your father is Mattathias. He and my father-in-law ..."

"My name," Judah told him, "is Glacon. I've come here to buy olive oil."

Amran's eyes widened questioningly.

Realizing the name Glacon meant something to him, Judah said, "Now, if you will excuse me, I must be on my way."

"Where are you staying in the city?"

"I am leaving today," Judah lied.

Amran nodded, apologized for having been mistaken and said, "You could easily be the twin brother of the man I once knew."

"Perhaps someday," Judah offered, "you will meet him." He nodded politely, turned and hurried away.

Meeting Amran did not sit well with Judah, but there was nothing he could do about it. He had to remain in the city for another few days to find out as much as possible about the Seleucid garrison. He had already seen Sostrates. But he wanted to discover how Sostrates utilized his troops, especially how many men were in the morning patrols that left the city and marched into the countryside.

That night, when Judah finally fell asleep, he dreamt about what had happened to Ismene. With a cry of terror, he bolted up. He was wet with sweat. His heart was pounding loudly. He reached for the pitcher of wine on the nearby table and poured himself a drink. He drank several more before he dropped off into a drunken stupor.

* * *

The same evening, Amran presented himself to Menelaus in his apartment at the palace. "I met Judah, the son of Mattathias, the Priest of Modin."

Since the murder of his brother and the subsequent appointment of Sostrates as the military commander of Jerusalem, Menelaus had devoted his time to three pursuits:

lechery, drunkenness, and intrigue against Sostrates. He gave up any pretense of worshipping Yahweh; now he sacrificed to Zeus in what had once been the Temple of the Jews.

Bleary eyed from too much wine, Menelaus looked at the man who had been his brother's drinking companion. He was having trouble making sense out of what he had just heard. After an enormous belch, Menelaus made an imperious gesture with his hand. "I have told you many times not to bother me with trivial matters. My time must be spent in philosophical contemplation and not on your chance encounters."

Amran moved closer to the couch on which Menelaus reclined. "My Lord," he said, "the man I met calls himself Glacon."

Menelaus started to tremble; his face blanched. He tried to speak but could not make a sound.

"But he is not Glacon," Amran explained. "He is Judah, the son of Mattathias, who was the Priest in the village of Modin."

Menelaus pushed himself into an uptight position.

"Judah and his father were with my father-in-law."

"I remember," Menelaus said, getting to his feet. "Mattathias was the old man with the white beard, he was the one who held the body of Eleazar in his arms."

"It was Judah, his son, who picked up my father-in-law's blackened staff. He had it with him when I saw him this afternoon."

"A giant of a man with blonde hair and a blonde beard?"

"Yes."

To clear his head, Menelaus rubbed his temples.

"Judah must know what happened at Modin," Amran said. "He must know, because he was there."

Hand trembling, the High Priest reached for his wine glass, brought it half to his mouth. Then changing his mind, he set it down on the table. "Now is not the time to drink," he commented, more to himself than to his visitor. He walked to the window. The western sky looked like a blacksmith's fire; it was red with the setting sun.

"So we've found one Jew from Modin," Menelaus said, "and I suppose you think that if there's one there's bound to be more?"

"Yes."

Menelaus was still at the window. He was not quite sure how to use the discovery to his advantage.

"My Lord," Amran said, "I don't think his use of Glacon was coincidental. But I'm sure it was an accident. No doubt it was the first name that came into his mind."

Menelaus turned from the window and walked back to the couch, though he did not sit down.

"They were known to be friends," Amran said. "They often wrestled and I remember having heard a rumor about a brawl in a tavern during which Glacon had helped Judah fight his way out. Something to do with a prostitute. I think her name was Ismene. I took the liberty of visiting the tavern before I came here, and I spoke with the proprietor. He remembered Glacon and Judah. They always came there, and Judah always went with the woman. I gathered that the Seleucid soldiers killed her because she obviously preferred to lie with Judah than with any of them."

"Then you think Judah might know where Glacon and that slave, Helen, might be."

Amran nodded.

Menelaus balled the fist of his right hand and several times pounded it into the palm of his left hand, saying, "To capture Glacon would be a gift from the gods."

"It would improve your fortunes immensely, My Lord," Amran replied. He glanced around at the small apartment occupied by Menelaus; it was far less sumptuous than his quarters had been when Antiochus had been in the city.

Menelaus sat down on the couch, and this time he took a sip of wine. Once before, he had made the mistake of acting, without giving too much thought to the consequence, and that had cost him a fortune; this time he would wait.

"You've done well," Menelaus told his underling. "Very well, indeed." And going to a small closet that stood on a table at the opposite side of the room, he removed several pieces of gold and gave them to Amran. "Now I want you to find out much more about Judah and Glacon. When we have enough information to prove that at least some of the Jews from Modin survive, we will use it to our advantage."

"Yes, My Lord," Amran answered humbly.

CHAPTER XIV

Though the sun was still bright on the top of the cliffs surrounding the lake, the camp itself was already shrouded in a rapidly deepening twilight. Everywhere on the eastern shore there were bright red flickers of fires.

Mattathias and his family occupied one of the largest huts in the camp. His sons and Glacon had built it. Though there was some discussion about whether Shulamith should be allowed to live in it, the matter was settled when Glacon interceded on her behalf, telling them that he and Helen would leave and give shelter to the woman, rather than let her be turned away.

Neither Mattathias nor his sons would hear of that, and so Shulamith became part of the household.

The late spring would soon become summer, and Glacon was beginning to worry about Judah.

Then, one evening when their meal was finished and the reddish light of the fire touched the faces of everyone around it, Johanan said, "It's time we talk, Father."

Mattathias, who was sitting across from his oldest son, did not reply but nodded, thus giving him permission to continue speaking.

Glacon softly cleared his throat. More strongly than eve, he felt that he was an outsider, and before Johanan spoke again, he said, "Perhaps I should leave your fire."

"No," Johanan said. "You're as much a part of this as any of us, perhaps more." Then he asked his father, "What are we doing here? I'm asking not only for myself, but for all the people of the village. Here in the wilderness we're nothing. We have nothing."

"We have our God," Mattathias answered gently.

175

"Father, even Judah has gone," Johanan said.

"He's in the wilderness; he walks with ..."

"No," Johanan declared. "He is gone; neither you nor I, nor anyone, knows where Judah is, or even if he still lives."

"Johanan is right," Simon said, his voice just loud enough to be heard.

And then Rebecca spoke up and told them, "Judah is dead; in a dream I saw him taken by the Seleucids and flayed alive."

A terrible silence fell over the members of Mattathias' household. "A dream can't be trusted," Eleazar finally said.

"Trust it or not," Rebecca responded, "Judah is dead."

"Because you wish him dead," Eleazar hissed, "that doesn't make it so. In my dream, Judah lives and is, even at this time, on his way back to us."

Rebecca uttered a disdainful snort.

For several moments, everyone was talking at once: some contending that Judah was dead, others proclaiming just as vociferously that he was alive.

Exasperated, Mattathias abruptly demanded silence. "Let Johanan speak," he said.

"Again and again," Johanan told his father, "I've asked myself what am I doing? Why have I come here?"

Mattathias nodded. His eyes went from son to son. It had never occurred to him that they did not know the answers to Johanan's questions, yet from the expression on all of their faces, it was painfully obvious they did not know. Uttering a deep sigh, he said, "We carry out God's words. We're his instrument."

"But how, Father?" Johanan pressed. He had in the back of his mind all these weeks what Joseph had told him about the book written by a man named Daniel.

Mattathias turned his eyes toward Glacon.

"What has Daniel to do with us being here?" Johanan asked, his voice now rising in anger.

Mattathias answered, "Eleazar said, "You don't know him as I do. 'He'll come to you by another name.'"

"Who, Father?" Johanan shouted. "Tell us who?"

"'And a mighty army shall rise up against the King and smite him,'"

Mattathias said, now looking back to his son.

Johanan rubbed his beard and in a low growl, he said, "We've followed the raving of a dead man. We're the victims of some witless elder who calls himself a prophet and has written . . ."

"A mighty army has risen up," Mattathias said gently.

"And all of us here are its soldiers."

Johanan shook his head. His worse fear had come to pass. Looking at his brothers, he asked, "What's to be done?"

"Nothing, until Judah returns," Eleazar responded.

"You'd walk through fire for him," Johanan said, "but his trust is in Simon and his love is for Simon."

Miriam tried to silence her oldest son.

"I only speak the truth," Johanan shouted. "I only say what everyone else knows. And Simon . . ."

"And Simon what?" Simon asked.

"And Simon would prefer to see his brother dead so that he could bed with . . ."

Simon sprang to his feet. Johanan gained his. Both of them had drawn their weapons.

Glacon leaped up and with his sword drawn, he rushed between them. "The first one to move," he told them, "will die."

They glared at him. But they knew he would make good his threat.

"Put up your swords," Glacon ordered. "Now, sheath them."

"A great army has risen up!" Mattathias suddenly shouted. He started to stand, and then with a gasp, he toppled forward.

Instantly, Johanan and Simon rushed to their father. Within moments, the rest of the family was clustered around the old man.

Glacon sheathed his weapon; the hard lines softened and he returned to Helen's side. In the dialect of her country, he said, "I love these people, but I don't understand them."

"Would you have killed one or the other of them?" she asked.

"Yes," he answered. "I'd have killed the first one who moved." Then he stood up and went to where the family was clustered around the fallen Mattathias.

Simon was bending over his father, listening to the beat of the old man's heart. "He still lives," Simon told the others, and then he directed his brothers to carry their father into the shelter. Before he followed them, he turned to Glacon and said, "You did the right thing." Glacon nodded.

"Judah will come back," Simon said.

"I'm sure he will," Glacon answered.

* * *

Judah learned the size of the largest patrol out of Jerusalem consisted of sixteen men, while the smallest was four men. They were never escorted by cavalry, and almost always spent at least one night out in the field before returning to the city the following day.

There were patrols out all the time, but they never kept in touch with each other. They moved along independent routes in full battle dress and sometimes took an ass along with them to carry their food.

On some days Judah would follow a patrol. He began to learn the different ways of the men to lead them. Some marched their men faster than others; some allowed their men to straggle.

Judah noted the appearance of each commander. If he ever saw the man again, he would instantly recognize him not only by his looks but also by how his men marched.

Without really evolving a plan of action, Judah soon found he had one. The garrison in Jerusalem was something more than a thousand men. It was too large a force for his own small band to attack. But his men could easily attack the patrols, one at a time or even several at a time, as long as they were separated by some distance from each other.

Satisfied he had what he needed to begin fighting the Seleucids, Judah began to think about returning to the camp in the Gophna Hills. He intended to leave the city on Saturday because the Seleucids would be less suspicious of him when he passed through the gates. Even they knew

Jews did not travel on the Sabbath.

Judah enjoyed his stay in the city. There were times when he was in a tavern drinking that he was sorely tempted to go with a woman who offered herself to him. But he always declined, though he was never able to explain why to himself, or to any of the men with whom he drank.

Now and then, he thought of Ismene and at other times he would think of Shulamith. The dead woman had been fixed in his memory forever. He had loved her. But whenever he thought about Shulamith he was filled with longing for her, for the warmth of her body and the way she moved under him. Knowing she was waiting for him made him feel good. To his surprise, he realized he was falling in love with her.

On Thursday night, Judah drank too much and staggered out of the tavern. Here and there a torch glowed yellow in the distance, but, for the most part, the streets were pitch black.

Judah's head was filled with swirling white clouds. He bumped into a wall and excused himself for being so clumsy.

Halfway down one street, a dog began to bark furiously.

"Quiet, dog!" Judah shouted.

The wine gave him a tremendous need for a woman: it was there twisting and hot in his groin. He stopped and considered going back to the tavern where there was a woman who had offered herself to him earlier.

"Maybe," he whispered aloud, "I should go back to Shulamith tomorrow instead of waiting ..." He had started to walk again. But now there were other footfalls besides his own on the dry mud of the street.

Judah guessed he had been followed out of the tavern. He forced the clouds out of his head, and he slipped into the first doorway he found.

"I don't hear him," a man said in a deep voice.

"He must've stopped," a second man answered.

"Remember, now," the fast man cautioned, "Menelaus wants him alive."

The second man did not answer.

Judah sucked in his breath and waited. If he were fortunate, the men would pass him by. Slowly he exhaled.

He saw the two men, now, moving slowly up the street. They were shades darker than the night itself.

They were very, very close. He wanted to leap out and crack their skulls. But instead he pressed back against the door that was behind him. To risk a fight could easily put all his people in jeopardy.

He was sweating profusely. His nose itched, but he dared not move.

The men moved past him.

"He's gone," said the one with the deep voice.

The other agreed.

Judah sighed with relief, slipped out of the doorway and hurried away. Rather than return to the inn where he had slept during his stay in the city, he went up to where the Temple was and, mingling, with the beggars, he slept amongst them.

Early the following morning, Judah left the city.

"Judah is here! Judah has come back! Judah! Judah!" the young man shouted as he ran from the mouth of the gorge toward the center of the ramp. "Judah! Judah is here!"

Over and over, Judah's name was repeated until the sound of it rose up and filled the great bowl of rock in which the Jews lived.

The people ran from their shelters to meet him.

"We thought you were dead," a man with gray hair shouted. "We didn't know what happened to you," a second man called out.

Other voices said the same thing in different ways. But Judah answered none of them, nor did he look at those who cried out to him. He walked to where he had left his family. They, too, lived in a structure made of wattles, but it had grown larger by far than all of the others in the camp.

Suddenly he stopped. His brothers were coming toward him.

Johanan and Simon together, and Eleazar and Jonathan behind them, followed by his mother, sister, Joseph and his sisters.

Judah did not see his father or Shulamith. He looked for Glacon and found him standing off to the right, not far from himself.

His brothers had halted and Simon, preparatory to speaking, cleared his throat.

But Judah's eyes went to slits and in a hard voice, he asked, "Where are the guards?"

No one answered.

"Where are the guards?" he thundered.

"Judah . . ." Simon began.

"Where are the guards?" Judah shouted.

Glacon stepped forward. "There aren't any, Judah," he said. "The men have refused to stand their watches. They claim we're safe here."

Judah nodded. He looked at the people and gathering a wad of saliva in his mouth, he spat.

"Things have changed here," Simon finally said.

"And the training," Judah questioned, "have the men claimed that it, too, isn't necessary because we're safe here?"

"I couldn't do the impossible," Glacon responded.

"You don't understand," Johanan said. "Many things have changed since you left"

Judah shook his head.

"Your father lies ill," his mother called out from behind her sons.

"He's an old man," Judah responded. "But all these people here are not old; he has a right to be ill. But what can you tell me of the illness I see here."

The people moved uneasily.

"Before you judge us so harshly," Johanan said, "will you listen to what I have to say?"

"Will what you say change the fact that we are Jews?" Judah asked.

"No."

"Will it change the fact we killed Apelles and his men?"

"No."

"Simon," Judah called, "have you told your brothers of your vision? Have you told these people we have no choice but to fight and become a new nation?"

"No, Judah," Simon responded.

Johanan took several steps toward Judah and then he stopped.

"Since I'm the eldest son, I, I . . ."

"Glacon," Judah shouted sternly, "send the men to their guard posts. Those who refuse to go, kill!"

An angry murmur arose from the people.

"Eleazar, Jonathan and Joseph, go with Glacon," Judah ordered.

"You can't do that to your own," the gray haired man shouted.

Many agreed with him.

"All right," Judah said, nodding. "We'd have come to this in time. Perhaps it's better now than later?"

Johanan was flushed with rage and turned toward Simon. "I'll tell him in front of all of the people, if you don't stop him," Johanan said. "Tell me what?" Judah asked.

"You, Simon, you're his favorite, you tell him," Johanan yelled. Simon stepped forward and said, "Everything that has happened to us happened because . . ."

"Because Mattathias wouldn't forsake the Covenant or the Law of Yahweh," Judah answered. "There is no other reason."

"But there is," Simon told him.

"The ravings of a madman," Johanan said. "Someone called Daniel, whose writings our father came to know through the old priest Eleazar. Writings prophesizing that a mighty army of Jews would rise up against Antiochus and topple him. Are we that mighty army, my brother?"

"We are and we will be," Judah answered. "There isn't any other way now. The act, the deed, the rebellion has begun. We began it in Modin. Now, listen to me, all of you. Now you must decide whether you'll fight to be a Jew or whether you'll die like a dog."

"Either way, we'll die," a red-faced man shouted back.

"Some of us will die but not all of us. There'll always be some of us left to carry on the beliefs of our people. But, here and now, you must decide what it will be. I've found a way to fight the Seleucids. It'll mean that some of us will be killed. But unless we're willing to fight, we might as well slaughter one another here and now."

The people did not move.

And Judah said in a more gentle voice, "How we came to be here doesn't matter, but what we do here does matter to us and to those who'll come after us. We'll strike blow after blow against the Seleucids, until like a hammer beating against a glowing piece of iron on the anvil, we'll beat them into a form of our choosing. We will, as Daniel wrote, bring down Antiochus and be free to worship the God of our forefathers."

The people began to shout Judah's name.

To silence them, he held up his blackened staff. When the shouting ceased, he ordered Glacon to mount the guard. Then, looking at Johanan, he said, "Take me to my father." Johanan nodded. He now knew his brother Judah was truly different from all other men. He was not even able to explain it to himself, but somehow he felt relieved that he did not have to lead the people. He knew that he could never have done what he had just seen Judah do. Simon fell in alongside of Judah but did not speak to him.

When Judah reached his mother, he stopped and hugged her gently. There were tears in her eyes and in a soft, stifled voice, she said, "He waits for you, Judah."

"As he has always done," he answered gently. Taking his mother by the arm, he entered the shelter with her.

She pointed to where Mattathias lay on a bed of reeds.

"Leave us," Judah said, letting go of her and walking slowly toward his father. A small oil lamp cast its yellow glow over the old man's face.

For a while Judah stood and looked at him. His father had never really been as tall as he had seemed. There was a certain manliness in his face, a characteristic that fitted him so very well and raised his stature in the eyes of the observer.

"Judah?" Mattathias questioned in a quavering voice.

"Yes."

"I heard them shouting your name," Mattathias told him.

Judah knelt down and took hold of his father's wasted hand.

"Will you lead them?" the old man asked.

"Yes."

Mattathias nodded approvingly. His eyebrows fluttered open, and he looked up at his son. "We never did speak about . . ."

"There's no need to," Judah responded, rubbing the old man's cold hand between the warmth of his own hands.

"All these years you've kept silent," Mattathias said, "but now you may speak about it."

"There's nothing to say," Judah answered.

"There's never really anything to say when a man's time comes," Mattathias told him. "These past few days I have spent so much time thinking about what I'd say to you. But what could I say that would remove the burden I placed on your young back, on your young heart?"

Judah shook his head and pressed his lips to the back of his father's hand.

"By doing what I did," Mattathias said, "I know I took Yahweh away from you."

"It never mattered," Judah told him. "I'd have never followed His ways."

"But now you lead His people," Mattathias responded, "surely He'll walk with you now."

"I lead them for you," Judah said, "because you walked with God."

"Will you regain the Temple?"

"I'll try ... I'll try."

Slowly, Mattathias moved Judah's hands to his lips and kissed both of them. "I always loved you," he whispered with tears streaming down his eyes. "But it was so very hard for me to show it. More than anyone, Judah, you know who and what I was."

"As you know me, Father," Judah answered.

Mattathias closed his eyes and for a few moments he was silent. Then he asked, "When my time comes, will you take my body back to Modin and bury it in the family tomb?"

"Yes, Father."

There was another long interval of silence before his father said, "I know now that I was, so that you could be. Yahweh had meant it that way from the very beginning."

"Yes, Father," Judah responded.

The old man smiled and whispered, "I'm tired now and would like to sleep."

"Sleep," Judah said softly. He let go of his father's hand, bent over and kissed him on the forehead. "Sleep well, my beloved father, sleep well."

* * *

After he had bathed and eaten, Judah sat by the fire. He silently stared into the flame and thought about his father. He would never again speak about him as he had earlier. But there was now the irrevocable bond between them that was far stronger than blood. For each of them to have voiced their love for the other had been more than he had ever dared hope would happen. The words spoken between them would always remain in his heart. He would treasure them as long as he lived.

When his thoughts drifted away from the conversation he had with Mattathias, Judah found himself thinking about the future. Though it was unknowable, the flames, as he stared into them, illuminated all of it for him.

Finally, he looked at his brothers and bade Eleazar to bring Glacon and Joseph to the fire.

When they were all assembled, Judah said, "When Mattathias dies, we'll bring his body to the family tomb in Modin. He has asked that this be done, and I gave my word that it would be."

"None here will oppose you," Jonathan responded.

Judah nodded; then looking at his oldest brother, he said in an even tone, "Had we remained in Modin, I'd have given my land to you. You would have become the rightful leader of our family. I mentioned all of this to you once before. But now I'll say it in front of all of my brothers, my trusted friend and my cousin, so there'll be no future misunderstanding between us. I command here and I lead. Because it must be that way, I'll slay the man who challenges either my right to lead or to command."

Johanan felt the blood drain from his face. His palms were suddenly moist and his throat very dry.

To Simon, Judah said in the same tone, "You've broken faith with me. I'm not interested in the reason, but it mustn't happen again. I need your counsel. We all need your counsel. None of us here have your wisdom. If we're to survive, then we must be able to think, as well as fight."

"I'll always stand at your side, Judah," Simon answered.

Judah looked at Glacon and nodded. There was nothing he could say to his friend. Between the two of them the understanding was deep. They knew what had to be done.

"As for what was said this afternoon about Daniel," Judah told them, "let it be known that Mattathias recognized the truth in what he had read and, because he walked with God, he became His instrument. In time that will become the truth."

"I'll see it's done," Simon assured him.

"Now what we do," Judah said, "depends on the willingness of every able-bodied man to fight. Our first goal is to get weapons for our men. Our second goal is to kill as many Seleucid soldiers as we can, while suffering as few casualties as possible." Through most of the night, he spoke to them about the patrols and how they moved through the countryside, who commanded them, and how the actions of the troops depended on the officer in charge of them.

Judah left nothing to their imagination. He told them about the land, where the passes to Jerusalem were and which one could be used to harass the enemy. He said, "We'll take our wounded if we can, otherwise we'll kill them. If we can take our dead we will, if not then we'll either bury them where they fell or abandon them. We must be as hard on ourselves as we will be on our enemy."

"What about additional food for the people here?" Jonathan asked.

"For now that must be put aside until every man is well-armed. Then we'll take from those Jews who have turned against us. And there are many, too many."

"And will we take prisoners?" Eleazar questioned.

"No, no prisoners and no mercy. I assure you none will be shown to us," Judah said, glancing at Glacon to confirm what he had said.

"If you're taken by the Seleucids," Glacon explained, "you'll consider yourself fortunate to be killed quickly. No doubt you will either be sold into slavery, tortured and then killed, or flayed alive."

"Do you think the men in this camp are up to the rigors of such a harsh reality?" Simon asked.

"If they aren't," Judah answered, "they'll perish, and so will their God."

Simon nodded. Since Judah's return, he had recognized a change in his brother. He seemed stronger in his determination to win than he had previously been. He was keenly aware that Judah never spoke about God in any way that indicated his attitude had changed toward Him. He was certain his brother did not walk with God, but he was equally uncertain that God did not walk with his brother. Such a possibility was more disquieting than anything else that crossed his mind as he listened to Judah outline his plans for the war against the Seleucids.

From now on, Simon knew he would have to prove his love for his brother and regain his faith. There was still that vision of what the future might hold for the entire family if Judah's war proved to be successful.

"We'll no longer train here," Judah told them. "The training will be accomplished in the doing. The waiting is over."

"When do we begin, Judah?" Joseph asked.

Judah stood and said, "Much sooner than you think." Then he turned and went into the shelter. He stopped for a moment and looked toward his father. The old man was breathing easily.

An instant later, Judah pushed aside the curtain that separated the area where Shulamith slept from the rest of the shelter. Since his arrival, he had not said one word to her, but several times they had exchanged glances.

"I've been waiting for you," she told him in a low voice.

The space was so dark it seemed her voice and the darkness were one and the same.

"There were things that had to be done before I came to you," he answered. Slipping out of his clothes, he stretched out alongside of her. Like him, she was naked and he pressed her warm body against his.

"I missed you," she told him, easing his penis into her body.

"And I was lonely for you," he replied. He kissed her lips and then the nipples of her breasts.

They began to move fiercely against one another.

Judah could feel her body tense and then she made a soft, almost purring sound.

Then, her body shuddered and she raked his back with her fingernails. "I love you, Judah," she gasped out. "I love you."

His passion poured out and he spun away into a place of exquisite color and ineffable pleasure.

Later he heard her ask, "When will you leave again?"

"Tomorrow evening," he answered, pressing his face into the mounds of her breasts.

"Judah," she said, "I'm going to have a child."

He raised his head and looked at her.

"I don't know whether it's yours or . . ."

He laid his fingers across her lips and said, "It will be mine. I'll give it my name."

She drew him to her and said, "I pray to God it is yours, Judah."

"It'll be ours," he told her, kissing her lips.

"It'll be ours." Then, with a sigh, he put his head down on her breasts and slipped into a deep and pleasant sleep.

CHAPTER XV

There were four men in the Seleucid patrol. They were on their way back to Jerusalem, after having spent the night just south of the village of Mizpeh. Though in full battle dress, they moved along easily, talking and laughing despite the heat of the late morning.

Judah and his men followed the Seleucids. Always keeping to their rear, Judah sometimes moved parallel to them. On this first raid, Judah had taken Eleazar with him and three other men who had been chosen by lot.

There were farms on either side of the road, and already the fields were filled with burgeoning crops of grain. Many of the farmers had outwardly accepted Zeus in order to live. But before the harvest, Judah knew, they would have to prove to him or to the Seleucids whether they were still Jews or had indeed forsaken their God for Zeus.

"How long will we continue to follow them?" Eleazar asked.

Judah squinted up at the sun and said, "When it's somewhat past its midpoint."

"Why then?"

"When the time comes, you will see for yourself," Judah responded.

The heat made the road shimmer in the distance and bathed them in their own sweat. And always in front of them they could see the small cloud of pale brown dust hovering over the Seleucids.

Because Judah chose to keep off the road, nothing marked the movement of his men, except the imprint of their footsteps in the earth of the fields over which they trod.

Eleazar soon began to notice that the road was beginning to rise above the land on either side of it.

"Faster, now," Judah said, "I want to close the distance between us." And he broke into a lope.

The roadway began to curve, its height lessened—and then Eleazar realized that they would soon cut directly in front of the Seleucids. But it was hard to think of anything except the heat.

A stone wall came into view. It was waist high. When they reached it, they stopped.

On Judah's order, two of them vaulted over the wall and hid themselves in a ditch on the other side of the road.

Breathing hard, Eleazar nodded to his brother.

"When you hear my shout," Judah said to those with him but loud enough for the other men to hear, "You go."

The Seleucids were just then moving along the high section of the road. From where Eleazar was, they looked like dark specks against a blue sky.

Judah pointed to the sun and he said, "By the time they are here, it'll be in their eyes . . . it will be the first few moments of the fight that count most."

"Yahweh will be with us. Our cause is just."

Judah, seeming not to have heard, took several deep breaths. "Are you afraid?" Eleazar asked.

"Perhaps even more than you are, Brother," Judah answered, reaching out to tousle his brother's hair. He had always known how much Eleazar had tried to emulate him, but until this moment, he had never felt the intensity of his brother's love. He could see it burn in his dark gray eyes. To give Eleazar something of himself to hold onto, he said, "If I fall, you lead the men back to our people and see to our father."

"Yes, Judah," Eleazar replied.

They smiled at each other and waited in silence for the Seleucids to come.

The dark specks became larger and very quickly took the form of men. They were still talking and laughing. They spoke in Koine and most of what they said was about various women each of them knew or had known.

When the troops came to where the wall began, Judah motioned his own band to move farther along the stone barrier. His heart was pounding and the palms of his hands were so sweaty that he wiped his right hand on his clothing several times to make sure he would not loose his hold on the hilt of the sword.

Judah glanced at Eleazar; his brother's face was white, his jaw set and, like his own, his breath was shallow and rapid.

"Now!" Judah shouted, leaping over the wall and bringing his sword down on the helmeted head of one of the soldiers. The blow dropped the man to the ground but did not kill him.

He rolled free of Judah's slashing stroke. Bounding to his feet, he was ready with his sword to fight.

Eleazar killed his antagonist on the first thrust, pushing his blade into the chest of a man, whose green eyes lingered long in Eleazar's memory.

Then the fight extended to all the Seleucids and all of Judah's men. Again and again, the swords clashed, making the quiet afternoon ring with the sound of metal striking against metal. Groans and curses filled the air

One of the soldiers tried to pick up a spear, but he was struck down.

Judah still battled with his opponent. Each man slashing or stabbing at the other and nimbly leaping away from a mortal wound. The man's face was set with determination. His face was wet with sweat. He looked much like Glacon.

Suddenly Eleazar was at Judah's side.

The Seleucid could not fight the two of them. He went for Judah, and Eleazar slashed across the man's sword arm, crunching through the bone. A wordless scream came out of his mouth.

Judah thrust his weapon into the man's stomach and, with a swift upward movement, disemboweled him.

Three of the four Seleucids were dead and the fourth was wounded; he threw down his sword, raised his hands and asked to be spared.

He was a young man with brown hair and brown eyes. His face was very white and his lips trembled.

Judah looked at Eleazar; he was about to tell his bloodstained brother to kill the man. But instead he rushed at the soldier, drove his sword into the man's heart. Then to his own men, he said, "Take their aims, then throw their bodies into the ditch at the side of the road."

Silently, the men obeyed; they were afraid of him, even Eleazar could not believe what he had seen his brother do.

Judah quickly led his small band back to the safety of the Gophna Hills and re-entered the camp at night.

The people gave thanks to God that all of them had returned safely. With shouts of joy, they celebrated the small victory.

Judah made his way through the happy throng of people and went to his father. Kneeling beside him, he said, "Mattathias, the second blow has been struck."

The old man smiled but did not open his eyes.

After he left his father, Judah washed the blood and sweat from his body. Freshly dressed, he joined the family. He ate sparingly, but he drank a great deal of wine. Then taking Shulamith by the hand, he went into the shelter, and left the telling of what had happened to the others who had been there with him.

Now, Judah needed to be with Shulamith, and in the throes of passion with her to cast death away from himself.

There were other raids. Some were led by Judah and some by Glacon. Throughout the summer, Greek patrol after Greek patrol was set upon by bands of well-aimed and well-trained men.

At first, the Seleucid commanders complained to Sostrates that they were dealing with bandits, who came and went like phantoms. But soon they realized that the phantoms were Jews.

Each raid brought new aims into the camp and, sometimes, fresh food. Soon, it became clear to Judah and his men who among the farmers they could depend upon, who would give them water, food, and shelter when they needed it. These households they guarded, but the others who would not help, or who would give information about them to the Seleucids, they treated as their enemies, killing either the eldest son or the head of the house to avenge a betrayal or a refusal to help when it had been asked for. As the fields of grain ripened, Judah's raids became more daring. Larger units were attacked; often there were several engagements in progress at the same time.

The people in the camp and those on the outside who were still loyal to their God, began to call Judah, Maccabaeus: Judah, the Hammer. And those who fought in his army were called Maccabees.

Many, many Jews joined the ranks of Judah's army, until he had a force of more than a thousand men.

Simon developed a network of spies that brought Judah information from every part of the empire. Within a day of their movement, he knew where various units of the Seleucid army had been sent. Sometimes runners brought the information; other times signal fires burned at night to indicate that military movement had taken place or was in progress.

The summer passed into a beautiful autumn. The Maccabees celebrated the Feast of the Tabernacles and food flowed to them from the Jews whose farms lay close to the Gophna Hills. By the efforts of Simon and Johanan, the people never again had to live on the fruits and nuts of the trees.

On the last evening of the religious celebration, Judah climbed to where his father had stood on the day he had brought them to the lake.

Judah leaned on his blackened staff and said, "We've fought and we've survived; we'll continue to fight and we'll survive. But we must fight wherever and whenever we're able to. We'll fight on the Sabbath . . ."

An immediate shout of disapproval came from the Maccabees.

"Our enemy must not rest," Judah declared, making his voice reverberate between the cliffs around the lake. "We won't go to our death willingly, as so many of our people have in the past. The Seleucids know who we are. They know where we are, but they won't come for us because we've made them fear us."

"But the Sabbath . . ." Simon began.

"It's as good, if not a better day to fight than the rest of the week. Better because the Seleucids won't expect us to give them battle on that day."

"It's against the will of God," a man cried out.

"Let His wrath be on me," Judah answered. "Let Him hold me and only me to account for breaking His commandment."

The people fell silent. They looked at each other but could not speak. No man asked for God's wrath, no man!

"We mustn't shrink from doing anything that'll give us our freedom," Judah told them.

In solemn stillness, they stared up at him. Judah said nothing more. He made his way down the slope, and when he came to his people, they opened a way for him. He was asking them to go against God's own law, and they were frightened. But it was far better for them to be frightened now than dead at some later time.

That night at the fire, his mother asked, "Are you sure you can take God's wrath, Judah?"

"I won't know until I have felt it," he answered. "But I do know that we can't set one day aside and say on that day we won't fight, because on that day the Seleucids will fight, and if we don't, we'll die. Then, Mother, all of what we've done and what we hope to do, will die too."

"But God's law . . ."

"I've taken His wrath upon myself," Judah said quietly. "There's nothing more that has to be said about it."

Miriam shook her head; in so many ways Judah was a stranger to her. She did not understand him as she understood her other children. It was even difficult, God forgive her, to love him. He was hard, a hard man, harder than any man she'd ever known. She looked at Shulamith and could not understand why any woman would choose Judah over Simon.

* * *

Winter came, bringing with it numbing cold, wind driven rain, sickness, and death. Day after day the sky was dark gray or filled with masses of twisting clouds.

To the Maccabees, the Gophna Hills became a place more desolate than the great wilderness through which their forefathers had wandered before God brought them safely to the Promised Land. No one escaped the suffering, and only the strong managed to survive. The battle was not against the Seleucids, as much as it was against the terrible harshness of the land that only a few months before gave them safety.

Judah was forced to curtail his raids on the Seleucid patrols. He was told by Eleazar and Glacon that there was a rising anger against him.

Some of the people claimed that, for violating the Sabbath, God had sent His wrath against all of them, and others said the Seleucids by some magical power had turned the weather against them.

Judah took a deep breath and looked at the doubters, but he did not answer. He did not care what they said or how angry they became, as long as when it came time for them to fight, they fought.

Mattathias died unexpectedly and with his last breath, he exclaimed, "Hear, oh Israel, the Lord is our God, the Lord is one." His family and friends gathered to mourn him.

But Judah could not weep with the others. He went out into the night and climbed to the top of the highest cliff above the lake. The wind howled around him and rain lashed his face. He stood in the midst of the raging storm and called the name of his father, Mattathias Ben Hasmon, over and over again, until the name became louder than the sound of the wind and the rain, until the name filled the space between the walls of the surrounding cliffs, until all of the Maccabees heard it and wondered if God was summoning the spirit of His faithful to Him.

The following morning, Judah and his brothers carried the body of their father to its final resting place in the family tomb in Modin. They moved slowly, oblivious to the cold and the rain. By nightfall, they were outside their village and a short time later, they placed Mattathias' body in the family tomb, offered a prayer for the dead and resealed the tomb. They spent the remainder of the night in the charred ruins of what once had been their home.

The following morning the sun was bright, the wind was no more than a gentle breeze. Shortly before they arrived at the gorge that led to the camp, Simon asked them to stop. He leaned against the sun blasted rock of the defile and said, "It's inconvenient to speak about certain things in the presence of others. Our cousin Joseph for one and Glacon for the other. Neither of them are part of our immediate family, Glacon even less so than Joseph."

Judah nodded and told him to continue.

"Once, I mentioned it to you, Judah."

"Your vision?" Johanan asked.

"Not so much a vision," Simon responded, "but rather an examination of some of the things that might happen if we're successful in our struggle to preserve our God. We'll rule Judea; we'll be likened to kings and other lords. One of us will be the High Priest."

"But that isn't our family line," Jonathan objected.

"It will be," Simon answered, "because it can't be any other way. Judah, by issuing his command to fight on the Sabbath, has already altered the Law in a way that previously was left to the High Priest."

Judah agreed but added he had done so for military reasons only.

"The point," Simon said, "was that he did it. Regardless of why we rebelled against Antiochus, we did rebel and if we win, then we hold all that we have won."

"We've won nothing yet," Judah responded mildly.

Simon raised his hand and with a smile he told his brother, "We've won a great deal, Judah. The right to worship Yahweh, to carry out His laws and even the place where we are camped is ours and ours alone."

Judah shrugged; he could not think of himself in any capacity other than the one he was in. "I'd make a poor High Priest," he responded, almost laughing.

"But not a poor king," Eleazar said.

"A poor king too," Judah answered, slapping his younger brother on the back.

"As Judah has said," Simon told them, "we've much to win yet. But the possibilities are there if we do win."

"I'll let you think about them," Judah said. "But I'll tell all of you here and now that if we rise to such exalted heights as Simon thinks we might, then Glacon must rise with us."

"As you wish, Judah," Simon answered.

"And what about Joseph?" Eleazar asked.

"I think he might be part of the family, closer by marriage than he is now," Johanan said.

Judah looked at his brother questioningly.

"You mean you weren't aware of his interest in Rebecca?"

"No."

"I think she's more interested in him than he is in her," Jonathan said.

Judah had still not spoken to his sister and, in truth, had ignored her. "It might be a good match," he said.

"Would you agree to it?" Johanan asked.

"If I agreed," Judah answered, "I've no doubt that she wouldn't."

"He's well liked by the men," Eleazar commented.

"Simon," Judah said wryly, "you find him a position in our new kingdom; I'm much too busy trying to keep us from getting killed." Then he started to walk again.

The others followed him, and Judah could hear them talking about the future and its possibilities, but he paid no attention to what they were saying.

* * *

Two days before the beginning of the Passover Feast, a sudden perversity of weather brought the return of the cold, driving winter rains. Many of the Maccabean units were caught by the change and were forced to take refuge wherever they could. And many were betrayed to the Seleucids, who came heartily down on them, killing all they were able to find.

But even before this sad news reached the camp, Shulamith went into labor and could not, because of the way the child had turned, give birth to it.

All through her agony, Judah never left her. He sat very still and held her hand. When the pain became unendurable for her, he let her bite on his hand until it bled. For one full night and one full day, Shulamith was wracked by pain, and then suddenly, she clutched Judah's hand and said, "I love you, Judah; I came to love you!"

"And I love you," he told her.

Then Shulamith died and the child in her died, too. The following morning she was buried on the north shore of the lake.

Judah stood for a long time and looked down at the mound of newly turned black earth covering the body of the woman with whom he had shared his bed. Tears were useless. Grief was useless, and yet he wept and grieved silently for her. She had given him all that a woman could give a man. He shook his head and, with a ragged sigh, Judah walked away from the grave and did not look back.

The death of his woman and child did not auger well for the future. He knew that the people would interpret it as a clear indication that God had indeed set his wrath against him.

* * *

Menelaus stood before Sostrates. He had taken the liberty of bringing Amran with him, and now was in the throes of doubt about his decision.

Sostrates glowered up at them from the map spread out over the table. "Your request to see me failed to mention you'd have another person with you."

"It wasn't an intentional omission, General," Menelaus answered deferentially.

Sostrates nodded. Being posted by Antiochus to command the garrison of Jerusalem had not turned out as he had envisioned it. There had been that incident at Modin, and then the raids by Jews who had taken to calling themselves Maccabees. His position was in fact becoming a nightmare. The Maccabees could move about his territory at will. He had lost a third of his garrison to them. He was trying to think of a way to explain to his king that a rebellion was in progress without having to use the word *rebellion.*

Sostrates carefully regarded Amran; he seemed familiar somehow.

"General," Menelaus said, guessing at the Seleucid's thoughts, "Amran is a frequent visitor of mine." With a smile, he added, "He's a man with many extraordinary connections."

Sostrates stood up; doubtless Amran was a Jew, too, and by the great god Zeus, he was being plagued by the Jews, even his dreams were filled with them. He strode across the room and looked at the gray sky through the opened shutter; inside himself he was far grayer than the sky. "Tell me what you want." the Seleucid officer demanded, without deigning to look at his visitors.

"My Lord," Amran said in a low voice, "I came only to be of service."

Sostrates whirled around, squinted questioningly, first at him and then at Menelaus. "How can he be of service to me?"

"He brings information," Menelaus answered, "about the Maccabees."

With three huge strides, Sostrates moved from the window to where the High Priest and his friend stood. He glowered at them and pushing his thick forefinger into Amran's chest, he said, "I'm ready to listen, Jew. But tell me first what you want in exchange for what you give?"

Before Amran could answer, Menelaus spoke. "He came to me first," the High Priest explained, "and when he told me what he had heard, I brought him with me for you to hear it from him."

"Speak then," Sostrates ordered.

"I've heard it said in the taverns," Amran said, "the spirit of the Maccabees is waning; their leader Judah has taken the wrath of God on himself and has suffered the loss of a father, his concubine, and her child. There's much illness in their camp and even more discontent."

Sostrates lowered his hand and returned to the table. Bending over the map, he said, "Yet, only yesterday they attacked one of my patrols and killed three of its men."

"Judah, their leader, forces them to fight."

Sostrates rolled his eyes up at Amran and said, "Judah Maccabaeus . . . Judah, the Hammer."

"It'd be a good time to strike them," Menelaus commented. "I've already tried to send men into the Gophna Hills; none of them has ever come out."

Menelaus was quick to recognize a change in Sostrates' tone. Not that it was any more conciliatory than it previously had been, but rather that it was indicative of more thoughtfulness than before.

"Are you sure of what you heard?" Sostrates asked, looking at Alum.

"I heard similar words expressed several times. My Lord, many of the Maccabees come to Jerusalem; they've friends here and outside of the city."

Menelaus blanched at what Amran had just said; he fully expected Sostrates to go into a rage. But nothing happened. The General simply returned to studying the map.

"I can write to Apollonius in Samaria and explain that there are signs of more trouble with the Jews," Sostrates said. His brows knitted together. "Though I'm sure he knows something of the situation here and is only waiting to have it acknowledged in writing from me."

Neither Menelaus nor Amran had anything to say.

"He'll know there is a rebellion," Sostrates commented to himself.

"Ask him for men to strengthen your garrison," Menelaus offered. "Tell him there are rebellious Jews and you need more men to quell them, before the situation requires more attention than it warrants from the King."

"Apollonius isn't a fool," Sostrates said with a forced laugh, "he'll know I'm in trouble." He uttered a deep sigh. "But I'll be in more trouble if I fail to ask for help. I need more men. With them, I've a chance of regaining control of the countryside."

"You must warn Apollonius there are Maccabean spies everywhere," Amran said.

"I'll mention it to him," Sostrates answered; then he added, "You've done me a service. I won't forget either of you."

"It's our pleasure to serve," Menelaus answered.

Sostrates offered them wine, but Menelaus graciously declined, telling the Commander he did not want to keep him from his work. Then with Amran at his side, the High Priest departed from the Seleucid's quarters. For Menelaus, this meeting augured well for his future dealings with Sostrates. He turned to Amran and said, "We've done very well by ourselves."

"So it would seem," Amran answered with a laugh, "so it would seem."

* * *

The rains departed, taking with them what was left of spring and leaving the fierce heat of summer in their wake.

Judah increased the number of his raids, and they were more successful than ever. The people soon forgot their fear and anger against him.

One afternoon a man named Ezra entered the camp. He was tall, with dark hairy aims and sharp, amber-colored eyes. He had been in the camp on several other occasions and spoke with no one other than Judah.

There were many stories about him, but none of them were true, and Judah had never asked him any questions about his past or his present condition. But it was whispered by some in the camp that he was really the prophet Daniel.

He went directly to where Judah stayed with the rest of the family. He did not hesitate or stop to nod to Simon or Eleazar. He saw Judah standing at the shore of the lake and he called to him.

Judah turned, saw who it was and immediately started toward him.

"I came in the usual way," Ezra said. "I doubled back twice to make sure I wasn't followed."

Judah nodded.

"Apollonius is on the move," Ezra told him.

"How many men?"

"Some two thousand."

"Soon begins the real test," Judah commented.

"You've three days at the most," Ezra told him. Then he asked,

"Will you fight him?"

"If not now," Judah answered, "then never." He gestured back toward the camp. "Not too long ago, I almost lost my hold on them. A battle will strengthen our purpose and give them hope for the future."

"And if you should lose?"

Judah looked off in the distance and said, "Then Yahweh will have lost, and Zeus will have won."

"That mustn't happen," Ezra responded passionately.

"That's why we must fight Apollonius," Judah said. "I'll tell my brothers and Glacon to prepare the men."

"God watch over you," Ezra said. He turned and walked through the camp to the gorge. When he reached it, he looked back at Judah and waved his hand high above his head.

Judah responded; then he went to Eleazar and told him to bring his brothers and Glacon to where he was.

Tell them," Judah said, "I summon them for our first Council of War."

"Before I go," Eleazar said, "tell me who that man is."

"His name is Ezra."

"Yes . . . yes, everyone knows that. But who is he, really?"

With a shrug, Judah answered, "I never thought to ask him."

"Aren't you curious?"

"Not enough to ask," Judah said.

Eleazar laughed and, shaking his head, he went off to fetch his brothers.

CHAPTER XVI

The gray light of a new day began to spread over the eastern sky. Judah moved back from the edge of the rocky defile. Gathering his cloak around him, he joined Glacon, who was seated on a flat rock. Neither of them spoke; everything that could have been said had already been said many, many times.

Within the next few hours, all their words would resolve into a bloody battle between the Maccabees and those under the command of Apollonius. Eight hundred against a force of more than twice that number. Most of the Maccabees were poorly armed. A few had swords and spears taken from the Seleucid soldiers that they had killed. Others came by bows and arrows the same way. And there were many who were armed with a sharply honed sickle. Several, perhaps as many as fifty, would use only the rocks they found. All of them had seen action with Judah and were especially chosen by him and Glacon for this battle.

Judah stood up and stretched. "After this is over," he said, "I'm going to sleep for a week, maybe even a month."

Glacon nodded.

"Too bad we don't have any Greek fire," Judah commented. "It'd have made us somewhat more equal."

"You can still pull back."

"Apollonius must be stopped," Judah said resolutely, "before he reaches Jerusalem."

"Then you must depend on your God to stand with you." Judah's expression conveyed no such conviction.

"If I live through this," Glacon told him, "I'll ask your God to accept me."

"You wish to become a Jew?" Judah questioned, completely surprised by what his friend had just said.

"And Helen, too," Glacon responded.

"I'll mention it to Simon," Judah said. "He will know the proper procedure. You understand, it'll mean you will have to be circumcised?"

"Yes," Glacon answered.

For a while Judah remained silent. Then in a low voice, he said, "Many Jews would rather be Greeks, and here you are a Greek wanting to be a Jew. Why?"

With a wry smile, Glacon said, "Logic. The more I thought about Zeus and the other gods, the more absurd they were and the more reasonable your Yahweh became . . . and the more meaningful His laws. If for no reason other than that He gave your people His laws, He should be worshipped."

"He's already with you my friend," Judah told his companion.

"As He's with you," Glacon responded.

Judah shook his head but did not explain. Instead, he pointed to the rising sun and said, "I think we should see to the men."

Glacon agreed.

Narrow and twisting, the defile was between nine and ten stadia long. From the north, where Apollonius would enter, the ground between the craggy walls was graded steeply and irregularly uphill. The combination of all of these features made Judah choose the place for his first real battle with the Seleucid army.

He had walked along its entire length many times. On either side of the narrow pass, he had scouted out the best places to conceal his men. And now they were all there ... waiting for the enemy.

He had divided his force into four groups. Eleazar commanded the one on the western side of the defile, and Johanan commanded the group on the eastern side. The group he would lead would enter the defile from the south and attack the forward units of the Seleucid army. The fourth unit was under Glacon's command. It would come into the rear of the enemy force as soon as the last Seleucid soldier had entered the defile. The battle would commence when Glacon ordered three blasts on a ram's horn to be sounded. Judah had left Simon and Johanan in command of two different units. Simon would cover his retreat, if the Seleucids should prove too much for his men. Johanan guarded their camp in the Gophna Hills.

They had gone over these details more times than Judah wanted to remember. Glacon had taught the men how to fight with a spear, how to use a sword and even how to cut a man in half with a single stroke of a sickle.

In voices just above a whisper, the men greeted Judah, and he answered them with a wave of his sword.

It was warmer now, with the sun above the eastern hills. Judah removed his cloak and, making a roll of it, he left it at the base of a huge rock. Then he walked toward the southern end of the defile, where the men he would lead into the coming battle were waiting for him.

The rocks at the top of the western side of the pass became yellow in the sun. The heat made them shimmer. The Maccabees strained to hear the coming of the Seleucid army. But they could hear very little more than the pounding of their own hearts.

Judah was beginning to regret he had ordered his scouts to join Simon's small force after they had reported Apollonius was no more than thirty stadia from the defile. Without his scouts, Judah was blind. He could do nothing but wait. Foolishly, he had given the advantage of surprise over to his adversary. He vowed never to make the same mistake again. Even if it meant risking the lives of several men, he must at all times be kept informed of the enemy's movements.

He feared Apollonius might have chosen the long way around to Jerusalem. If that had happened, then he and his force would have to fall back to the camp. He would have to devise another plan that would enable them to encounter an army larger and better equipped than his own.

The men around Judah began drinking from their water bottles.

"Save it for later," he cautioned them. "Later, you will need water as much as you need the air your breath." To keep saliva in their mouths, he told them to suck on pebbles.

As the morning wore on, the heat was unbearably fierce.

Judah became more and more restless. Alone, he walked along the length of the defile and examined the emplacements on either side of it.

Eleazar had devised the idea of rigging several stages against the walls of the pass. These platforms were loaded with rocks. At the proper time, the stages would be cut away and tons of rock would drop on the Seleucid troops, crushing many and wounding many more.

Judah returned to his own group. He sent a runner to Glacon, asking him if he saw any sign of the enemy.

The runner returned and said, "Glacon told me to tell you that you'll hear them long before you see them."

Judah nodded, thanked the man and, turning away, he walked once more into the defile, but this time he only went a short distance. Glacon had once told him that the worst part of any battle was not the fighting itself but the waiting for it to begin.

He glanced back at his men. They too were uneasy. Some of them, like Bozrah and Zeitlin, he had known all his life. Bozrah once had a wild sense of humor, but lately he was more subdued. Zeitlin was an excellent carpenter. It had been said of him he could build anything out of sticks. Now, when he was not fighting, he spent most of his time cutting shafts for spears.

Judah looked up the defile. The men he had brought to this place came because of him. But it was Simon who had led them all. Though the Jews had given him the name Maccabee, Judah without Simon would be good only for fighting, for killing. Judah recognized that Simon held a greater vision of the future than he did. Then, realizing that he was sweating profusely, Judah returned to his men at the opening of the defile. There, at least, it was somewhat cooler.

"I think I hear something," a young man said.

Judah turned to him. He was Sarah's brother Yavneh. His jutting chin was just beginning to show signs of a black beard.

"Like distant thunder," Yavneh explained.

Within moments, the sound of the Seleucid trumpets and drums floated over the hills and through the defile.

Though it would be some time yet before the first phalanxes entered the defile, Judah ordered, "To your places."

The men fell back to their concealed positions to the left and right side of the pass's opening.

"Wet your mouth with water," he told them.

The blare of the trumpet and boom of the drum became louder. But under those warlike noises was an even more terrifying sound; the slow steady marching tread of two thousand disciplined troops. The earth seemed to tremble under the impact or their footfalls. Two thousand separate men moving as one man was enough to blanch the dark faces of the men who were listening to the oncoming engine of destruction.

"They're only men," Judah whispered to the men nearest him. "They may sound like something more, but they aren't."

No one answered him.

The trumpet sounded a series of several signals.

"They're changing their formation," Judah said. "They will be in ranks of four."

The tread of the enemy feet was louder now.

"Remember," Judah said, "we'll fight our way through to Apollonius. Between him and us are a thousand troops."

"We'll do our best," several of the men responded.

Judah concentrated now on the ever-growing sound of the oncoming army. It was frightening enough to quicken his heart and dry his lips. More than anything, he craved wine. His stomach felt as though it was in the grip of a giant hand. Sweat poured into his eyes and several times he was forced to use his hands to clear his vision.

He could hear the Seleucid commanders urging their men to quicken their pace. They seemed anxious to be out of the defile as quickly as possible.

"Soon," Judah told his men, "very soon now!"

The voices of the oncoming army were very loud and very clear. Now and then, there was laughter.

To be certain his men remained silent, Judah signaled to them with his hand and then crossed his lips with his finger.

The very act of waiting, of remaining silent and immobile, taxed his strength almost beyond endurance. Every muscle in his body tensed. It was as if he were held by the tight, unyielding coils of some serpent. The physical pain was excruciating.

Two of the men near him stood up and urinated. They started to apologize, but he gestured to them to remain silent.

A fine yellow dust rose above the defile.

Then, suddenly, the three blasts from the ram's horn burst over the defile.

"Now," Judah shouted. "Now!" He raced forward into the furnace heat of the defile.

Someone behind him cried out. "Hear, oh Israel, the Lord is our God, the Lord is one!"

Judah and his men plunged into the first ranks of Seleucid troops. The soldiers did not have time to lower their long spears, or draw their swords.

Judah cut his way through several men. He swung his sword in long vicious strokes, taking an arm off, severing a head, slashing a man in half. Within the first few moments, he was splattered with blood.

The stages on the sides of the cliff were cut away. Tons upon tons of rocks fell to both sides of Judah's charging men on the screaming Seleucid soldiers below. Their ranks stalled. The men in the rear could not move forward and found themselves under attack at the northern end of the defile.

The troops began to throw down their spears and started to draw their swords.

Judah urged his men on. He parried one attack, and then he drove his blade into the man's stomach. He fought with another and killed him with a quick thrust into his neck.

Here and there, at the fringe of his vision, he saw some of his men fall.

The defile was filled with the wild shouting of men trying to cut each other to pieces.

More rocks slammed down on the Seleucid soldiers. Some were on the bloodstained ground with their heads smashed. Others suffered broken shoulders or severe cuts and bruises; they were easy prey for the Maccabees.

Then, suddenly, the Seleucid resistance stiffened.

Judah knew he was getting close to Apollonius. He fought harder. His breath came in chest-heaving draughts.

A man blocked his way. He was tall. His face was pockmarked and he held a sword in his hand.

"Come, you lousy Jew," he shouted, "come and die!"

Judah moved toward him. Their blades clashed, and Judah felt the shudder travel along the length of his arm. They circled one another. Then, out of the corner of his right eye, Judah saw another soldier coming at him. He whirled toward the second attacker. With a swift downward stroke, he severed the man's hand at the wrist. Then he turned back to the man in front of him. His movement was not fast enough. Searing pain flashed across his chest. To counter, sword probing, he lunged.

The man dropped to his knees and tried to pull the sword out of his stomach.

Judah wrenched the weapon free and pressed forward into the attack. His wound though not deep, was bloody. He fought his way around one of the turns and saw Apollonius astride a gray stallion.

The Seleucid commander was trying to rally his men. But there were few left in front of him. Almost a thousand men had been killed or wounded by the onslaught. The bombardment of rocks from above had taken a terrible toll.

"Re-form," he shouted. "Re-form!"

But the men seemed unable to move. Word came to him that his force was suffering heavy casualties in the rear. He knew that, within the narrow confines of the defile, he could not hope to maneuver what was left of his units into any sort of cohesive fighting force. His only hope to save himself and as many men as possible would be to break out through the southern opening. The ferocity of the attack from that quarter had already spent itself.

"That way!" Apollonius yelled, waving his sword toward the southern portion of the defile.

Another surge of rocks came crashing down on the remaining units. This was quickly followed by a flurry of arrows. More of his men fell.

The first rank of the unit behind him finally lowered their spears. They started to move. The second rank put their spears into fighting position. Two more ranks followed.

His men were rallying! Apollonius gave the order for a forward movement at a run. Then, without warning, there were swarms of men coming at them from the sides of the cliffs.

The fighting had quickly become a ferocious melee.

Then he saw a tall, blonde man hack his way toward him. In an instant, he realized he was looking at Judah the Maccabee; Judah, the Hammer. He remembered having seen him on the day when the old priest Eleazar had been put to death in front of the Temple. He had picked up the old man's staff.

Above the din of the battle, Judah shouted to Apollonius to fight him.

Apollonius was a big man. He swung out of his saddle and, letting go of his horse, he moved toward Judah. Without another word passing between them, they began to fight.

Judah, despite his wound, was more agile than the Seleucid General and, like a hunting cheetah, he slowly circled him, dashing forward for a quick jab and retreating with equal swiftness.

The fighting continued to rage around them. The Seleucids were trying desperately to shake the Maccabees from them, but the effort cost them more and more men.

Sensing the threat from nearby Seleucids, Judah rushed forward. Apollonius' blade caught him in his left shoulder. Judah went down on his knees. The pain blurred his vision. He glanced up and saw Apollonius over him. He drew himself almost into a ball, and then, with a wordless shout, he bolted up and under the Seleucid General—lunging his sword into him with such force that it went in to its hilt and the point came out of Apollonius' back.

Judah picked up the Seleucid commander's gold-hilt sword and with the rest of his men, he continued to fight until he and Glacon joined forces.

No quarter was given and none was asked. There were many Seleucid soldiers who managed to fight their way out of the defile, but the Maccabees had killed practically all of the two-thousand-man force that had been sent against them.

Judah ordered his men to strip the bodies of the Seleucid troops of their weapons and their armor. Before the sunset, he and his army had melted away. They had won a great victory and now were hurrying back to their camp to celebrate.

Another attack was quickly mounted by the Seleucids. It was led by General Seron, commander of the Seleucid forces in western and southern portions of the empire. He had received instructions from Antiochus to settle the matter of unrest in Judea with dispatch and to avenge the death of Apollonius, who had been a faithful officer to the King.

Seron was a small, thin, energetic man with a handsome face, dark brown hair and heavy lidded brown eyes. He wasted no time, and in a matter of days he was on the move with a grand phalanx, consisting of four thousand men.

The moment his forces left the city of Ptolemais, northwest of Jerusalem, the information began to move along a network of Maccabean spies until Judah was apprised of the new danger rapidly approaching him.

To avoid repeating Apollonius' mistake, Seron kept his force close to the coast, where the terrain was flat and open and where there would be no possibility of an ambush. Despite the intense heat, Seron drove his men. He wanted to accomplish the task as quickly as possible, and then perhaps he might be in a better position to ask the King for a command in the forthcoming war against the Parthians. There had been a time when he would not have had to ask . . . then the King would have anticipated his want and would have been happy to gratify it.

Day by day, the distance between the Seleucid army and Jerusalem lessened. But sooner or later, Judah realized, Seron would have to swing his army toward one of the several passes leading to the city.

Then, late one afternoon Ezra entered the camp. Judah had seen him come through the mouth of the gorge and ran to him.

"They have swung toward Lod," Ezra said.

"We will meet them at Beth-Horon," Judah answered in the choked voice.

"Yes."

"Will you be with us?"

Ezra shook his head. "No," he answered. "I do what I must do, and you do what you must do. But I can't kill, Judah."

Judah nodded.

"God be with you and keep you safe," Ezra said. Then, he turned and disappeared from sight.

"We'll meet them at the pass of Beth-Horon," Judah shouted. "At the pass of Beth-Horon. Glacon, form our units. We must be in position by daylight. Hurry, hurry! We leave here before sundown."

Judah wore Apollonius' gold-hilt sword across his back and carried Eleazar's blackened staff in his right hand. He walked along the lines of men. He knew all of them by name. Their faces were set with determination, but deep in their eyes he could see the shadow of fear, of death. He knew they saw the same thing in his eyes. He would have signaled them to begin moving, but Simon came running up to him and breathlessly said, "You must speak to them; you must give them some words of hope."

Judah hesitated. But then he looked toward the women and children who stood clustered together under the gathering gloom of the high cliffs above the camp. The women clutched their children tightly to them; some were no more than infants at their mother's breast, while others were old enough to understand that the men were going off to fight and some, perhaps their father or brother amongst them, might not return. They were frightened.

Judah saw his own mother. She was looking at him. Since Mattathias' death, she had become an old woman who was waiting now only to join her husband. He realized suddenly how much she must have loved Mattathias. It was incredibly strange to think of them at that particular moment as lovers, and yet Judah knew they had been. He remembered having listened to them in the dead of night, listening to the sound of their movements and their exclamations of pleasure.

"Speak to them, Judah," Simon urged.

And Judah walked to where his mother stood. Drawing her to him, he embraced her. "Come with me," he whispered, leading her away from Rebecca and the other women of the house. "Come stand with me," he said, "while I speak to the people."

Miriam went with him.

Judah stood between his men and the women. He glanced up toward the top of the cliff, where the sky flamed with a brilliant red sunset. Then looking at his men, he said, "Our mothers, our wives, our true loves, our sisters and our children will be waiting for us when we return. Don't let them wait in vain. Return to them. Your God is just. Don't fail Him!"

"Judah!" Simon shouted, raising his sword to salute his brother.

"Judah! Judah! Judah!" the men cried, brandishing their weapons.

"They love you," his mother said softly, as he walked with her to the women.

Turning his palms out, he answered, "No more than I love them." He kissed her gently on the forehead and hurried away.

Moments later, Judah raised the blackened staff and the Maccabees began to move toward the mouth of the gorge. He summoned Jonathan and told him to send out scouts. Then to Glacon, he said, "We should be at the pass sometime after midnight."

"I'll see that everyone is in position long before daybreak," his friend responded.

"How do you think it'll go?" Judah asked.

"God will be with us," Glacon answered with conviction.

"What will be your answer," Judah questioned with a chuckle, "once you're circumcised and are finished with your instruction?"

"No more than what I've already told you," Glacon replied, "since I can't imagine myself believing more than I do now."

Judah said nothing more about the matter, though he could not help but wonder at his friend's love for a God who, at best, must find it strange to be worshipped by a former enemy and at worst did not even exist for Glacon or, for that matter, for anyone else who was not a Jew. That was what tormented Judah most about God: he could not believe in

His existence. Despite the Covenant and the laws, he could not believe, though he desperately wanted to. Desperately!

Maccabees marched unerringly through the black gorges of the Gophna Hills. There was hardly any conversation between the men, though now and then a few spoke in low tones about the coming battle.

Judah ordered the pace quickened.

The men were trotting.

Suddenly, they were out of the hills and so close to Modin they could see the dark, empty burnt-out shells that had once been the homes of many of them.

Out of the darkness, one of the scouts appeared and reported to Judah, "Seron's army is camped for the night less than five stadia from the pass."

Judah passed the information to the rest of the men. He wanted them to know as much about the situation as himself. Though he led them, they were the ones who would win or lose the battle. Each one of them was a man fighting for his God. They were not being paid to fight. If they had to die, Judah wanted his men to feel that God had chosen them, and not because they were at the mercy of someone else's blunder or that they had known less about what was happening than they should have.

A thin crescent moon came up. It was very yellow and shed its little light over the open plain.

Simon fell in alongside of Judah and suggested that they slow their pace.

Judah agreed and he gave the order to resume walking.

Simon remained close to Judah. When their breathing became regular, Judah said, "Our mother might not live much longer."

"She grieves for our father," Simon responded.

"If anything happens to me," Judah told his brother, "lay her to rest next to Mattathias."

"Yes Judah," Simon answered.

"Strange, until recently," Judah said, "I never really thought about them as ever having been lovers."

"They were," Simon replied. "I assure you they were."

With a laugh, Judah said, "I heard them too, Simon."

And Simon also laughed.

The terrain began to slope downward.

The Maccabees reached the pass of Beth-Horon before midnight. Immediately, Judah, his brothers, and Glacon began to deploy the men.

Eleazar and Jonathan took positions with their men opposite each other in the middle of the pass, where the slope suddenly becomes very steep. They laid several lengths of rope between them, carefully concealing the lines by spreading earth over them.

Simon's and Johanan's men took the lower reaches of the pass and sat opposite one another.

Judah and Glacon with their men remained at the upper end of the pass; they would prevent any of the Seleucids from breaking out of the defile.

Judah had kept Joseph with his unit. All of his brothers and Glacon had nothing but praise for the young man's prowess in a fight, especially Eleazar, who had told Judah that their cousin was striving to attract his attention.

"He desperately wants to command," Eleazar had told Judah one afternoon when they were alone.

"And no more?"

"Perhaps to be closer to you than he is."

"He's related by blood and might soon be related by marriage," Judah said. "I already have four brothers . . . what more can *he* hope to be?"

"To be as close to you as Glacon," Eleazar replied forthrightly.

Judah looked at his cousin. Joseph was resting with his back against a huge boulder. His spear was within easy reach. He did not appear to be troubled by anything.

Judah smiled, and for a moment he wondered if the young man was thinking about Rebecca. Then he frowned. There was something about Joseph that disturbed him. Something . . . but, whatever it was, Judah willed it away and sat down, leaning against a rock and closing his eyes. He drew his knees up and, crossing his arms, rested his head on them. He took several deep breaths and feeling his body dissolve, he began to drift into a light but restless slumber where dreams of Ismene and Shulamith resided, where physical yearning welled up with such force that it abruptly woke him.

Judah got to his feet and he went quietly to where the pass emerged on the plain that would bring the Seleucid army to Jerusalem, if he and his men could not stop them. He shook his head and urgently said to himself, *"We must stop you, Seron, we must!"*

Dawn came, graying the sky at first, then turning the eastern portion saffron. Judah awakened Glacon and Joseph. They in turn roused the other men.

The darkness dissolved. The light of the new day starkly outlined every boulder, every piece of shrubbery that concealed a Maccabean.

As soon as the sun was above the horizon, its heat flashed over the land and the men who shivered from the cold during the night, now dripped with sweat.

"We had better cover when we fought Apollonius," Judah commented to Glacon.

"Each battle is a different experience," his friend answered, "just as each woman a man lies with is different."

A scout came dashing up the pass. "Seron's army has broken camp," he shouted. "They're coming!"

Judah ordered silence. From the distance came the sound of the Seleucid horns and drums. After a while, they heard the tread of the army, the beat of each footfall as the soldiers raised a cloud of dust around them.

Seron was directly in front of his lead phalanx. He rode a brown stallion. His scouts were out in front of him and there were several protecting units on his flanks. The pass was wide enough to allow a sixteen-man front on his phalanxes. The first five ranks moved with their long spears down, ready for action.

Halfway up the pass, Seron dropped to the rear of his first phalanx. The pass suddenly narrowed, forcing him to order his protective flanking units to halt and allow the phalanxes to make their way up the pass.

He was moving his men as swiftly as possible and hoped to be inside of Jerusalem by nightfall. But the ascent was becoming steeper and his men were in full battle dress. Sweating and bumping against one another, the soldiers broke their marching step and even used the shafts of their spears as staffs to help them up the steep incline.

Judah crouched behind a rock. Below him he saw the first units of Seron's army move steadily toward him. The sun shone on their breastplates and their black-plumed helmets were pushed low over their eyes to protect them from the glare of the sun. The sixteen-man front was a ragged line of struggling, breathless men.

Judah pointed to the man with the ram's horn.

A single shrill trill slashed the stillness of the morning air.

In an instant, Judah and his unit rushed headlong into the lead phalanx of Seron's army.

The Seleucids screamed as the first rank went down on the Maccabean spears. The second rank desperately tried to raise their shields and form a defensive line, but they were scattered by a barrage of arrows and stones.

The next three ranks were forced back. Many of them lost their footing.

Judah dropped his staff and, drawing his sword, he rushed forward with Glacon and Joseph at his side.

Judah slashed into a fair-haired man, nearly cutting him in two. Then he ran into the wild melee surging around him.

Seron's first phalanx gave way. They dropped their shields. The men tried to run backwards. He screamed at them and killed two with his sword but nothing would stop them from running away from the battle.

Suddenly, a sharp unbearable pain pulled a scream from Seron's lips. He fell forward over the neck of his mount with an arrow in his side. He was pulled to the ground. Through the blur he saw a tall blonde man standing over him. The next instant the point of the sword rushed toward his body. He screamed. The point of the blade tore through his chest. Blood welled up in Seron's mouth. He was left to die.

The second phalanx was thrown into confusion by the retreat of the first. Their officers tried to form them into battle array, but more men were pouring down from the head of the pass.

Above the screams of the men another shrill note sounded. The Maccabees broke off fighting.

From each side of the pass came a rain of missiles. Rocks broke the faces of some of the Seleucids or struck them with such force that they were felled. Before they realized what was happening, the Maccabees were attacking their flanks.

Above the cries of the wounded and the wild yelling of the men who hacked at one another, many of the Maccabees shouted, "Hear, oh Israel, the Lord is our God, the Lord is one."

"Jews," some of the Seleucids screamed, "Jews!"

"The Maccabees!" others yelled. "The Maccabees!"

Eleazar and Jonathan pulled on the ropes. Drawing them taut across the pass, they blocked the retreat of the Seleucids from the upper half of the pass.

The remaining phalanxes could not move forward. Dropping their shields and spears, they turned and fled.

Waiting for them were Simon and Johanan's men, who closed with the escaping soldiers and slaughtered many hundreds of the fleeing men.

The Seleucids blocked by the ropes stretched across the pass made several efforts to fight their way out of the trap. But each time the Maccabees forced them back, first toward Judah's units and then toward one side or the other of the pass, where Eleazar and Jonathan's men were waiting for them.

The pass was filled with the screams of the dying and the shouts of those in a rage. Sword crashed against sword!

Judah killed and killed, until the men he killed were no more than a blur, and he was stained with their blood.

"After them," Joseph shouted, vaulting over the rope barrier. "After the rest of them." Many men followed him.

"Come back," Judah shouted. "Come back."

Joseph and those with him ran down the defile and out onto the flat plain; then suddenly they found themselves facing the sixteen-man front of a phalanx.

The Seleucids had stopped running; their officers had managed to re-form what was left of them. They were ready to fight for their lives.

Breathing hard, Joseph realized he must turn and run. Signaling to the men behind him, he ran back into safety of the pass.

Judah was waiting for him.

"I didn't think they'd re-form so quickly," Joseph said, gasping for breath.

"You didn't think," Judah responded, his voice hard with anger. "You wanted to prove yourself, even if it cost the lives of the men you led." He turned away and walked back up to the head of the pass. He would never trust Joseph again, and he knew Joseph would hate him for as long as he lived.

When Judah reached the top of the pass, he picked up his blackened staff and signaled his men to gather in front of him. When they were there, he said, "Our dead are few, but we can't take them back with us. We must reach the safety of our camp." And gesturing to the bodies of the Seleucid soldiers, he said, "strip them of their arms. We'll use them for our own purpose."

With childlike simplicity, one of the bloodstained men called out, "Judah, did we really win?"

"We won," Judah answered. "We won another victory for Yahweh!"

The men began to cheer and slap each other on the back. They shouted Judah's name again and again. Several of them lifted Judah to their soldiers and carried him, despite his protests, all the way back to the Gophna Hills.

CHAPTER XVII

After Seron's defeat, the Maccabees were able to move with impunity anywhere in the countryside surrounding Jerusalem, while the men of Sostrates' garrison were limited to making short forays that never took them beyond the sight of the city itself. When night came, the Seleucids shut themselves up in the Citadel, leaving the streets deserted.

Sostrates suspected that if a relief force did not come by the end of the summer, or at the very latest, by early fall, Judah might make a serious attempt to take the city. As it was, bands of Maccabees entered it almost nightly and delivered harsh punishment to those Jews who had become Hellenized. To give his plea for help more urgency than a letter to the King would convey, he had sent Tyropus to Antioch to speak on his behalf to Antiochus. But, as yet, he had not received any word that either Tyropus had safely reached Antioch or that the King had decided to send yet another relief expedition to Judea. He could do nothing but wait, and the summer was very hot and seemed to be interminably long.

In the weeks that followed Judah's victory, more and more Jews threw off their pretense of becoming Greek and joined the Maccabean forces. The camp in the Gophna Hills was too small to hold the multitude that flocked to it. The Maccabees were now an army, and Judah appointed officers over thousands, hundreds, fifties and tens.

One afternoon, at a meeting with his brothers and Glacon, Simon broached the subject of attacking Jerusalem. They sat at a long wooden table protected from the sun by a canopy of wattles. Glacon was on Judah's right and Eleazar at his left. He sat opposite Judah.

"We could take it," Jonathan said with enthusiasm.

Judah moved his eyes from Simon to his youngest brother, who had, for all his youth, proved himself exceptionally able in the field and in camp. He had a way with men that made them follow him.

"We'll take it sooner or later," Simon commented.

"What do you say, Glacon?" Judah asked, now facing his friend.

"It could be done," Glacon answered. "But we would be wiser to wait until we could be sure of holding it."

Simon frowned. He accepted Glacon only because Judah loved him as if he was another brother.

"You seem to question our ability to fight," he said.

"We haven't yet fought our last battle," Glacon responded.

"The Temple must be retaken," Simon said. "We can't wait until we have fought our last battle. Even though you've accepted our God as yours, you can't feel the way we do about the Temple." Simon realized he was being less than gracious to Glacon, but he was speaking the truth.

"I know what you yourself taught me about the Temple, the old one and the one that now stands," Glacon replied. "But whether I feel toward it as you do has no bearing on the military consideration of whether it should be taken now."

"I promised Mattathias I'd regain the Temple," Judah said, "and I won't go back on my word. But I, too, think it'd be a mistake to take it now. It would be a terrible blow to our people to lose it again."

"But what makes you say that we'd lose it?" Simon questioned.

"I'm not sure," Judah answered. "But I don't know what Antiochus intends to do about Seron's defeat, and he must do something. He can't afford to have a rebellious force in his midst while he's fighting in the East. Until we know what he's going to do, we must wait as impatiently as Sostrates waits for the future to become the present."

Though Judah's answer explained the military reason for not proceeding at once against Jerusalem, Simon was certain the religious implication of retaking the Temple should have prevailed.

But rather than risk a confrontation with Glacon, for he was really the source of the opposition, Simon accepted the decision with a nod and even said, "Perhaps you're right. Perhaps my zeal sweeps my reason before it."

"Perhaps," Judah responded and immediately took up the subject of forming several light cavalry units to act either as scouts or flank protection for the infantry units.

The summer wore on. The heat became fiercer than it had been in years. The size of the lake diminished and the green foliage on the shore opposite the camp burned to a dry brown.

Almost every day, several of the old people and many of the infants died.

Miriam was among those who were felled by the summer heat. She had in past weeks shriveled to the size of a child. Her face was crisscrossed by deep lines, and she even lacked the strength to leave her pallet.

Her family was with her when she breathed her last breath. Though she could hardly speak, she took each of their hands in turn, starting with Johanan and managed to whisper how much she loved them.

"See to it," she charged Simon, "that your sister makes a good marriage."

"I will," he answered, his voice choked with sobs.

And to Judah, she said, "You were always more your father's son than mine. I'm sorry I couldn't touch you as I touched my other children. I tried, but I could never reach you. But you were mine, and I loved you because you were mine. Don't be angry with me, Judah, or think ill of me."

"Never, Mother," he tearfully told her.

With her feeble hand, she brushed his cheek. "You'll weep for me?" she questioned.

"Yes," Judah answered.

She nodded and asked for Glacon. When he came and told her he was there, she said, "Take my hand."

Glacon glanced at Judah, who nodded.

"If I had another son," she said haltingly, "I'd have wanted him to be you."

Glacon kissed her hand.

"Judah once mentioned to me you never knew your mother."

"No," he said in a low voice. "I never knew her."

"Pity. She'd have loved you as I've come to, as I know my husband loved you."

"I'll think of you as—" he hesitated; he did not want to insult her real sons.

"As your mother," she whispered, finishing for him what he wanted to say.

"Yes, as a mother," Glacon repeated.

Miriam nodded and with a smile on her lips, she died.

The very next day her children brought the body of their mother to the family tomb in Modin. But this time, they moved in daylight, and thousands of Maccabees followed. They prayed for the wife of Mattathias and the mother of Judah. They prayed that God grant her eternal peace and that

He also grant them victory in their struggle to uphold the Covenant and live by His laws.

On the way back to the camp in the Gophna Hills, Judah made it a point to walk alongside of his sister. And he said in a voice meant only for her to hear, "I wish to end this long silence between us."

"Then die," she answered in a harsh low voice." And without a word more, she quickened her pace.

Judah's step faltered; his heart began to pound.

Eleazar hurried to Judah's side and asked if anything was wrong.

"The heat," Judah answered, "the heat."

"You are very pale."

"It'll pass. I feel better already," Judah assured him.

"Why not take some water?"

Rather than enter into a discussion about it, Judah accepted his brother's water bottle and drank from it.

Then with a nod, he said, "That was what I needed; it was foolish of me not to realize it."

Rebecca's response to him greatly disturbed Judah; and several nights later, long after everyone else had gone to bed, he sat alone by the fire to think about it. He remembered that Joseph had been, or perhaps still was, interested in her. But he did not see any evidence of it, or perhaps he was just not looking.

Joseph, despite what he had done at Beth-Horon, was a good soldier, so good that Judah, contrary to his own feelings about him, had given him command of a thousand men. Joseph and Eleazar were obviously good friends.

Judah reached down, broke off a small piece of dried grass and chewed on it. The prospect of Joseph coming any closer to him than he already was did not sit well, but neither did his sister's antagonism. Her response to his bid for some sort of reconciliation was almost enough to make him hate her.

In disgust, Judah tossed the blade of grass into the fire. Touched by the flames it became a flame and was consumed.

He stood up and stretched. Though he should have been tired, he was not, and he knew it would be useless for him to try to sleep. He walked down to the lake. In the darkness, its surface looked like a black mirror, reflecting a portion of a gibbous moon as it hung above the cliffs behind him.

Without giving much thought to what he was doing, Judah walked halfway around the lake, to where the trees began, stopped, stripped and dove into the water.

The sudden rush of water against his body delighted him. He swam to the middle, rolled over on his back and, floating, he looked up at the splendor of the night sky. After a while, he returned to the shore. But just as he stepped out of the water, he saw a woman. She was going toward water. Her body was very white.

"Who are you?" Judah asked. He was not in the least bit ashamed by his nakedness and did not rush to cover himself.

"Hepzibah," she said. "And you're Judah?"

"I'm Judah," he affirmed with a nod. He held out his hand to her and said, "Come, let us swim together."

She gave him her hand and let herself be led into the water.

Later, he made love to her. She had never lain with a man before and suffered some pain before she experienced any pleasure. Later, when they lay spent in each other's arms, she told him she had come with her family three days before from the town of Hebron and her father's name was Lapidroth.

Judah fell into a deep sleep.

By the time he awoke, most of the night sky had gone and so had Hepzibah. The whole episode was so much like a beautiful dream that by the time he saw her again several days later, he scarcely recognized her. Then, when he did offer a nod of recognition, she flushed and turned away.

* * *

The King's palace in the city of Antioch was very large and decorated in Grecian style with frets made of pink and green marble laid over white alabaster. Its gardens were carpeted with thick green grass and shaded with billowing willows, aspens and smaller oleanders. Close by flowed the Orontes River, whose width was greatly reduced by the intense heat of the summer.

The halls and chambers of the palace were filled with people from various parts of the world and with the officers who helped the King develop his battle plans. All of them had served with him from the time he became their king and many of them would go with him when he left to fight the Persians and the Parthians beyond the Tigris and Euphrates rivers.

But the usual bustle that preceded any military venture had all but ceased since word came of Seron's defeat in Judea and his death at the hands of the Maccabees. To make matters worse, Tyropus had recently arrived to plead on behalf of Sostrates for yet another expedition to be sent to help him hold the city of Jerusalem and suppress the Maccabees, who were, he said, nothing more than a mob of rebellious Jews. That they had destroyed two large forces was unthinkable, yet it had actually happened, and because it had, the King was in a rage. He prowled his sumptuous rooms alone, without regard to whether it was day or night and oblivious to the splendor that once had given him so much pleasure. His eyes were blind, turned inward toward his own sense of agony, of doubt, and self-admitted fear for the future.

Antiochus would speak with no one and, when he was told of Tyropus' arrival, he ordered him bound with chains and cast into a loathsome dungeon. That incident had taken place several weeks before, and since then life in the palace had changed drastically. People spoke in whispers and moved about as quietly as possible. Nothing could change either for the better or the worse until the King would emerge from seclusion.

"Who is this Judah?" the King asked.

"The son of Mattathias, the Priest of Modin. He was the man who held Eleazar in his arms that day in front of the Temple. It was Judah who picked up the dead man's staff. I'm told he carries it wherever he goes, even into battle."

Antiochus did indeed remember that scene. Even without closing his eyes he could see the whole episode, as if it were actually happening in front of him.

"On that day," he said, "I remarked something to the effect that we were witnessing the first of many battles between the Jews and ourselves. But I'll soon put a stop to that."

"Help must be sent to Sostrates as quickly as possible," Tyropus told the King. "It's possible for the Maccabees to take Jerusalem."

Many in the room murmured that it would be impossible for Jews to do something like that. And several scoffed openly at the idea.

"To be sure that it will not happen," Antiochus told them in a tone that did not conceal his anger, "I'll have them completely destroyed, all of the Jews in Judea and Jerusalem will be put to death."

He stood up and, fixing his eyes on Lysias, a trusted member of the royal family and his Viceroy, he called him by name and said, "To you, Lysias, I entrust the task of destroying the Jews; to you I give the honor of being guardian to my son while I battle our enemies in the East; to you I entrust the work of uprooting and destroying the strength of Israel and the remnant of Jerusalem, to blot out all memory of them from the place, to settle strangers in all their territory, and allot the land to settlers."

"I'm deeply honored, My Lord," Lysias said, stepping away from the small group of generals with whom he had been standing. "I'll do my utmost to carry out your commands."

Lysias was a tall, slender man, whose hair was already turning white. He had political skills as well as military ability. Everyone respected him; even his enemies admitted that he was one of the most qualified men in the kingdom and among those most loyal to Antiochus.

"I'll assign half my army to you, Lysias," Antiochus said. "And when you are finished with them, send half of what you have to join me in the East."

"Yes, My Lord," Lysias answered, and then he asked permission to choose his subordinates.

Antiochus granted it with a nod.

"Ptolemy to oversee everything, and Nicanor and Gorgias to command in the field."

"You couldn't have chosen better men," Antiochus said with a broad smile of pleasure. "Now I can go about the business of fighting a real war. Tyropus, my dear friend, spend a few days with us and then return to Sostrates. By then my scribes will have prepared a written report for you to take back to Sostrates that you will find reassuring."

"He'll be most heartened, My Lord," Tyropus answered.

"Tonight," Antiochus told his court, "we'll celebrate our forthcoming victories against all our enemies."

The Seleucids hailed their King and loudly acclaimed the wisdom of his decision to finally destroy all of the Jews forever. It was a visible sign that Zeus had imbued him with a new sense of purpose and the power to achieve it.

CHAPTER XVIII

The Seleucid army marched down the coast, turned east to Lod, bypassed Beth-Horon, worked their way south to Geezer and once more swung east to Emmaus, where they finally stopped. There they built a fortified camp, protected by breastworks and constantly patrolled by fully armed, mounted troops.

General Nicanor, a lean man with green reptilian eyes, had no intentions of going directly into Jerusalem and running the possible risk of having to fight the Maccabees in the passes, as Seron and Apollonius had done with such calamitous results. His intent was to force the Jews out in the open and then overwhelm them with the sheer weight of his army.

General Gorgias agreed completely with his commander. Gorgias was more convivial than Nicanor and therefore better appreciated by his subordinate officers. He looked more like a prosperous merchant than a general. He was a short, heavyset man with a round face, black, flashing eyes and a ready smile.

Many members of his family were in business, and an uncle on his mother's side, named Apollodorus, was a wealthy slave dealer. Because of this family tie, Gorgias, as they walked through the encampment, offered the suggestion to his commander that it might be foolish to kill all of the Jews.

Nicanor did not give the slightest indication he heard what Gorgias said. He seemed completely preoccupied with the Valley of Aijalon, which lay close by and where, according to the holy book of the Jews, one of their ancient heroes, Joshua by name, caused the sun and the moon to stand still. He did not believe that story, any more than he believed the Jew's unseen God could exist.

"Some of the Jews," Gorgias said, undaunted by his superior's lack of response, "might be spared and sold at a handsome profit. Say, half of all we capture. Selling them into slavery would essentially destroy them."

"Have you already discussed the matter with your uncle?" Nicanor asked, still looking out at the broad sweep of the valley.

"Apollodorus made the suggestion to me in a recent letter," Gorgias explained. "He spoke to General Lysias about it, who left the matter completely in our hands, though I'm sure the General would be pleased to receive some token of our appreciation should we decide to . . ."

"Since there'll be no booty and nothing we can claim for ourselves other than the victory," Nicanor said, "we might as well make the expedition as profitable as possible. But I'd much prefer having other slavers in addition to your uncle come and bid for the Jews."

"I'll send word to my uncle," Gorgias responded.

"And I'll notify the slavers in Jaffa, Jamnia and Ashkelon," Nicanor said. "I think they should gather here within a week. I want to have everything about this matter settled before we go against the Maccabees."

"I agree with you most heartily," Gorgias answered.

* * *

Within a matter of days, fifty slavers arrived in the Seleucid camp. Among them were representatives from Gorgias' uncle, Apollodorus. All of the dealers brought their personal slaves with them and women for the officers of the army. They also brought a large supply of iron fetters and a sufficient quantity of gold and silver to pay for their purchase.

Nicanor's men set up special tents for the slavers and made certain they were well fed. He purposefully withheld his presence from them and insisted that Gorgias do the same.

"Let them wonder about us a bit," he told his subordinate general. "I wouldn't want them to have the impression that we are too eager. To them this must appear as some courtesy we're willing to extend to them, or perhaps that it has something to do with the wishes of Antiochus himself. The more official it seems, the higher they will bid."

Gorgias laughed approvingly. Then their conversation turned to the military situation.

"Our spies," Nicanor said, "haven't seen any major movement of the Maccabees. "They're still in the Gophna Hills and in the camps close by them. Judah appears to be watching us as closely as we are watching him."

"Some of our sentinels have received arrow wounds," Gorgias told his superior. "I'm told more of them than before are now in their camp at Mizpeh."

"That base covers Beth-Horon to the north of Jerusalem and Sha'ar Hagai to the south of the city," Nicanor commented.

"If we overran it," Gorgias suggested, "we might force Judah to give battle."

"It's certainly worth thinking about."

"I'll see if I can come up with some sort of a plan," Gorgias offered.

Nicanor nodded and then told his junior commander to hold the slave auction the following night. "Have our guests well fed and give them as much wine as they want."

"Perhaps we might have them eat, drink and do business at the same time?" Gorgias suggested. "It might even be a good idea for the women to be there."

Nicanor rubbed his chin and commented, "A festive atmosphere might make the bidding more active."

"And it would give our officers a chance to enjoy the women."

"Excellent!" Nicanor exclaimed. "I'd have all of the men take their pleasure with the women, but there are too few of them and too many men. We'll let them use the Jewish women we capture. If in fact we tell them the women are theirs, it should give them more incentive to win than to just stay alive."

"The slavers are more interested in the men than in the women," Gorgias explained "We'll have to kill the women anyway; they might as well be used for a good purpose before they die."

"If the slavers should want some of the women," Nicanor said, "we could always put aside whatever number they ask for."

"Absolutely!"

* * *

"Ninety to the talent," Judah said reflectively. He repeated it several times without looking at Ezra, who sat across the open fire from him. Then he commented, "That would be about nine men and women for every six hundred drachmas."

"Men," Ezra responded. "They won't take any women. The women are to be given to the soldiers and then killed, the way they were in the hills to the southwest of Jerusalem."

Judah's jaws clamped so tightly together that a sudden pain tore at the muscles on both sides of his face. Through clenched teeth, he explained, "I'd slaughter the women myself before I let any one of them fall into the hands of the Seleucids."

Ezra remained silent.

"They have twenty thousand men," Judah said. "That's twice what I have all together and three times more than the number in this camp. I can't move until I know their intentions."

"Neither Nicanor nor Gorgias appear to be in a hurry to reach Jerusalem."

"If they were," Judah responded, "it'd be much easier." Then he said, "They hold us so very cheaply, it almost makes me suspect they don't think of us as men, much less men who are willing to fight and die for their beliefs. That's their biggest mistake, Ezra, and not the loss of any past or future battles. They fail to see us for what we are."

Ezra drew his cloak more securely around him before he said, "They hope you and the people will lose heart."

Judah spat into the flames. His spittle made a hissing sound the moment it struck a red glowing faggot. "The people fight for their God and the Law He gave them. They fight to honor the Covenant between our forefathers and Him. To lose heart would be the same as dying."

"Would it be the same for you, Judah?" Ezra asked in a low voice, looking at his host through the reddish flicker of the flames. Since he had first come to Judah, he had never spoken to him about Yahweh, but this time he felt that he must. He had to know what drove this man to become his champion.

Judah extended his large hands toward the fire, but not for warmth. He wanted Ezra to look at his hands as he said, "They're well suited for what they do."

"And that's your purpose, your reason?"

"Perhaps to do what Mattathias would have done," Judah answered, "had he been young enough."

"What about your love for Yahweh?" Ezra questioned.

With a look of resignation, Judah replied, "I love my people; I could never find any reason in my heart to love Yahweh." Then he added, "I'm sorry, Ezra, I couldn't tell you what you wanted to hear. But I did tell you the truth."

"The truth was all I ever wanted," Ezra said. "The truth, Judah, is all that Yahweh ever wants." He stood up and told Judah he would return as soon as he had new information about the Seleucid's movements. Then he disappeared into the wilderness.

* * *

Ezra did not bring word of the Seleucid's movements; it came from Judah's own reconnaissance units. Just after sundown, when the weather turned raw and blustery, four riders galloped into the camp at Mizpeh. They reported to Glacon that several thousand men, including cavalry, had left their encampment at Emmaus and were heading in their direction. From what they could gather, the force was being led by Gorgias, at least they saw his banners to the rear of the lead phalanx.

"The Seleucids aren't much when it comes to night fighting," Glacon commented, after he had related the information to Judah.

"They won't have to do any fighting," Judah answered with a smile; then he assembled his brothers Johanan, Simon, and Jonathan and told them about Gorgias' movement. "But while they're *here,"* he said, "we'll be *there.* We'll attack the remaining force at Emmaus. Johanan, Simon and Jonathan take fifteen hundred men each, and I'll take fifteen hundred men. Jonathan and I will attack from the east, while Simon and Johanan will do the same from the west. Glacon and Eleazar will be with me. We must move swiftly. Light fires in the camp and feed them with enough wood to burn throughout the night. Gorgias must think we're here."

All through Judah's camp, the men prepared for the coming march and the battle at the end of it. As soon as the army was assembled and ready to move, he shouted to the men, "Nicanor and Gorgias have already sold you into slavery. One talent of gold for each ninety men. One talent for ninety of us!"

The Maccabees grumbled angrily that they would be the ones to take prisoners.

"There'll be no prisoners," Judah roared. "We don't want slaves." He told them what the Seleucids planned to do with the women.

The men were silent. There was not one among them who did not remember what the Seleucids had done some two years before to the women of the Hasidim outside of Jerusalem.

"We mustn't let them fulfill their purpose," Judah exhorted his army. "We must stop them!"

"We will," the men shouted in response. "We will, Judah. We will!"

When they fell silent, he raised his staff and ordered them to begin the trek to Emmaus. While on the march, he sent word to each of his brothers to tell their men to move as quietly as possible, that surprise would put victory within their grasp.

Glacon looked up at the ragged clouds and commented, "The wind is wild tonight."

"The men will fight well," Glacon said. "You've more than given them reason to."

"That was why I said nothing about the slavers until I was sure it would do them the most good."

Glacon clicked his tongue appreciatively.

* * *

The Seleucid forces were skillfully guided through the passes by Hellenistic Jews who knew the country. Gorgias had his point men out and several units of cavalry covering his flanks.

The cold, blustery night made it difficult for Gorgias' men to keep the pace. They used their huge shields to ward off the buffeting wind but a sudden change in its direction would turn their protection into a small wild sail that they would have to fight in order to bring it back under control. They did not march in step, for fear that their rhythmic footfalls would be heard by the Maccabees.

Gorgias had chosen his best men for the task. All of them had seen action in one or another part of the Kingdom. His plan for a night attack had come none too soon, since Lysias had become impatient with his and Nicanor's lack of action and was already on the march from Antioch with another twenty thousand infantry and four thousand horsemen.

Nicanor had made it quite clear that Lysias had lost faith in their ability to handle the situation.

But Gorgias knew if his action was successful, then Lysias' coming to Judea could only appear to be the act of a foolish man, probably one uncertain of his own standing with the King.

The march for the Seleucids seemed endless; they twisted through deep gorges whose sides at the top became so narrow that only a ribbon of the sky remained visible from below.

Gorgias ordered silence and his troops obeyed.

Most of the night was gone before they saw the flickering fires of Judah's camp at Mizpeh.

Gorgias ordered a halt. He sent his scouts forward.

Minutes later they returned and told him that the Jews had not even posted guards.

Gorgias ordered his men to encircle the camp. Cavalry units were to rush in first; the infantry would follow. Everyone would move on the blast of the trumpet.

The army dispersed and silently ringed the camp. In one fell swoop, the Maccabees would be destroyed. Gorgias' heart thumped with excitement. A crack in the eastern sky showed the gray of dawn. He looked at the fires in the Maccabean camp; they had all but burnt out.

"Sound the trumpet now," Gorgias ordered. "Sound the attack! Now!"

A single quavering note shimmered above the enemy camp. Shouting wildly, the men of Gorgias' army rushed forward.

The cavalry charged ahead of the slower phalanxes. With lances held low, they swept into the camp, scattering glowing embers on the windy fury of their gallop.

Behind the swift assault of the horsemen came the rush of the phalanxes, whose lead units were caught in the swirling dust of the riders. They stabbed at everything, but there was nothing.

"Nothing," the soldiers cried. "Nothing! Nothing! The Jews have vanished!"

The cavalry wheeled around and, at a walk, re-entered the camp, while the soldiers looked questioningly at each other. Then realizing that somehow their enemy had managed to escape, they grumbled at their officers, who had made them march all night for nothing.

Gorgias summoned his subordinate officers and, breathing hard with anger, he said, "These Jews have run away from us . . ." He glanced up at the sky. "It's light enough to follow them. They can't be too far from here. Send out the scouts and the cavalry. The rest of us will remain here, ready to move as soon as word comes to us."

His commands were acted on immediately. But he was deeply troubled by the fiasco that had just taken place. He could expect no consideration from Nicanor, who was already more than concerned about Lysias' attitude toward himself. Besides, Nicanor had only agreed to the night operation because he could not think of any other ploy that would draw the Maccabees into battle.

Gorgias had expected the night attack to be completely successful, and as part of the operation, Nicanor had agreed to march his force straight to Jerusalem, where they would join their two forces together again to make one complete victorious army.

He looked around him; the men had rekindled the fires left by the Jews to deceive them and were warming themselves. Many of them were sleeping, and several like himself were just standing and waiting for word from the scouts.

By dawn, Judah's men were in position to attack the camp at Emmaus. They crouched low, and when the first light of the day cracked through the edge of the eastern sky, the Maccabees rushed at the Seleucid camp, shouting, "Hear, oh Israel, the Lord is our God, the Lord is one!"

But as soon as they broke from their concealment and charged for the breastworks, Judah saw that Nicanor's forces were moving out of the camp. It was too late for the Maccabees to stop the attack.

As Nicanor formed men into battle array, he realized that the men attacking him were the very same Maccabees that Gorgias was supposed to have destroyed. His phalanxes wheeled into the open country in front of the encampment.

Judah ordered his unit to strike at the cavalry and sent runners to his brothers to press their attacks on the flanks and the rear of the Seleucid phalanxes.

Judah wielded his gold-hilt sword with great stabbing thrusts at the riders that loomed above him. He caught glimpses of the riders; here a scared face, there a tuft of brown beard.

The horses reared and the smell of fresh blood made the animals scream with terror.

Judah took a spear in his shoulder and tore the iron head from his bleeding body. Another horseman came charging down at him and, leaping aside, Judah brought his sword down on the man's back, slicing through him.

Glacon mounted one of the riderless horses and rushed at the Seleucid cavalry.

Judah called him back, shouting "Glacon, order our own cavalry units into action."

Within minutes the Maccabean horsemen charged into the fray. Their spears brought down many of the Seleucid riders.

Judah mounted a riderless horse, and with Glacon at his side he galloped to where Simon was fighting.

"Keep them from forming up," Judah shouted to his brother. "Bring the men into close combat with them."

Then Judah swiftly rode to Johanan and, dismounting, he hurried to his brother's side. "Bring your men around to the rear. We must cut their escape off. They mustn't be able to retreat into the camp again."

"Judah," Johanan shouted, "I won't be able to hold them long."

"Close with them," Judah shouted back, as he swung into the saddle again.

With Glacon, he galloped back to where Jonathan and Eleazar were fighting.

Most of the Seleucid cavalry was unhorsed and were fighting on foot. Half of the Maccabean horsemen had been killed or wounded. Jonathan and Eleazar were spattered with blood.

Everywhere there were dying horses.

"They're running, the Seleucids are running," the Maccabees shouted to one another.

"After them," Judah yelled. "Keep after them!"

Nicanor ordered his men to fall back toward the coastal plain. Thousands of them dropped their weapons and fled. Those who stood and fought were cut down by the pursuing Maccabees; they chased the enemy to Gazar, to the lowlands of Idumea, Azotus and Jamnia before Judah summoned them to return to the camp at Emmaus.

"The day still isn't done," Judah told his men. "We must burn this camp and ready ourselves for Gorgias." He looked up at the sun. It was flecked with the dark wings of the vultures; he hated those carrion birds as much as, perhaps more than, he hated the Seleucids. He turned toward Glacon and said, "Burn everything."

"What should we do with the slavers?" Eleazar asked, as they entered the encampment.

Judah stopped. He spread his hands, halting everyone. There in the center of the camp, Ezra was mounted on a small cairn of rocks. He was impaled on a spear and the end of the bloody spear shaft was imbedded in the rocks. He flailed his arms and legs.

Judah staggered. He shut his eyes.

No one moved.

Judah opened his eyes and motioned all of them to remain where they were. He walked slowly to where Ezra flailed at the empty air and several times he softly called to him.

Blood came from Ezra's mouth when he opened it to cry out, "Hear, oh Israel, the Lord is our God, the Lord is one."

"Ezra," Judah whispered, fighting back the sob in his throat, "oh, Ezra, Ezra."

"Kill me," Ezra screamed. "Kill me, Yahweh, kill me!"

Judah's vision blurred. Tears streamed from his eyes. He nodded and lifting his sword, he plunged it into Ezra's heart. Then with his own hand, he lifted Ezra's body off of the spear and, carrying it in his arms, he set it gently on the brown earth, which was quickly stained red by the gush of blood from Ezra's pierced body.

Judah looked up at Glacon. Choking, he said, "I never really knew who he was, or where he came from. But he was one of us, Glacon. Perhaps he was even more than all of us." Judah shook his head, then, with a ragged breath, he ordered the slavers be brought to him. When they were assembled, he pointed to Ezra's tortured frame and said, "Look at him, each of you and then look at us. Don't shrink from looking at the body or at us. You have seen the last of what you'll ever see."

Fifty voices offered gold and silver to be spared.

"Blind them," Judah shouted. "Blind them and send them back from whence they came."

The slavers screamed for mercy. Judah's men did not move.

"Blind them" Judah shouted and taking his sword, he stabbed its point into the right eye of the slaver nearest him. "I'll do it myself, if you shrink from it."

"Mercy," the slavers cried. "We plead for mercy!"

Judah pointed his sword at Ezra's bleeding body and he said, "I give you more mercy than you gave him."

Simon came forward but Judah waved him back, "If necessary," Judah told his men, "I'll blind all of them. But, blind they will be."

The Maccabees rushed forward. The screams of the slavers rose above the sounds of everything else that was happening. Soon, the air was filled with columns of black smoke and the stench of burning tents.

With his own hands, Judah buried Ezra, and with stones he built a cairn to mark the site of the grave.

By late afternoon, the Seleucid camp at Emmaus was a smoking ruin, and Judah deployed his men along its approaches to wait for Gorgias' return and the beginning of another battle.

But Gorgias never returned. His scouts saw the destruction wrought by the Maccabees and reported it back to their General. Rather than risk defeat, Gorgias and his army fled in panic to the safety of Philistra.

Judah left Emmaus and brought his army back to the camp in the Gophna Hills. The wound he had taken in the shoulder was not serious, but the death of Ezra affected him greatly. Several times he tried to pray but found he could not. He could not speak to Yahweh and Yahweh would not speak to him.

CHAPTER XIX

Winter was rapidly approaching, and before the cold, wind-driven rains struck the land, Lysias wanted to reach Jerusalem. The defeats suffered by Nicanor and Gorgias had subjected him to letters of sharp rebuke from Antiochus.

Lysias' plan was to use Jerusalem as his base; then with large units move into the Gophna Hills. There was nothing dramatic or elegant about his intended maneuvers. He was going to use brute force and nothing more to crush the Jews and end their kind forever.

He marched his army down the coast to Ashkelon, moved southeast through Gezara and finally made for the pass at Beth-Zur that lay on the road from Hebron to Jerusalem. He kept his army intact.

Judah followed the movements of Lysias' army, and when it reached Gezara, he knew it was heading for the pass at Beth-Zur. Judah chose a place about ten stadia north of Beth-Zur. He committed his entire force to the action, except for several units that were left to guard the camps. The men were posted on either side of a gully. They took their positions at night.

Toward morning, a strong, wet wind brought the promise of rain.

The sky was filled with low, scudding clouds.

In the distance, they could hear the sounds of trumpets, as Lysias' army began to break camp and ready itself for the final march to Jerusalem.

The portion of the defile through which the Seleucids would have to pass before they could reach the open plain above was too narrow to allow a sixteen-man front. They would be forced to change into a column of twos.

Judah told his men, "Once the Seleucids are out of the pass, they won't expect anything; they won't be on the alert. We'll charge them at the sound of the rain's horn."

The Maccabees lay crouched behind the huge boulders that lay strewn on either side of the gully. Moment by moment, the sound of the Seleucid army became louder.

The wind blew swirls of sand across the mouth of the defile.

The Maccabees could hear the shouts of the Seleucid officer urging their men to move faster.

The first few Seleucids came out of the pass. They continued to move forward. The gully proved too narrow for them to form a four-man front and they continued to move in a column of twos.

Judah turned to the man with the ram's horn and nodded.

One sharp note sounded and the Maccabees loosed a shower of arrows. Many of the Seleucids fell. And then the rest of Judah's army fell upon the emerging column.

Judah slashed his way to the mouth of the pass. Glacon followed him. Between the two of them they killed many of Lysias' men. Then Judah fell back, allowing more of the enemy to enter the gully. These were quickly cut down by the other Maccabees.

The Seleucid soldiers dropped their weapons and fled back into the pass.

Judah's men slashed at them from either side of the gully; now a swift foray with swords; then a terrible charge with spears and always with volleys of arrows.

259

Shouting in tenor, the forward units of the Seleucid army completely disintegrated, and they ran aimlessly, colliding with those units still in the defile.

Judah ordered his men to keep at them from the heights above the pass from where they hurled rocks and rolled huge boulders down on the enemy soldiers.

More and more of Lysias' units turned and ran. Many of them fled back into the previous night's camp before the last of the remaining phalanxes had left.

Lysias saw his army destroyed. There was no hope of regrouping to mount a counterattack. He and all his officers joined the fleeing soldiers.

"Now," Judah shouted to his men, as they watched the enemy disappear under a cloud of dust, "now, we'll go up and retake Jerusalem."

The Maccabees shouted with joy; they had truly won a great victory!

* * *

As they made their way from the Gophna Hills toward Jerusalem, a cold-edged wind drove against the Maccabees. They were an army now of several thousand men. They were well armed from the store of enemy equipment they had captured at Beth Zur, after having defeated the Viceroy, Lysias, there.

Though Judah did not use any of the roads, he knew it would be impossible for him to conceal the movement of so many men from the Seleucid spies.

Now, all the Jews who lived in the villages and farmed the land around the city were friendly to the Maccabees. In the past, Judah had been forced to deal harshly with some of the families, killing the father or the oldest son to prevent them from betraying his own sympathizers to the Seleucid authorities. Almost from the beginning of his war with the Greeks, he also was forced into fighting those Jews, who like Menelaus, preferred to accept Zeus rather than keep Yahweh and His laws.

"It feels more and more like rain," Eleazar commented. He was dressed similarly to Judah and all of the other Maccabees. In addition to his other clothing, Eleazar wore a Seleucid breastplate, helmet and sword. Since he had taken to the Gophna Hills some two years before, he had become lean and hard.

"What do you think, Glacon," Judah questioned, looking to his right, "will we have rain?"

The former Seleucid officer scanned the dark sky. "Ugly," he said, "When it comes, it'll be a hard rain."

"Will we fight if it rains?" Eleazar asked.

"Yes," Judah answered. "We must take the city as quickly as possible. Lysias won't waste time. As soon as he re-forms, he'll be at us again, or we'll be at him."

Simon came up.

Eleazar moved way from Judah's side to allow Simon to walk between them.

"Joseph, our cousin, asked to be allowed to lead one of the assaults," Simon said. "This is the second or third time he made the same request."

Judah glanced at his brother. Though he had developed a deep affection for Eleazar and had come to admire all of his brothers, his ties to Simon had grown stronger. Each had learned to sense the other's moods; sometimes even the other's thoughts. From the very beginning of their trek from

Modin into the wilderness of the Gophna Hills, they had worked together.

Simon saw the expression on his brother's face, and for an instant he felt as if Mattathias had come back from the grave to glare angrily at him. There was dark smoke behind the light blue places in his eyes; and there were even two vertical ridges on his forehead.

"Then Joseph has also spoken to you about it?" Simon asked.

"Yes," Judah said. "I told him that unlike Uriah, he doesn't have to ask to be put in the front rank to prove his courage. He fights well but not well enough to be among the first."

"He's ambitious," Simon responded.

"None of us," Judah told his brother, finally facing him again, "can afford the luxury of personal ambition, such an extravagance might cost him his life."

"He doesn't think you recognize his courage," Simon said. "Is that what he told you?"

"Not in so many words," Simon answered. "But the meaning was clear."

Judah looked past Simon to Eleazar and he said, "Joseph is your friend; do you think him ready to lead an assault?"

"We haven't spoken much since Beth Zur," Eleazar answered.

Judah surmised that the falling out between the two young men had something to do with him, but he did not press Eleazar for an explanation. Instead, he moved his eyes back to Simon and said, "You tell our cousin, I place more value on his life than he does. He'll fight when and where I order."

"I've already indicated as much to him," Simon said, "but I wanted to be sure of your thinking."

Judah laughed and good-naturedly slapped his brother on the back. Then he said, "This won't be like the other battles."

"We'll be exposed," Glacon commented, "until we reach the stones."

"God will be with us," Simon answered, "as He has been in all our past encounters. He knows we come to Jerusalem, not so much to conquer the city as to win the Temple back for Him."

They fell silent and continued to walk at a very fast pace.

Judah glanced back at the thousands of men following him. They were spread out over a large area. Despite Glacon's pleas, Judah refused to move them in phalanxes.

"Certain things," he once had said to Glacon, "we must copy from our enemy in order to stay alive. But we must do many, many things on our own, otherwise the longer we fight, the more we'll become like them and the less we remain like ourselves."

The Maccabees moved on a broad, inwardly curved front. The two ends were guarded by small cavalry units. Then, in each portion of the arc there was a specific group of fighters. Some were spearmen, others fought mainly with the sword, and still others were bowmen and stone slingers. And far out in front of the army ranged its scouts. Many were mounted, while others moved on foot in groups of two and three.

The bite of the wind sharpened. A cold, stinging rain swept in from the sea. Judah ordered the pace quickened.

Two riders came close to them but they did not stop.

"From Sostrates," Glacon commented.

"Yes, from Sostrates," Judah echoed.

"Are we going to try to capture the Citadel?" Eleazar asked.

"We'll have more than enough to do to take the city," Judah answered. "The Citadel will fall of its own weight. Once we take Jerusalem, the fortress will be cut off from the rest of the world. We'll take it without a fight."

The city suddenly came into view, and the men shouted with joy. Judah ordered the army to swing south. After a brief march, they turned north and faced the city.

In front of them lay the walls that Sostrates had smashed when he had forced Menelaus on the Jews. Now those same stones would provide excellent cover for the Seleucid soldiers.

Judah signaled the army to come to a halt and sent Eleazar for Jonathan, Simon, and several of his other commanders. When they were assembled, he pointed to the stones and he said, "Part of the attacking force will have to drive the Seleucids out of their hiding places."

"I'll do it," Jonathan volunteered.

Judah nodded, and then he said, "Glacon, swing to the left, around the stones, and block off any retreat to the Citadel . . . Eleazar, go with him. The rest of us will go to the right and fight our way to the Temple . . . If we reach it, we might have to fight our way into it . . . Should that happen, have the assault ladders ready to lay against the walls of the Temple . . . Are there any questions?"

"How long will we remain in Jerusalem?" Jonathan asked.

Judah looked at Simon.

And Simon said, "First, let us get there. Then we'll decide everything else."

Jonathan, realizing his brothers divined the reason for his question, cast his eyes downward and flushed.

After a short prayer offered by Simon asking God to grant them victory, Judah dismissed his commanders, but he had Jonathan remain with him for a few moments. Then to his youngest brother, he said, "I won't stop you from what you must do. If I loved a woman, I would want to see her, even if she were a Greek."

Again Jonathan's face reddened, and he tried to speak but Judah told him, "Perhaps if she loves you enough, she will leave her God and accept yours."

"I hope she will," Jonathan responded.

"For your sake, Brother, so do I," Judah said, and with a firm clasp of his hand, he sent Jonathan back to his men.

Once more, the army began to advance. But, even as it moved, the various units rearranged themselves into a battle formation that would permit them to carry out the three-pronged attack Judah had evolved.

The bow shaped front of the army straightened. Cavalry units detached themselves and swung behind the attacking force to guard its rear.

The air was suddenly rent by three blasts from a ram's horn. "The Maccabees began to run. Over and over again, the men shouted, "Hear, oh Israel, the Lord is our God, the Lord is one!"

They raced across the open space separating them from the stones of the wall.

The rain lashed them and then the air was filled with the swishing sound of hundreds of arrows loosed by the Seleucid soldiers hidden behind the rocks.

The arrows arched high in the air and came down with a soft thwack.

Men screamed, fell, and bled to death. But the Maccabees continued to run.

More arrows swooshed toward them. Some found their mark. More of the running men went down.

Then there were another three blasts on the ram's horn. The Maccabean army divided into three segments.

Judah led his group toward the Temple, while Jonathan continued to drive toward the stones and Glacon's force raced off to the left.

The action confounded the Seleucid Commander, Sostrates. He had expected a frontal attack, and he was completely prepared for it when it came. But now his bowmen had three different targets to fix their sights on. In their confusion, they stopped shooting altogether.

Jonathan shouted for his men to run faster. He saw the stones in front of him and, here and there, he caught sight of a Seleucid helmet. His men reached the stones. In the next instant, the enemy force leaped up and, casting their bows down, met them with their swords. Blade clanged against blade in the fierce and deadly struggle to dislodge Sostrates' men from their positions. Within minutes, the rocks were slippery with blood and the spaces between them were filled with the dead and dying men.

Glacon's units found little resistance. They ran up the long valley and through the crooked streets that separated the western and eastern portions of the city and took up positions to block off the retreat of the Seleucid soldiers who were fighting at the stones.

Judah and Simon led the dash to the Temple.

But Sostrates was determined to keep the Maccabees from their goal. Under his own command, two phalanxes moved against Judah's force. They came with spears held low.

Judah ordered his ranks to open. He attacked the Seleucid force on its flanks. He cut his way through several lines, leaving nothing but death in his wake. His men followed him.

The Seleucids fought back. Their spears caught many of the Maccabees, but the attack was too ferocious for them to stop it.

Their lines could not hold against the deadly slashing strokes of the Maccabees.

Then, from the stones came wild screams of triumph. Jonathan had fought his way through the Seleucid ranks. The enemy soldiers who could still retreat began to run toward the Citadel.

When the men with Sostrates realized what was happening to their comrades, they wavered. Some broke and ran.

"Keep at them!" Judah shouted, driving his sword into the chest of a long-faced man with a scar on his cheek.

The Maccabees drove deeper into the two phalanxes.

Sostrates attempted to rally them. He killed two that tried to run away. And then was surprised to hear his name being shouted. He turned and saw a lean, bloodstained man confronting him. He knew he was facing the Jew called Judah, the leader of the Maccabees. He gathered a mouth full of saliva and spat. Then he lunged at Judah.

Judah sidestepped Sostrates' thrust. With a slashing stroke to the right, he cut through the neck of the Seleucid commander. Sostrates' head dropped into the mud, while his body slipped forward, close to where Judah was standing.

The Seleucid troops that broke and ran from Jonathan's onslaught found themselves under attack from another force of Maccabees. The battle that followed was swift and bloody.

Judah let his soldiers finish off what was left of the two phalanxes that had tried to stop him from retaking the Temple. With Simon at his side, he entered the outer precincts of the holiest of holy places. He walked slowly.

To stop him from going farther, Simon put his hand on Judah's arm. "We are filthy with sweat and the blood of other men."

"And this place stinks from the offerings of swine made to Zeus," Judah answered.

"There's still killing going on outside," Simon said. "You can hear the screams of the men."

"I gave them their Temple," Judah responded. "I paid for it with my blood and the blood of many thousands of men."

"Judah," Simon told his brother, "God gave you the strength to do what you did."

Judah lifted his eyes and looked at the building in front of him. In the rain its red bricks looked as if they were drenched with blood. "I gave it to them Simon," he said in a low voice. "I gave it to them with this." And he raised his bloody sword aloft.

"And now, Judah," Simon responded softly, "you must be prepared to give them a miracle."

"I don't believe in miracles," Judah said.

"The Temple is not enough, Judah; our people must have something that they will be able to carry down through the ages with them."

Judah shook his head.

"It must be, Judah."

"If you say it must be, Simon," Judah responded, "then it will be. But at this moment, if I could make a miracle happen, I'd have my father here to see this, to know that the Temple belongs once more to the Jews."

Simon nodded and gesturing toward the walls, he said, "The battle is over; there is no more screaming."

Judah walked toward the inner precincts, and, this time, Simon did not stop him. He knew that, even if he tried, he would have failed. For a short while, Judah had to have the Temple to himself so that he could share it with the spirit of their father.

CHAPTER XX

Under Simon's direction, the Temple was cleared, cleaned and purified, according to the Law. Even the stones of the altar, defiled with the blood of sacrifices made to Zeus, were removed and in their stead unhewn stones were used to rebuild the altar.

The men who had fought so hard to regain the holy place of their faith put down their weapons. With a joyous vigor, they worked to restore the Temple, making day of night with hundreds of torches so that darkness would not stop or even impede the restoration of their beloved Temple.

As Simon watched the men toil, sometimes standing with Johanan or Eleazar, in the flickering reddish-yellow glow of a torch, he was deeply troubled. More than any of his brothers, he understood that the retaking of the Temple was the beginning of a new era for all of the Hasmoneans and for all of the Jews. There had to be something to mark it for the generations to come, an act that the people could perform again and again in the centuries to come that would recall what had been done by Maccabees. The more Simon thought about the problem, the more the solution eluded him.

The work in the Temple was finally finished. Then, on the twenty-fifth day of the ninth month, they rose early and offered upon the newly made altar sacrifice of burnt offering according to the Law. On the anniversary of the day when the heathen had profaned it, it was reconsecrated with hymns of thanksgiving, to the music of harps and lutes and cymbals. All the people prostrated themselves and uttered praises to Heaven that their cause had prospered.

On that day, the sun was bright in a cloudless sky. And when Judah and his brothers came out of the Temple, the people swarmed around them, shouting each of their names and commending them to God.

Judah removed his prayer shawl from his head and laid it across his shoulders. His brothers followed his example.

Then, unexpectedly, Glacon separated himself from the group who had been in the Temple. He stepped in front of Judah and held his hands high over his head to silence the people. "All of you know me," he said, "and many, many of you have fought at my side. I and my wife came to you because of all the men I have ever known, I knew Judah would protect us, if need be with his life."

The people listened intently to what Glacon was saying; they knew he was among the bravest of their soldiers.

"I came to one man," Glacon told them, "but I found a second father in Mattathias and a second mother in Miriam, may God grant them eternal peace. I found even more than the love of these people, I found your God and your Law." He turned to look at Judah. "I pledge until the end of my life the use of my sword to keep faith with Judah, with you, and with our God."

The multitude shouted their approval of what Glacon told them. They had come to love and respect him as much as he had grown to love and respect them.

Once more, Glacon raised his hands for silence. Then reaching into his robe, he brought forth a beautiful piece of blue silk that had been folded into a square. "This is the work of my wife Helen. It is our gift to all of you and especially to Judah. It is what we all believe." He flung it open for everyone to see. A large white Star of David was embroidered on its center, and below it in golden thread was inscribed, "Who resists tyrants obeys God."

Irving A. Greenfield

Even as the Maccabees cheered Glacon's gift, Judah came forward and embraced his friend, "It'll be our flag, the flag of our people.

Wherever we go, it'll be with us and its likeness will fly over the Temple for everyone to know our purpose!"

A joyous period of dancing and singing followed. The people took hold of Judah and drew him to dance with them; then they did the same to all of his brothers and finally they brought Glacon into the dance too.

When the celebration was over and all of the people had left the precincts of the Temple, Simon gathered his brothers together and asked them to enter the Temple with him. There, it was darker than in the swiftly gathering twilight that was already spreading over the land and erasing the last vestiges of day. Only a few candles burned. He gestured to his brothers that they sit at a small table set along the west wall. Then he said, "All that is lacking is a miracle."

Judah shook his head and, holding forth Glacon's gift, he said, "This is enough of a miracle." He was deeply touched by his friend's gesture and the response of the people to it.

Slowly and in very precise terms, Simon explained what he meant by a miracle. "All we've done must never be forgotten by the Jews of the future. They must know that without the Maccabees they would have been denied their God, the Covenant would have been broken between the Jews and God, and they would be without His Law."

"I told you," Judah said, "our miracle is that we've come here at all and perhaps that we might yet win the struggle. Antiochus won't let us keep what we've won without trying again to take it from us."

"But I thought," Johanan complained, "when we retook Jerusalem and reclaimed the Temple, our battles would be over."

Eleazar reminded him of the Citadel.

"But surely," Johanan said, "they'll see the hopelessness of their situation and surrender."

Judah did not reply.

"What the Seleucids do or don't do," Simon commented with exasperation, "is not the problem now. Now we must give the people . . ."

Jonathan stood up and walked to where an eight-branched oil lamp stood. He looked up at it for a long time; he walked around it, and then turning to where his brothers sat, he said, "Tell the people there was only enough oil for one night but that it burned for eight."

"Tell them what you want," Judah responded.

Simon went to where Jonathan was standing, and he too examined the eight-branched oil lamp. It looked surprisingly like a tree. All of the branches were of different lengths or went in different directions.

From the dark sheen on it, it seemed to have been newly wrought. Most probably by one of their own craftsmen. Indeed, the bowls on the top of each branch appeared to have been hammered out of Seleucid spearheads, bending them in such a way so that they now looked like long-stemmed buds.

"We could say," Simon suggested, placing his hand on a stem, "that only one cruse of undefiled oil could be found, one cruse that still bore the seal of the High Priest Onias."

"And what of the truth?" Judah asked.

Simon returned to the table and he said, "We will give them a greater truth, something their children and their children's children will be able to do for all time. They will be able to celebrate our victory and the rededication of this Temple by lighting a candle each night for eight nights. By next year we can even name it *The Festival of Lights* and it will be known as that for all time."

Judah remained silent.

Simon pressed him for a response.

"I don't walk with Yahweh," Judah said with a voice of resignation. "I can't answer, other than to say that, if it's what our people need, then they must have it."

"It is what they need," Johanan told him.

Eleazar and Jonathan agreed with their oldest brother.

"Trust me," Simon said to Judah.

Judah nodded, but the good feeling he had when Glacon had handed him the flag was gone. He no longer felt comfortable in the Temple and, though he had given it back to his people, Judah knew he would never again enter it. He was a stranger in the house of the Lord, even as Moses, after he fled from Egypt, had been a stranger in a strange land.

"I'll see to it," Simon said.

Again, Judah nodded; then he stood up, and he walked out of the Temple into the beauty of a crisp, star-studded night. He paused in the courtyard, looked up at the sky and in a whisper, he said, "My brothers walk with You, even Glacon walks with You but I, . . . I must walk alone. Perhaps, if I could really believe You're there, then I'd try to walk with You." He glanced over his shoulder at the dark form of the Temple. "We are indeed strangers to one another," he uttered with a sigh, "and such we always will be."

For days the people spoke about little else except the miraculous burning of one cruse of oil for eight consecutive days.

* * *

It was Judah who finally asked Jonathan if he had yet seen the Greek woman. The question came unexpectedly.

They had spent most of the afternoon talking about the future plans for the Maccabees. No sooner had they established themselves in Jerusalem than they began to receive calls for help from other communities of Jews from all parts of the Seleucid kingdom. Some of these entreaties came in the form of letters to Judah, and others were delivered by envoys who pleaded with him to succor their people.

Judah called his commanders together to discuss the situation; the meeting was held in a large tent just outside the Temple grounds. Nothing had been decided during the long hours of discussion, and after Judah had dismissed the others, he asked Jonathan to stay a while longer with him. It was then that he asked about Iphegine, though he did not know her name.

Jonathan shook his head.

"And why not?" Judah asked, knowing his brother's passion for her.

"She's no longer there," Jonathan replied.

Judah stood up and walked to the brazier to warm his hands. He waited for his brother to offer more of an explanation before he should ask for it.

"Her servants told me that, about a year ago, she exchanged marriage vows with a merchant," Jonathan said. "They fled to Seleucids after we defeated Nicanor."

Judah did not look at his brother; the tone of Jonathan's voice was enough to tell him what he wanted to know. "The hurt will pass," he said softly. "It'll become a dull ache and then that too will change until it becomes no more than a twinge."

"God forgive me," Jonathan told him, "I'd have rather been told she had died than to know she lies in another man's arms and knows his weight on her body."

"No!" Judah cried, turning around to face his brother. "No. Not if you truly loved her."

There was the same smoke in Judah's eyes that Jonathan had remembered seeing in their father's eyes when he had been inflamed with anger.

Then Judah told him in a less fearsome voice, "Be thankful she lives and perhaps has moments when she remembers her passion for you and yours for her."

Jonathan stood mute before his brother; he did not know what to say. Since Modin, he had not thought about Judah in any way other than as the man he appeared to everyone. Judah was their leader, without him they would have perished in the Gophna Hills or would have been killed by the Seleucids. At times, Jonathan even found it difficult to remember they were brothers. And now, looking at him in the soft glow of a dying winter's day, he was confronted by a man whose feelings for a woman had been deeper and more passionate than in the past he would have ever imagined them to be. Judah seemed to be a man without feelings, or if he did have any, they were totally directed toward the killing of Seleucids and the preservation of the Maccabees. Without the killing, none of them would have survived. If Judah knew nothing else, he knew better than anyone, even better than Glacon, how to kill.

Only when Judah offered Jonathan wine and said, "Simon is pleased with his miracle," did this disquieting subject of conversation come to an abrupt end.

"He should be," Jonathan answered, accepting a beaker of wine from his brother's hand. "It will be remembered; everyone says it will."

Silently, Judah saluted his brother with his own beaker of wine, and after he sipped from it, he said, "Simon has always had more of an insight to the future than any of us."

Jonathan nodded and drank more wine.

Then Judah said, "Our battles aren't yet over. We must fight the Seleucids wherever they seek to destroy our people and their God. We're no more than a deep thorn in Antiochus' small toe. But Simon sees our family as rulers, lords of the earth." He drank more wine. "Johanan wants nothing more than to be a farmer. Eleazar has become my shadow, which does me honor, but is of small use to me. And then we come to you, Jonathan, tell me what you want?"

"Like you," the younger brother replied, "I'm blinded by the future."

"And haunted by the past?"

"I never knew a woman like Iphegine," Jonathan answered.

Judah repeated her name, and then he said, "I will take you with me to Gilead and you'll be at my side when we fight the Seleucids there. Will that please you, Brother?"

"Yes, Judah, it will please me very much," Jonathan answered, realizing that sometime during the discussion with the other commanders or after it, Judah had made up his mind to expand the military operations of the Maccabees.

* * *

Judah sent Simon to aid the Jews in Galilee, and Johanan went with him. He left Glacon to guard the Temple and the city of Jerusalem. On Eleazar's request, he assigned Joseph, their cousin and his friend Azariah, to protect their camp in the Gophna Hills. And Eleazar would become the liaison between Glacon and Joseph. Then, with an army of eight thousand men and with Jonathan as his captain, Judah went straight for Gilead.

Every day, reports of newly won battles came to the camp in the Gophna Hills. Simon won a battle and saved thousands of Jews, and Judah's victories were without parallel. Though the people rejoiced at the success of their army, Joseph and Azariah fretted about it; their life was dull and routine. Joseph felt that Judah had purposefully out of malice assigned him to be keeper of the camp. He had hoped his growing friendship with Rebecca would have been noticed by Judah, but it obviously had not.

Then, one evening, when the wind howled and sleet beat against the shelters, Joseph sat with Rebecca in a corner of the large room that had formerly served as the kitchen. The large hearth on one side provided a feeling of warmth and security from the savagery of the weather.

"I have received word," Joseph said, "that Judah has within the last few days captured Bozrah."

"Does that make you sad?" Rebecca asked, raising her crescent-shaped eyebrows.

"Only because I'm here and the fighting is somewhere else," he responded.

"Oh—"

"It isn't that I don't want to be with you," he hastened to explain. "I think I've made my feelings clear to you and, had you agreed, I'd have asked your brother for your hand in marriage long ago."

"Which of my brothers would you have asked?" she questioned. She moved her fingers over the base of the brass oil lamp on the table in front of her, but looked at him with her piercing black eyes.

"Judah, naturally."

"But Johanan is the oldest," she said.

Joseph rubbed his small dark beard. He was too close to the family not to know of the immense distance between Judah and Rebecca and what had caused it. She had often shown to Judah disrespect that he would not have tolerated from any other person.

"If not Johanan," she questioned, "why not Simon, since he too has shown that he can win battles?"

"Are you telling me to ask for you in marriage?" Joseph responded.

Rebecca could feel the sudden flush in her cheeks. This was the moment she had prayed would come, though not for the reason Joseph would ever suspect. She extended her hand so that the tips of her fingers touched his. Then, she said in a low voice full of feeling, "You, too, could become a leader of our people. You, too, could bring victories to us and defeats to the Seleucids. Judah is no more than a man, and you are more of a man than he. Everyone knows that his only virtue is his ability to kill. But you deserve more, much more than you have received from the hands of my brother, Judah." Her breasts rose and fell with the mounting passion of her words. "I have heard the men praise your courage in battle, and I've seen Judah ignore it, and why? Because he's afraid it will outshine his own and the people might turn against him and choose you in his stead."

Joseph grabbed hold of her hand and brought it to his lips.

"Will Azariah stand with you?" she asked.

"He, too, feels we have been purposefully placed far away from the action," Joseph told her.

"Then go to him and tell him you will lead an army against the Seleucids, that the two of you will share equally in the glory of the victory. I heard it said that Gorgias has gathered an army in Idumea. Its borders are within striking distance of this camp. With only a thousand men, you can win a great battle."

Joseph was fired by Rebecca's words. His heart raced, and his face became flushed with excitement. "Many men here feel they have been left here to serve no good purpose, while others are fighting for the glory of God," he said.

Rebecca nodded understandingly.

"Judah couldn't turn away from a victory," Joseph said. "Even he couldn't do that."

There was a long silence between them.

Joseph uttered a deep sigh, as if he were being wrenched away from a wonderful vision by the realization of what it would take to make that vision his reality.

To stiffen his resolve, Rebecca pressed his hand against her breasts and, looking straight at him, she said, "I'll uncover myself for you and have you lie against me. I'll take your seed into my body and pray to bring forth sons to be like their father."

Still holding his hand, Rebecca stood up and led him to her sleeping pallet; there she removed her clothes and, standing naked before him, she said, "Do with me what you want; even make of me your whore, but swear to me you'll become greater then Judah."

Joseph swore he would take an army against Gorgias.

Satisfied, Rebecca lay down on her pallet and spread her thighs for Joseph to come between them.

* * *

Judah stood with his back toward Eleazar. A short distance in front of Judah was the beginning of the slope leading to Mount Zion, where not too long ago he, his army, and the Jews he had rescued in Gilead, celebrated their victory over the Seleucids. The top of the mountain stood out in sharp relief. The day was bright with sunshine, the sky peppered with small white puffs of clouds. The moment Judah saw Eleazar race into camp astride one of Glacon's swiftest horses, he knew he was there to give tidings of some disaster, and he dreaded that it might be the loss to Gorgias of almost a thousand men.

"Tell me," Judah said in a low growl, "exactly what happened." He still did not look at his brother.

Eleazar could not find the words. His throat and lips were dry, and he could not help but feel that he was responsible for what had happened. It was at his behest that Joseph and Azariah were given command of the men in the camp.

"My orders to them," Judah rumbled, "were clear. I said, 'Take charge of these people. On no account join battle with the Seleucids until we return.' Was that so difficult for them to understand?"

Eleazar fell to his knees and sobbed, "They were already on the move when I arrived in the camp. Until the afternoon, I knew nothing about what Joseph was planning. A rider came from the camp with a letter from Joseph telling Glacon of his intention. I raced to the camp and Rebecca told me that Joseph had gone to win a great battle. Later, I learned that she had lain with him."

Judah turned abruptly toward him and spoke their sister's name with such asperity that Eleazar lapsed into silence again.

Jonathan entered the tent and, seeing Eleazar on his knees, asked what the trouble was.

"Joseph and Azariah went against Gorgias and were defeated," Judah told him. Then to Eleazar, he said, "Stand up and tell us what happened."

Eleazar got to his feet. "After I was told Joseph was marching against Gorgias, I raced to stop him. But I was too late. I reached them just before they went into battle. I saw it all, Judah. I saw it all."

"Tell me exactly what you saw," Judah said, and then he asked Jonathan to bring wine and food for their brother.

"Wine," Eleazar told him. "I have much more need for wine now than for anything else."

Judah nodded, and when Jonathan brought an amphora of wine and three drinking cups, Judah poured wine into one and, handing it to Eleazar, he said, "Now tell us what took place."

"It was mid-morning," Eleazar explained. "Our forces were moving toward the Seleucids. The country was flat. Joseph had drawn his men into phalanxes like those of the Seleucids. From where I was I could see the black plumes on the helmets of the enemy. There were perhaps eight phalanxes moving toward Joseph. They moved as one. The sound of their tread carried to where I was. It was a steady beat. Gorgias had a drum keep the rhythm. The night before, it had rained so the ground was still wet enough to be free of dust." He paused to take several gulps of wine. "I saw the flash of the Seleucid spears in the sunlight. A trumpet sounded, and the first five ranks in the phalanx lowered their spears and raised their shields. A volley of arrows came from Joseph's force but they did no damage. The two phalanxes came closer and closer. And then . . ." He shook his head. Jonathan urged him to drink again. "Joseph ordered the ram's horn sounded," Eleazar continued. "Our men began to run toward the Seleucids, but the enemy never broke step; they kept moving. Then a trumpet sounded three, perhaps four times and several of the other phalanxes wheeled out to the sides." Eleazar used his hands to demonstrate the movement. "Before Joseph could react, he was inside of an open-ended square. The flanking phalanxes turned, and their five-front ranks lowered their spears. It was these phalanxes that did the most damage. There was a tremendous shout from our men when they realized that they were running headlong into a trap. Again, the Seleucid trumpet sounded, and the ends of the two flanking phalanxes came together to form a V. Our men were inside of the V. The killing did not take very long. There was shouting and screaming. Some of our men managed to fight their way out of the trap. Perhaps twenty or thirty, but the rest lay dead. And then the strange silence came over the open field. Overhead the vultures were already beginning to gather."

"And what of our sister?" Judah asked.

"I don't know," Eleazar answered. "When I returned to the camp, several of the survivors had already arrived there. I went to speak with Rebecca, but she wasn't in the shelter. I asked if any one had seen her, and I was told she had left the camp."

"Did Joseph or Azariah survive?" Jonathan questioned.

Eleazar shook his head.

"I'll go back to Jerusalem," Judah said, "and those men who followed Joseph and Azariah will be taken before the people and killed. As for our sister . . ." He stopped, took a deep breath and told his brothers, "I never want to hear her name mentioned in my presence ever again. Is that clear?"

"Yes, Judah," each of his brothers answered softly, "Yes, Judah."

CHAPTER XXI

Judah marched his army hack to Jerusalem. Simon had already returned from his successful operations in Galilee. There was nothing either of them could say to the other about the defeat at Jamnia.

Simon made an attempt to plead for the lives of those men who had survived the catastrophe.

But Judah would not be swayed.

Finally, in desperation Simon cried, "Vengeance is Mine, saith the Lord, and do you, Judah, dare take that burden on your shoulders?"

"Look around you, and tell me how much less is on my shoulders? How much less have I taken on myself to build this army?"

"And if Rebecca were here, would you demand her blood, too?" "Yes," Judah thundered, "I would, and to free everyone from the guilt of shedding it, I'd kill her myself."

Simon became pale.

"And if need be," Judah told him in a dark voice, "I'll kill all of those twenty men who went against my orders. I have killed many, many more than that."

"But they were our enemies," Simon whispered, "while these are our own."

Judah shook his head; he did not want to continue the discussion. He was tired and heart sick over the treachery of Joseph and Azariah. "Will nothing move you?" Simon asked.

"Nothing will bring back to life all of the men who died to preserve the Covenant and the Law."

"You know that can't be; the dead are dead."

"Then let those who should have died be given to death," Judah growled. "I'll hear no more about them. I didn't send them to Jamnia. They knew my orders, and they chose to disobey them."

"Judah . . ."

"No more!" Judah exclaimed, holding up his right hand. "No more!"

Simon turned and went away from his brother. He understood Judah's wrath, but he could not condone the execution of twenty men to satisfy it. He pursed his lips, and he hoped that somehow the men would be spared.

But they were not. The men were hung in front of the entire army and their bodies were left for the vultures and the crows.

After the executions, Eleazar made several attempts to apologize to Judah for having taken up Joseph's cause.

"I don't hold you responsible for his actions," Judah told his brother each time he came to him.

But the answer did not satisfying Eleazar. And he was troubled by dark thoughts. He felt as if he were enveloped during the daytime in the vapors of a dark cloud and at night, when everyone slept, he could not sleep. If he did drop off, it was only to become invested with the battle he had witnessed at Jamnia.

Eleazar could find no joy, no reason to laugh. He became gaunt. His eyes held the look of a man possessed by demons. He tried to assuage his pain with women but found little pleasure in them. The best he could do was to drink himself senseless. He avoided seeing Judah, and he preferred, instead, to spend his time drunk in the taverns of the city or in the confines of his own tent.

Judah was aware of Eleazar's lamentable state and would have tried to help him, if he were not himself possessed by a black humor. Many, many times he galloped out of Jerusalem and rode hard until he reached Modin. There he dismounted and prowled about the burnt-out shells that had been the homes of the villagers. Sometimes, he went to the family tomb and stood for a long time looking at it.

He did not know why he returned to the village, but whatever the reason, he could not deny its force. He even returned to the place under the wall where he and Mattathias had buried Dion. All that was left of the tax collector now were his bones.

There were nights when Judah would not return to Jerusalem. He would spend them in Modin remembering his youth. The boy he had been then and the man he was now seemed total strangers to each other. He wondered if indeed he had ever been a child.

He seemed to be so old, older than Mattathias had been when he had died. Such an age, Judah realized, was not chronological. It came to him like winter comes to the earth after it has endured the fullness of the other three seasons; it came to him from all he had done in the past few years. Each new battle that he fought, Judah knew, would age him even more. That was the way it would be. There was no other way for him and, with a gesture of resignation, he accepted it, half-believing, wanting desperately to believe, yet always doubting that what he had done and what he would yet do was Yahweh's way for him.

* * *

Simon knew Judah would be in Modin, and, with Jonathan at his side, he rode back to the village. He did not tell his youngest brother why they were going to Modin, but when they came within sight of it, he said, "Judah spends as much time here now as he does in Jerusalem. If we can't find him in the city, I know he'll be here. When he was younger, he couldn't leave fast enough."

Jonathan patted the neck of his mount; the animal snorted appreciatively and Jonathan commented that the horse enjoyed being stroked. Then he said, "Joseph, Rebecca and all the men that were killed at Jamnia weigh more heavily on Judah than you might think, or than he'd want you to think."

"And on Eleazar," Simon answered, "who holds himself responsible for all of it."

"I tried speaking with him," Jonathan said, "but it didn't help him.

I know Judah told him that in his eyes he was blameless."

Without any further conversation, they entered the village and rode slowly down the main dirt road that led to the square. The sun was high and greatly foreshortened their shadows. Small swirls of dust rose beneath the hoofs of the horses.

Simon raised his hands to his mouth and called to Judah several times.

"I'm coming," Judah answered, leading his mount toward them from the direction of the house where they had lived. "I'm coming!"

Simon waited until Judah was very close before he said, "Antiochus is dead; he had appointed Philip Regent to his son Antiochus the Fifth, now given the added name of Eupator to honor the deeds of his father."

Judah stopped and blinked up at him. Since that day in front of the Temple when Antiochus had ordered the bloody death of Eleazar, Judah, in some dim way, had always thought of the King as his enemy; the generals that had come against him, even Apollonius, whom he had slain with his own hand, had always stood between him and Antiochus.

"It is said," Simon told him, "that he died horribly."

"In battle?"

"No, of some disease that gnawed at his bowels and made him scream in pain."

Judah swung into the saddle.

"There are now two Regents for the new Antiochus," Simon said, as the three brothers turned and, at a walk, started back to Jerusalem. "Philip, for the time being, will remain in the East." He paused, reined in and waited until his two brothers stopped. "Lysias is gathering an army to return here," he told them in a quiet voice. "He hopes to hold his power by first gaining control of Judea, and then turning against Philip."

Judah rubbed his beard.

He had expected Lysias to try again but not so soon.

"He is coming with elephants," Simon explained. "Elephants and twenty-five, perhaps even thirty thousand, men."

Judah let out a low, sad groan. "We would have good use for those thousand men that were lost at Jamnia," he said, looking straight at Simon, "We would have very good use for them now."

The gray smoke behind the blue circles in Judah eyes warned Simon to keep silent.

"Has Lysias put his army in motion yet?" Judah asked.

"He will now, any day."

Judah touched his spurs to the side of his mount and began to move forward. Without looking to see whether his brothers had immediately followed, he said, "The army must be brought together. Food supplies must be gathered into the Temple and at Beth Zur."

Simon and Jonathan flanked their brother, and Simon asked, "Are you sure he will come that way again?"

"With elephants," Judah answered, "there isn't another way. Simon, I must know every move his army makes. Lysias is not apt to make the same mistake again and we cannot afford to make one." Then turning to Jonathan, he said, "Sober Eleazar up, tell him I need him at my side. Tell him I hold nothing against him and love him as I love the rest of you."

"Yes, Judah," Jonathan responded.

"Ride ahead of us," Judah said.

Jonathan spurred his mount and raced away.

"This won't be like the other battles," Judah commented.

"Will we be able to hold the city?"

"First, we'll have to fight the battle and win it," Judah replied with a sudden stiffening of his shoulders. "Our men will fight, but that may not be enough; it may not be enough to stop the elephants."

The Maccabees came together again in Jerusalem. Those who had gone back to their farms and villages returned to serve under the flag of Judah.

Glacon trained the new men in the art of war.

Each day, runners brought news of Lysias' further progress. He was moving down the coastal road. His force was even larger than Simon had first told Judah. With him, Lysias also had five thousand cavalry and three hundred chariots.

The closer Lysias' army came, the more anxious the men became. All of the women, children and the elderly were taken under escort back to the camp in the Gophna Hills. The force there was put under Johanan's command.

"If we are completely overrun," Judah told his oldest brother on the day of their departure, "don't let the Seleucids take the women and children into slavery. You know what you and your men must do to them?"

Johanan nodded.

"Say it to me," Judah told him, "so there can be no mistake between us."

"They must be slain," Johanan responded in a tight voice.

"If they must be slain, will you slay them?" Judah asked.

"Yes, Brother, we'll slay them. And then we will ..." he hesitated, and then with a sad, meditative nod, he added, "We'll fight until there is not one of us left."

Judah embraced Johanan, and he said, "The fruit and wombs of our people are all in your charge. Other than those you take, your God has nothing more. If we die and they die, then the Covenant between Him and our people is over for all time."

"Live," Johanan said, "live, that we all may live and keep our Covenant with Him."

After Judah watched the women and children leave the city, he went into his tent and drank several beakers of wine, but even that did not stop the dull ache in his breast.

In the early morning of the next day, when half of the sun was above the mountains in the East and the night mists had not been fully dispelled, Judah was summoned from his tent. His name rang through the camp and roused him from sleep.

The possibility that Lysias might have been sighted sooner than had been expected leaped into Judah's mind and, grabbing hold of his sword, he rushed out into early morning light.

Eleazar, Simon, and Jonathan ran from their tents, too, and, seeing Judah, they went to him, while he in turn raced toward the guards, who were still shouting his name.

"There," the man gestured with his spear, "look, there, just above the door of the Citadel."

Judah turned. Now the full light of the sun was over the mountains, and the gray stones of the Citadel were turned to gold by it. There, hanging by her two arms was Rebecca.

She was naked. Between the bare thighs the Seleucids had tied a huge wooden phallus.

"Is she alive?" Eleazar asked haltingly, his voice choked with anger.

"Would it make a difference, if she were?" Jonathan asked.

No one answered him.

"Judah," Rebecca suddenly shouted. "Judah . . . Judah, I have whored for them. Judah, I have let them use me and found more pleasure in their lust than . . ."

Judah grabbed the spear from the guard. Before his brothers could stop him, he rushed forward and hurled it at his sister.

Rebecca saw it coming, and she screamed.

The spearhead made a dull thud as it pierced her chest. She screamed again, and then her body went limp. The Seleucids cut her free and she fell to the ground. Immediately, the vultures swooped down on her body.

Eleazar started to run toward her, but Jonathan threw himself at his feet, hinging him down. "One death in the family is enough," Jonathan said.

Judah turned, and he walked back to his tent.

The people gazed at him with fear and pity in their hearts.

He did not look at them. He did not even know they were there. He was numb. He felt nothing and heard nothing. He sat down, set his elbows on the table and then put his hands against his closed eyes. Whirls of red spread inside of his lids, huge whirls of red, red blood!

CHAPTER XXII

On the day of the battle, winter was already in the air. The sky was overcast with dark gray clouds. A strong wind blew from the west, carrying with it to the Maccabees the sounds of the Seleucid army waiting at Beth Zur, where a year before Judah had routed Lysias' army.

Judah's stand was to be made at Beth Zechariah to the north, a third of the distance between Beth Zur and Jerusalem. There, the land was flat, and Judah planned to attack the advancing army in the open, hoping a direct frontal assault would cause so much confusion in the enemy ranks that his own force would be able to scatter them.

Judah had left Glacon and a thousand men to defend the Temple. Every other man was with him.

Simon commanded a force to harass the enemy. It hid among the huge boulders that stood on either side of the road between Beth Zur and Beth Zechariah. Eleazar and Jonathan were with Judah.

For several days before Lysias began his march through the pass, Judah and his brothers had gone to the heights to the south and west of the pass to survey the enemy force. It was larger than any previous army that had come into Judea. The distance between its lead units and those in the rear was so great that neither Judah nor his brothers were able to see the end of it.

Judah had put his men into position the night before the battle. His scouts had told him that Lysias had already sent his light units and several cavalry detachments to cover the heights above the pass.

Now, in the gray morning, the sound of Lysias' army filled the narrow defile with the tread of thousands of feet, the blare of horns and the terrible trumpeting of the elephants.

The Maccabees at Beth Zur waited and shivered in the cold dawn.

Then, very slowly, the first Seleucids came out of the pass. The column of twos quickly formed a line of four. And when the entire phalanx was in view, it marched toward them. Behind it came an elephant with a wooden turret mounted on its back.

The Maccabees were terrified and beseechingly mumbled prayers to God to protect them.

But Lysias ordered his army to bypass the garrison at Beth Zur, leaving only a few detachments to surround and besiege it. He moved forward to engage Judah.

Lysias' purpose was to destroy the Maccabees and retake Jerusalem. He would not allow himself to be detained by the men at Beth-Zur. His army was like a mighty liver; it flowed around the garrison and left it in its wake on its way to Beth Zechariah.

Simon, realizing he would soon drown in the sea of men coming toward him, ordered his command to fall back to where Judah was.

"They come," Simon breathlessly told his brothers, "they come with their elephants in the lead. Thousands of them, Judah, thousands!"

Judah looked toward his men; he could still order them to retreat into the Gophna Hills. There was still time to change his plan. But he shook his head. To allow Lysias to march into Jerusalem unopposed was unthinkable.

Judah shouted to his army, "We'll be ready for them when they arrive. They want our city and we want our lives; they want to destroy our kind forever, and we want to live and see our children flourish and their children do the same."

The men shouted his name and waved his flag for him to see. "There isn't any other choice," he told his brothers. "If we don't fight here, then we'll never fight again, and all that we are will die. All our battles have been that way."

The loud blasts from the elephants silenced Judah. With a wave of his hand, he dispatched Eleazar and Jonathan to their positions. Then to Simon, he said, "Take your men to the center directly behind me. The others will open their ranks for you."

Simon nodded and directed his men to where Judah wanted them. Judah listened to the rhythmic tread of the Seleucid soldiers. As many times as he had heard it, he was still not used to it.

Trumpets sounded. The enemy pace quickened.

Judah ran his tongue over his lips. He wished Glacon were there beside him. He glanced back at his men. Fear marked their faces; several of them could not hold their water and a few had lost control over their bowels. He did not blame them for being afraid; he too was filled with fear; his stomach was knotted with it.

The wind brought the heavy stink of the elephants to the Maccabees. It was unfamiliar, yet all of them knew it was the smell of death.

The Seleucids were suddenly in front of them. A low, inarticulate sound of terror came from the Maccabee ranks.

The elephants led the army; four of them moved together. Each of them held a wooden turret on its back with four archers. And every one of the beasts was protected by many soldiers dressed in coats of scale armor and bronze helmets, and these men were flanked by several horsemen. Between each of the four elephants were light infantry units. But the army's main force was made up of the heavy infantry units, already in phalanx formation. Lysias had moved his cavalry units to cover the flanks of the army.

The Seleucid force came slowly up the road, and then the sound of the elephants rose above all of the other sounds made by the army.

The gray sky brightened unexpectedly. The wind shifted and was blowing from the East. Within a short time, the sky was very blue and the sun bright. The gold and bronze shield of the advancing army scintillated in the brilliant sun, sending blinding bursts of light into the eyes of the waiting Maccabees.

Judah's plan was to let the elephants pass through his ranks, killing as many of the men who guarded them as possible. Then he would hurl his own compact formations at the Seleucid phalanxes, in the hope they would break them into smaller units. He was depending on the ferocity and skill of his men in close combat to force Lysias from the field.

The elephants drew nearer and nearer. A Seleucid trumpet sounded. The huge gray beasts came charging down on the Maccabees.

Judah ordered the blowing of the ram's horn. His men leaped up and rushed at the oncoming enemy. Within moments, the two armies collided and were locked in a fearsome struggle.

The elephants trumpeted wildly as they charged through the ranks of the Maccabees, crushing many of them underfoot and hurling others into the air with a sudden snake-like movement of their trunks.

Judah's men broke and ran. He tried desperately to re-form them. Several times, he managed to form some sort of a line but it always gave way. Judah slashed his way forward. The men he cut down were faceless. The screams around him were fearful.

Then, suddenly, Eleazar leaped forward and shouted, "There's Lysias! There, on that beast. Judah, I have always loved you. Judah, for all that has passed between us!" Eleazar ran toward the elephant, cutting every man down who tried to stop him. He rushed under the animal and thrust his sword into its neck. The animal screamed in pain, dropped on the knees of its forefeet, a torrent of blood spewed from its neck.

Eleazar tried to scramble out from under the stricken beast. But he couldn't move fast enough. With a dying gasp the huge animal rolled over on its side, crushing Eleazar under its enormous weight.

Judah tried to fight his way through to the body of his brother but was driven back. All around him, he saw his men fall. There were no longer enough of them left to make a stand. He fought now to escape, and he shouted to his men to break off the fight.

Wet with sweat and gasping for air, Judah managed to kill or wound all of those who tried to kill him, and finally he was clear of the terrible slaughter at Beth Zechariah. Those men he could find, he led through the defiles and passes until they reached the safety of the wilderness. There, Judah paused for a while.

More men joined him.

Jonathan came. He had taken a sword cut across his arm, and the wound was still bleeding.

He asked if any of the men had seen Simon, but all of them answered with a silent shake of their head.

"We must move," Judah told the survivors of the battle. "We must move, or Lysias' scouts will find us." And lifting Jonathan across his back, he carried him through the long, cold night to the camp deep in the Gophna Hills.

As soon as they arrived, the women took the wounded and cared for them, while he carried Jonathan to the family shelter, where Johanan, his wife and child lived.

"Eleazar is dead," Judah told his oldest brother. "He was crushed by an elephant."

"And Simon?" Johanan asked, helping Judah to put the youngest of them on a pallet.

Judah did not answer. He bent over his brother and dressed the wound.

"What will happen now?" Johanan asked.

"We'll fight," Judah answered. He stood up and said in a loud voice, "We'll go back to the beginning, to the way we were when we fled from Modin and came here." He was about to tell them that he wanted to sleep, when the door was flung open, and Simon staggered in. He, too, had been wounded. The spearhead was still in his left shoulder. Judah ran to him and caught him in his arms. "I brought as many as I could," Simon gasped, "as many as I could save." Judah pressed Simon to his chest. "Eleazar is dead," Simon said. "Yes, I know," Judah answered softly. "I saw it happen." He wanted to add words that would express the depth of his grief. But they would not come. His grief was too deep. Too deep and too painful.

"And Jonathan?" Simon questioned.

"Here, safe."

"Thank God for that," he whispered. "Thank Almighty God for that." Then he fainted.

* * *

Lysias entered Jerusalem and after ending the siege of the Citadel, he immediately asked for the surrender of the Temple.

Glacon refused.

In a fury, Lysias vowed to kill every one of the survivors after his soldiers had taken the Temple by storm. And he immediately ordered his officers to mount an attack. He watched the movement of his men from the palace window.

Menelaus, the High Priest of the Jews, stood slightly to his left, and other dignitaries were close by, including Dryas, the priest to Zeus, and the former king's friend Tyropus.

So excellent were the Maccabean bowmen, that Lysias' troops could not even bring their scaling ladders close enough to lay them against the Temple walls.

Two attacks were made and two attacks failed.

"Have our men withdrawn," Lysias said to one of his subordinates, "and let them try again tonight." After dinner, Lysias and his entourage went to the palace windows to watch the Seleucids make a night assault on the Temple. They could see the wavering light of hundreds of torches rush toward the dark walls of the Temple. They even heard the ferocious yells of the attacking troops, and then the night seemed to be filled with a sudden whirring sound, like that made by the startled flight of a huge flock of birds.

Then there was screaming, and many torches dropped to the ground.

Another swooshing flight of arrows.

More screaming. Cursing. And many more torches lay on the black slope that led to the Temple.

"Stop the attack," Lysias shouted. "Stop the attack!"

For a while, the line of torches seemed suspended in the blackness of the night; then they moved back toward the palace. As they came closer to those who stood at the window, a sullen, sweaty soldier emerged from the yellow, flickering chrysalis surrounding each torch.

But there were over a hundred torches still burning on the side of the Temple Mount, marking the places where men had fallen in agony and screamed as their lives fled from their bodies.

By morning, the vultures and the crows were already feeding.

After the failure of the previous night's attack on the Temple, Lysias called his commanders together for a Council of War. He held the meeting in the main room of the palace, which he found singularly lacking in anything resembling comfort.

Since the walls of their objective could not be taken by storming them, they agreed that the wisest course of action would be to lay siege to the Temple and, with their huge catapults and battering rams, smash it to pieces.

"Once we breach its walls," Lysias told them, "I am confident our troops will have no trouble in overcoming any resistance. There will be no prisoners taken, even those who surrender are to be killed." He stood up, paced back and forth several times and then he said, "This time . . . we will level it, pull down every stone of the place so that nothing remains of it. In time, no one will remember that it was ever there."

Satisfied with his decrees, Lysias dismissed his officers and left his own quarters to seek out Menelaus, whose rooms, he had already been told by Tyropus, were luxuriously furnished and decorated with many beautiful objects that were brought to Judea from the entire world.

Lysias had already decided that no Jew, even if he were the High Priest of his people, could possibly appreciate anything of beauty. *Jews,* he told himself, *lack the capacity to experience sensual beauty. Their ridiculous unseen God forbids them to experience that kind of joy.* He could not understand why any people would be so willing to die for a God they could not see and whose laws were beyond conception for any rational mind. Yet, the Jew could not, or more likely out of obstinacy, would not acknowledge that Zeus was the only God and that their Yahweh was some impostor, for false gods like false men, came in various guises, even Yahweh's guise of invisibility.

Without bothering to knock, Lysias entered Menelaus' apartment, announced he was there and waited for the High Priest to present himself. As Menelaus hurried toward him, Lysias said, "I will send my soldiers to take those things that please me."

Menelaus stopped.

"Do you have any objections?" Lysias asked.

"Take whatever pleases you," the High Priest replied, knowing that the very dignified man, who had come to save him, now had come to rob him of everything of value. Perhaps, someday, even his life? That possibility sent a tremor through him.

"Is anything wrong?" Lysias questioned.

"No, My Lord," Menelaus said, "all things are as I should have expected them to be."

Lysias smiled.

And Menelaus forced his lips to assume the expression of a smile.

* * *

The defenders of the Temple answered Lysias' bombardments with deadly accurate fire from their own catapults. Each side suffered casualties, but the Maccabees defended the walls of their fortresses with such skill and daring that even Lysias grudgingly admired them.

But inside the Temple the men were hungry, their supply of arrows and stones was dangerously low.

Glacon had heard nothing from Judah, and he began to make plans to abandon the Temple at the time of the next new moon and to take his men to the camp in the Gophna Hills, where he knew some of the survivors of Judah's force must be.

Glacon called his captains together and told them of his decision. They did not take issue with it.

"We'll pray for rain," he said, "for a heavy, blinding rain storm . . . the less the Seleucids can see, the greater the chance for all of us to escape . . . but we won't destroy any part of the Temple." Then with a hint of a smile playing on his full lips, he added, "We'll leave it to remind them it belonged to the Jews before we came and will belong to them long after we have gone to our eternal rest."

The men nodded.

"Now we must make every effort to hold out until the new moon comes," Glacon said. "There must be no slackening in our return fire. Nothing to give the Seleucids a hint of what our intentions are."

"We'll keep them so busy," one of the captains said, speaking for all of the others, "that they'll begin to think we have been reinforced and rearmed."

"If we do that," Glacon said, "then we'll live to fight with Judah again."

And by the following day, Lysias' officers reported to him, "The Jews somehow managed to bring more men and armaments into the Temple, and the siege might last for months, perhaps as long as a year."

Lysias was in a fury; he had not anticipated having to spend his time laying siege to the Temple and, more to the point, he had been receiving disturbing reports about Philip's plans. His rival had told several of his intimate friends that he planned to pull his armies out of the East and bring them to Antioch, where he intended to claim his rightful place, or if need be to take it by force of arms. This information was secret, having been brought to him by his own spy. It weighed heavily on him. At stake was a kingdom, while in Jerusalem he was wasting valuable time and men trying to subdue a handful of intractable Jews. The importance of one far outweighed that of the other.

For the next few days, Lysias pondered his situation, balancing one plan of action against another and disregarding both because neither one would enable him to extricate himself with grace. It would have been easy for him to just leave. One order to his army would immediately put them in motion. But if he left that way, then he had no doubt that the remnants of Judah's army would quickly retake the city. And everything would be as it was before he came. That, to him, would mean, and he had little doubt that others would view it in the same way, an incredible waste of men and material. No, he had to find a way to leave and by leaving give the appearance of having won a total victory over the Jews. To accomplish that, he had to have the Temple.

Self-assured when dealing with his own countrymen or men from other nations, Lysias found himself unable to cope with what he secretly referred to as his entanglement in an unseen web, spun by the unseen God of an incredibly stubborn people. He needed to discuss the situation with someone whom he could trust. That condition alone ruled out all of his subordinate commanders, since any discussion of the situation would have to include revealing what he knew about Philip's movements. And despite the gravity of the situation, he would have preferred to delay a test of loyalty among his command, whether to himself or to Philip. There would be time enough for that when he would confront Philip on the battlefield.

Lysias' eyes fell on Tyropus as his confidant. After all, Tyropus had already been that to Antiochus, and he had a long period of association with the Jews. He probably knew more about them than anyone else within reach, so Lysias extended a dinner invitation to Tyropus.

The two men faced each other across a magnificent table whose top was inlaid with ivory and rare woods. Tyropus knew, as did everyone else in the palace, that Lysias' had appropriated for himself the treasures of Menelaus' apartment, leaving the High Priest nothing of any value.

All through the sumptuous dinner, the conversation between the host and his guest ranged over many, many subjects. Both men were well read and enjoyed the pleasures of philosophical discussion.

Lysias led the conversation through several different subjects until he came to the concept of man in his relationship to the gods. That provided him with the precise place from which he could launch into a discussion of his immediate problem. "I think," he said, pouring more wine into the golden cups, "that the Jews' particular relationship to their God has caused them more grief than pleasure."

Tyropus remained quiet for a few moments. His experience with various members of the court had given him the ability to quickly ascertain when a superior was seeking something from him. He sipped some of his wine before asking, "I think, My Lord, I can speak frankly with you?"

"By all means, do."

"The Jews are no different from any other people. Strange in their ways, yes. But no stranger than we are to them. They don't care for us and we don't care for them."

"Our differences have cost us a great many men," Lysias commented sourly, "not to mention the arms. Their writings have been seditious. Antiochus, himself, showed me what was written by one of them who called himself Daniel."

"Don't misunderstand me," Tyropus was quick to explain, "I have no love for them, but neither do I have any love for a struggle that is interminable. Your own siege of the Temple is a case in point. I'm sure that by now you expected it to be over."

Lysias ground his teeth together and with a reluctant nod, he said, "You see only part of my difficulty."

Tyropus raised his eyebrows.

"Have I your trust?" Lysias questioned, leaning forward to place his elbows on the table.

"It would be foolish of me to say that you didn't," Tyropus responded with a hint of smile on his thin lips.

"Suppose, when I depart from here," Lysias offered, "I make you Military Governor of Jerusalem."

"I can safely say," Tyropus told him, "that you have my trust."

Lysias revealed what he knew about Philip's movements, and he added, "Now you can understand my predicament. I must leave here as soon as possible."

Tyropus nodded and said, "And you must have your victory." "And I can't have it until I take the Temple."

"Something of a paradox."

"I'm between a kingdom and the Temple of the Jews," Lysias said heatedly. "In my place, which would you choose?"

Tyropus drummed the fingers of his right hand on the table. Then looking straight at the regent, he said, "My Lord, has it ever occurred to you that by giving the Jews what they want, you will be giving yourself what you want?"

"Go on," Lysias responded, "and explain yourself."

"The Jews want to worship their own God . . . let them . . . they object to Menelaus. Remove him and give them a High Priest they will accept. Let their Temple stand."

"But Antiochus ordered their destruction!" Lysias objected angrily.

"That Antiochus is no longer alive, My Lord. The circumstances have changed. Your men hold the city. Philip will try to claim the kingdom for himself. The Jews are but a minor detail. By giving them what they want, they will return to their former peaceful way of life. I think, My Lord, our previous King paid too much attention to them, and if I might add, with all due respect to his precious memory, committed two serious blunders."

"Tell me what they were."

"He should have chosen a High Priest from their priestly line," Tyropus said, "and he desecrated their holiest of holy places, the Temple."

Lysias drank a full cup of wine. It was to him obvious that his guest had given the matter some thought long before he himself had confronted the problem. "How would you go about carrying out your ideas?" he asked.

"With the greatest display of magnanimity on your part and that of your young king," Tyropus replied with a smile. "It must be done so the Jews feel as if they have won, and our people too should feel the same way."

"More wine?" Lysias offered.

"No, thank you, My Lord, I have already drunk more than I usually do. Oh yes, there's one other matter that I think needs to be called to your attention."

Lysias nodded.

"When you remove Menelaus," Tyropus said, "you must also remove Amran, his toady."

"It'll be done," Lysias replied and again offered his guest wine.

"I'm not much of a drinker," Tyropus said, "and I'd like to be able to remain awake for a while and think about the coming change in my status."

"Perhaps you would enjoy the company of a woman or a boy to divert you for a while?"

"Yes. Yes, this time I would like a woman," he answered with a laugh. "For me a woman provides pleasure without the strain of any emotional attachment."

"I understand," Lysias said. "But after marriage one becomes used to sharing one's bed with a woman, at least most of the time."

"That 'most of the time,'" Tyropus responded, "is what keeps me from marriage. I can abide a woman now and then but no more than that."

"I'll have one sent to you," Lysias told him.

The two of them stood up, and Lysias accompanied his guest to the door, where he shook his head and said, "You have done yourself well tonight, my friend, far better than you could have dreamed."

Tyropus left Lysias' apartment and as he walked through the halls of the palace, he whistled a lively dance tune.

CHAPTER XXIII

During the days immediately following the battle of Beth Zechariah, Judah tended his wounded brothers. He slept for brief periods and ate very little. He hardly spoke and then only to Johanan to ask him whether there was any news about the Temple or if more of the men who were with him at Beth Zechariah had returned to the camp. Practically all of the army had come back, and it was soon apparent to Judah that his losses were not as great as he had thought they were. Most of what had taken place had been confusion. His men had been routed more by the elephants than by the numbers of the Seleucids. He spoke of this to Johanan, telling him in short sentences how Eleazar had been killed.

"He did it to prove his love for me," Judah said, staring at the flames of a low fire. "He'd have proved it more if he were still at my side." Then with a sigh, he added, "He couldn't undo what Joseph and Azariah had done."

Johanan could not remember ever having seen his brother so dispirited. He was afraid that Judah might fall ill and said as much to him.

Judah denied it with a vigorous shaking of his head. "That isn't the way it'll be," he told him. "But we must be thankful we still have our army intact; we can still fight."

"There are already too many women who are widows," Sarah said.

Johanan motioned her to be silent. He was very disturbed by Judah's word. "That isn't for you to say," he told her.

But she insisted on speaking. "For all the years of our fighting and dying," she asked, "what have we to show for it?"

"Your lives," Judah answered harshly. "Your lives. You and all the others live because so many were willing to die. Even now, Glacon and the others with him . . ." His voice choked up. He could not go on and, letting out a melancholy groan, he left the fire and went to keep watch over his brothers.

Jonathan healed rapidly, but Simon's shoulder wound leaked pus and he was seized with a high fever. For several days, he hovered between life and death. Gradually the fever subsided, the wound closed, and he slowly regained his strength.

By the time spring came, Simon was on his feet again, though he tired very quickly. But when the Passover was celebrated, he was sufficiently strong to lead the people in its observance.

Every day, Judah sent men into the countryside around Jerusalem and often into the city itself to find out what was happening at the Temple. That the men were able to hold out for so long, under such heavy bombardment, was indeed a credit to Glacon and those men with him. Soon or later, Glacon would have to break off the fight and surrender or somehow manage to flee.

Then late one afternoon one of the men who had been sent to the city the previous day came running back into the camp. "It is over," he shouted, "the siege is over; praise be to God, we have won our greatest victory!"

Judah came forward with all of the people, and they formed a great circle around the man. Judah asked his name.

"Shobal," the man replied, "Shobal Ben Tahath." Then waving a large scroll of papyrus, he said, "It is all written down here, as Lysias sent it to his King. His soldiers are posting them all over the city."

Judah took the scroll and handed it to Simon, telling him to read in a loud clear voice.

And Simon read: "Now that our Royal Father has gone to join the gods, we desire that our subjects be undisturbed in the conduct of their own affairs. We have learnt that the Jews do not consent to adopt Greek ways, as our Father wished, but prefer their own mode of life and request that they be allowed to observe their own laws. We choose, therefore, that this nation like the rest should be left undisturbed, and decree that their Temple be restored to them and that they shall regulate their lives in accordance with their ancestral customs."

Simon lowered the scroll, rewound it and handing it back to Judah, he exclaimed, "I can't believe it is over!"

And the people, suddenly realizing the meaning of the words they had just heard, began to shout with joy. They fell on their knees and they praised the power of their God! "Hear, oh Israel, the Lord is our God, the Lord is one," echoed and re-echoed between the cliffs around the camp.

The women wept for joy and men congratulated each other on having, with the aid of God, accomplished the impossible.

* * *

The following morning, Glacon and the remnants of his forces marched into camp. They were hollow-eyed, gaunt-looking men with smiles on their faces and pride in their hearts.

The people swarmed around them, shouting their praises. Several of the men lifted the protesting Glacon to their shoulders. They carried him to where Judah stood and set him down.

The two men faced each other in silence. Tears flowed from their eyes, and they embraced.

Judah placed his right hand over Glacon's shoulder and, with his left, he raised his staff to quiet the people. "If you have ever loved a man," he shouted, so that his words reverberated from one side of the lake to the other, "love him; if you ever honored a man, honor him." And once more Judah embraced his friend.

The people called Glacon's name over and over again.

Gesturing to the men who fought alongside of Glacon, Judah said, "Love them and honor them. They have withheld from the enemy all that he sought to deny us. They have given us our lives and have made it possible for us to keep the Covenant."

The gratitude of the throng was like the sudden gush of a summer torrent. They rushed to the defenders of the Temple and embraced them, kissed them and more than one man was lifted to the shoulders of two other men and carried back and forth in front of Judah and his brothers.

Judah proclaimed three days and three nights of celebration. And for the first time since Mattathias had led the people from Modin, they drank, danced and ate with the wild abandon of men and women who were certain that when the sun rose and when it set they would still be alive the next day.

Judah, too, joined in the revels, drinking so much wine that the very top of his head was filled with extraordinarily soft white clouds. In the darkness of the first night, he found himself with a woman, whose face he could not see and whose name he had no need to know.

But more than pleasures of drink and passion, were those that came to him in those quiet moments, when he stood alone on some high place above the camp and looked down at the happiness of his people. They could never know how much they had given him, how much of what he now was had been wrought over the years by their needs. Without them, he would have been nothing. But with them ... he smiled whenever he thought about it . . . he had become a man, someone whom Mattathias would have been proud to acknowledge as his son.

During some portions of the three days and three nights of celebration, Judah and Glacon spoke about the present and the future.

Glacon told him, "Lysias is on his way north to fight Philip, and he's going to send a new High Priest to the Temple, whose name is Alcimus and whose line can be traced back to Aaron."

"And who was left in Jerusalem?" Judah asked, as they walked by the lake in gathering twilight.

"Tyropus," Glacon responded.

"A favorite of the former Antiochus," Judah commented.

"Yes. But more reasonable than most members of the court, as I remember them."

"Do you ever regret . . ."

"Never, Judah, never!"

Judah clapped his friend on the shoulder and apologized for having asked a stupid question.

"Now, let me ask you a question," Glacon said.

Judah nodded.

"What are we going to do now?" Glacon asked, making a sweeping gesture to indicate that he meant everyone in the camp.

"I'm not sure yet," Judah answered with a narrowing of his eyes. "I think we must wait, as we always have in the past, to see what the present promises about the future."

The two men continued to walk in silence for a while longer; then Judah stopped and putting his right hand on Glacon's left arm to halt him, he said, "I didn't expect to gain all we have fought for quite so easily."

"We were that much away from losing everything," Glacon answered snapping his fingers. "When Lysias entered the Temple and saw our state he was so furious for having given us terms that he immediately ordered his men to tear down the wall surrounding the Temple. I tell you, Judah, we couldn't have held out more than another day or two at the most. My hope was to wait for the new moon and then attempt to escape!"

Judah nodded and said, "I'd have done the same."

"I had the men pray for rain," Glacon told him. "The worse the night, the better it would have been for us. But Yahweh was with us; He brought us out with good terms and in broad daylight."

They began to walk again.

"Lysias would rather have us peaceful while he fights Philip," Glacon said. "And then, of course, he'll somehow have to come to some sort of an agreement with Demetrius, the son of Seleucis the Fourth, whom Antiochus had murdered. Either Demetrius will get the throne peacefully or he will fight for it. You see, Judah, the whole empire is really coming apart, and Rome, no doubt, will help to pull it down completely."

"Is Demetrius still hostage in Rome?"

"Probably. But I don't think he will remain there long," Glacon said. "He's the rightful heir to the Seleucid throne and he has many friends in Rome and in Antioch who'd be willing to help him secure it."

Judah rubbed his hand over his beard and commented, "You've given me a great deal to think about."

"I'm sorry," Glacon laughed. "I didn't mean to weigh you down with matters concerning the Seleucid Empire."

"Whatever happens to them," Judah responded, "concerns us.

Our fortune could be the reverse of theirs; our star could wax while theirs wanes."

"How?"

Judah held up his hand and said, "Not yet. I don't know, here and now. But soon, my dear friend, very soon, I'll have thought of a way to make an advantage of their disadvantage. But for now, all of us must wait. We must have the patience to be patient a while longer."

Their walk had taken them to a place almost directly opposite the camp. They stopped and looked across the lake. Already the huge fires that had been lit every night since Glacon's return were burning brightly, turning the darkness luminous with yellowish-red light. And the joyous blending of drum, lute, and song filled the air.

"Come!" Judah exclaimed, taking hold of his friend's arm. "Let us hurry back and join the celebration. I'm hungry, thirsty, and feel the need to enjoy myself."

The first days of summer came and the Maccabees were restless.

Alcimus was known to have left Antioch, escorted by the forces of General Bacchides. And because the new High Priest was directly descended from Aaron, practically all of the Hasidim accepted him.

The temper of the people at the camp had shifted from joyousness and pride to angry discontent. More and more of the men refused to attend the military drill session, claiming the war was over and there was no longer any need for anyone, except those who delighted in killing, to learn how to kill.

Judah was painfully aware of what was happening to his army. But until he could clearly present them with something they would understand, he said nothing.

From all sides, there were ominous rumblings of discontent. Veiled insults were made against him and his affection for Glacon.

Then, one sultry morning a deputation arrived at Judah's shelter and demanded to see him. Jonathan and Simon tried to reason with them, explaining that Judah was asleep and, since he slept so little, they were reluctant to wake him.

The deputation became boisterous.

One man pushed himself forward and in a low voice he demanded to know whether Judah sleeps with Glacon or Glacon's wife.

In a fury Jonathan drove is fist into the man's head, instantly felling him.

The man twitched for a few moments. Then he became still. Two of the others bent to their friend, and one looked up at Jonathan and said, "He is dead."

And the other added, "You have killed him."

They picked up the body of their fallen comrade and, carrying it throughout the camp, they cried out against Jonathan and Judah.

The people gathered in front of Judah's lodging and called for him to answer the charges against his brother and himself.

Judah had heard from Jonathan and from Simon what had happened, and, when he stepped out into the brilliant sunshine, he held his blackened staff in his right hand and raised it to silence the people.

Then he said, "I'll speak to everyone at once. Gather all our people together in front of that slope there." He pointed to the place from where he had once stood and spoke to them about their cause, and now he would do the same thing, but this time he was about to offer them something that had been taken from them over a hundred years before.

Judah made his way through the muttering throng. His brothers and Glacon followed him. But when he started to climb the slope, he turned to them and said, "Stay with the rest of the people until you've made your decision."

"But Judah," Simon told him, "we're with you."

"Listen to what I have to say," he answered his mystified brother, "before you tell me that you're with me. All of you, stay with the people."

When he reached a height where the cliff began, Judah stopped and turned around. Below him were the men, women, and children of the entire camp.

They were silent.

"The man my brother killed," Judah said, "slandered me. Accused me of an abomination that is, according to our Law, punishable by death."

From one place in the throng there were angry mutterings.

Judah could not make out the words but he heard their tone. "You," he shouted, so that his words would sound several times between the cliffs around the lake, "you men who stood before my brothers and insulted me, step forward now and before all of the people here, make the same accusation."

No one came forward.

"Let me tell all of you," Judah said, "so that there's never again a mistake made about it. My love for Glacon is no different from my love for my brothers. I have told you that before. And now I tell it to you again, the man who lifts his hand or his voice against Glacon lifts his hand and his voice against me. And I will kill him. Make no mistake about it! I'll kill him, or he will have to kill me. Those of you who came to slander me this morning will do well to remember my words."

Then, pointing his staff at Jonathan, he said, "I take the blood he shed on my hands. I take his guilt before your God on my shoulders. Let it be there until I die!"

A low whisper of fear ran through the ranks of the people. They looked up at Judah and saw him, tall and blonde in the brilliant sunshine.

By raising his staff, Judah silenced them. "Now, I'll speak to you about the future," he said. "I will tell you what we who are here might do."

"Judah," one of the men shouted, "we've done all that Yahweh could expect us to do."

"But I'm not He," Judah answered, "and therefore I can expect you to do more."

Everyone began to shout at once. Some accused him of blasphemy; others said he was mad. Even his brothers and his friends looked questioningly at each other.

Judah waited until the storm of noise subsided before he tried to speak again. Then he told them, "We still have an army; we can still fight."

"No, Judah," someone yelled, "we don't want to fight; we want to return home."

There was a riotous effusion of agreement for what had just been said.

"If we do that now," Judah explained, after they became quiet enough to hear him, "we'll go back to the old way. Before you start to shout again, hear me out. We can become a nation again. A true Nation of Jews, the way we once were before we were taken into captivity by the Babylonians. Now we've the strength to strike a blow for our complete freedom. Judea can be ours again. We can go back to Jerusalem and drive the Seleucids back into the Citadel or destroy them."

A stunned silence came over the people.

Simon stepped away from the others, and he said, "But we're less than ten thousand against tens of thousands. Against an army of elephants, what force have we?"

"The lords of the kingdom will fight each other for power," Judah answered, "and while they're fighting each other, we'll be able to drive their armies out of our land. We will form a Nation of Jews; we'll take back what was taken from us."

"Judah," Simon cried, "the people are tired of war; they want to live in peace. We've achieved all that we dared to hope for. Judah, we can do no more!"

"Once you told me of your vision," Judah shouted back at his brother. "You saw me and the rest of our family as lords. Where is that vision now? Where is that vision that sees to the future, when Jews rule themselves, when we no longer live by someone else's sufferance, when Yahweh is in the land of His chosen people."

Silenced, Simon retreated.

"Would you be King, Judah?" a man called from the throng.

"Before there is a King," Judah answered, "there must be a kingdom. We must first win that kingdom before we can decide who reigns over it."

"We've fought enough, Judah," another man called out. "How many more widows must there be before we live in peace?"

The argument between Judah and his people went on for hours. And the longer it continued, the more he realized that all too few of them grasped the idea that there was a possibility for them to make themselves into a nation. They were more interested in their own individual lives than in giving life to a country that would belong to them!

"Judah," one of the men finally said, "you're asking all of us to have your thoughts and to act as you do. We're not like you, Judah. We don't fight because we take pleasure in it; we fight only to hold what is ours. This kingdom you speak of isn't ours."

"It was yours," Judah replied, swept away by his anger. "It was yours and it can be yours again!"

"We'll fight no more, Judah," the same man shouted back. "We'll fight no more!"

Many, many people repeated those words again and again. Judah raised his staff, and eventually silence returned. He moved down from the slope.

The people opened away for him.

When he came to where the ground was flat, near the shore of the lake, he inscribed two large circles in the earth. "Those who'll stay with me," Judah said, "will put black stones in this circle." He set his staff over the other circle.

"Those who'll leave will put white stones here." Then he returned to where he had been on the slope and watched the two piles of stones grow.

The white stones were so numerous that they spilled out beyond the circumference of the circle.

Judah called the people to him again and said, "Those who remain with me do not need any words of cheer or comfort from me, and those who leave need only to know we'll be here when they need us; we'll be here when they come to us for succor, for as sure as the sun will rise tomorrow morning, they'll come. They'll come because the difference between Menelaus and Alcimus is only in name, only in name." Then, lowering his head, Judah made his way down the slope.

Twilight was already gathering between the cliffs around the lake.

CHAPTER XXIV

To Judah, those who elected to remain with him seemed more like phantoms than people. Where there had been ten thousand, now there was scarcely more than a thousand and some of them, through their loyalty was strong, were not among the best of fighters.

In the morning, when everyone else still slept and the mists of the night had not yet let loose their hold on the land, Judah would go where the circles of black and white stones were. And shifting his eyes from the black to the white and back to the black again, he would sadly shake his head. Though there would always be a preponderance of white stones, he would always find them of little importance when weighed against the black ones in the scales of his mind.

But before the summer was over, before the last harvest was gathered in, Jews were once again being killed by the Seleucids and by the gray haired, kindly looking Alcimus who, by his own hand, had signed the order to hang sixty Hasidim for having taken part in the Maccabean revolt. And the Seleucid General Bacchides had slaughtered many Jews in the village of Bethziath, where he had encamped for a night.

These tales of woe were brought to Judah by five men who returned to offer their services again.

Judah nodded and gathering all his people, he led them down to where the piles of stones were. "Now each of you take a white stone and place it with the black," he told five men.

They understood the significance of what he asked and did it with grace and dignity.

"Each man who returns to us," Judah told his people, "will add their white stones to our black ones, when there are enough of them, we will once more be an army."

With each passing day, more men returned; some came alone and others brought their families.

Many white stones were now mixed with the black ones, and Judah once again sent out raiding parties to harass the Seleucid garrison in Jerusalem and to prevent the High Priest from enjoying as many aspects of his office as possible.

Judah's men wrought havoc wherever they struck. And now they were so well organized by Simon and Jonathan that many units lived within the city itself. On an order from Judah, they would quickly carry out whatever mission he assigned to them.

* * *

The raids had a telling effect on the Seleucid garrison in Jerusalem, and Tyropus was at a loss as to how he might put an end to them without having to appeal to Antioch, where Demetrius now sat on the throne. After having escaped from Rome, Demetrius had caused the army to rebel against Lysias and Antiochus V, both of whom he executed. Tyropus, always conscious of his person, now noticed lines of care marking his brow and etching crow's feet at the corners of his eyes. He was sorry that he had accepted from Lysias the position of Military Governor; it was aging him with a rapidity that was frightening.

But, each day, the High Priest came to his office and exhorted him to send to Antioch for help, threatening to do it, if he did not.

* * *

From his spies, Judah knew about the arrival of Demetrius in Antioch and the subsequent deaths of Lysias and Antiochus V. He also knew that Tyropus was very hesitant about asking the new King for help and that Alcimus was demanding that he do what he obviously was reluctant to.

Judah realized that if he were to move more white stones to those already mixed with the black ones, he would have to prove to everyone that the Jews could have their own nation.

One morning, he took the first step toward achieving that end. He summoned his brothers and Glacon to Council of War.

They sat at a long table with a canopy over it to protect them from the sun. Judah and Simon sat opposite one another. Jonathan was to Judah's left and Glacon to his right. Johanan sat to Simon's right.

Judah began by explaining the information that had come to him about conditions in Antioch and in Jerusalem. Then he said, "Sooner or later, Tyropus or Alcimus will ask for help, and a new army will come to Judea to attempt to destroy us." He pointed to where the circles of stones were. "If we could prove to the people that others recognize us as a nation, then we'll have their support again, and all of the white stones will be intermingled with the black. With such an army we could keep the Seleucids at bay."

"And what would it take," Simon questioned, "other than a miracle, to do that?" Though he would never leave Judah, he had grave doubts about this new phase of the struggle and when they were alone, he counseled his brother to seek an audience with either Tyropus or Alcimus in an effort to end the strife. But Judah, though he listened, would not be moved toward that course of action.

"We need the help of a power stronger than the Seleucids," Glacon said.

"Rome!" Judah exclaimed, striking the table with his fist. "Rome will be our behemoth against our enemies."

"And what makes you think," challenged Simon, "that you can bend them to your purpose?"

"I don't know if I can or I can't," Judah answered. "But now they're the strongest nation in the world. Demetrius slipped away from them to become a king against them. In us they would find a way to remind Demetrius that he lives by their sufferance and that if he should displease them, they'd crush them, as a man might crush some bothersome insect."

"And who would you send to Rome?" Johanan asked.

"Glacon for one," Judah answered.

"I'd prefer to remain here, Judah," Glacon immediately responded.

"You've been to Rome," Judah told him. "You know its ways and you speak a form of Latin. You'd be there to take care of the other two representatives."

"And who would they be?" Jonathan asked.

"Simon," Judah said, "you choose them. Two good men, who can be trusted to give us the best possible representation to the Romans."

"But by what authority do we do this?" Johanan asked. "We aren't recognized by anyone. We are, if the truth be said, outlaws."

Judah agreed. "But that's what we always were," he said. "We were outlaws the instant Mattathias struck down Apelles that afternoon in Modin. Perhaps by the law of the Seleucids we were outlaws from the time of our birth because we were born Jews. Being an outlaw in one set of circumstances doesn't make you an outlaw in a different set of circumstances. We don't live outside Roman law; we live outside of Seleucid law."

"The Seleucids will accuse us of . . ."

"Treason," Judah interrupted. "And that," he added coldly, "they've already done many times. Now, Simon can you give me the names of two men for this mission?"

"Eupolemus, son of John, and Jason, son of Eleazar," Simon answered.

"Good men," Judah commented, "very good men, indeed. But say nothing to them until we've drafted a letter to the Roman Senate. It's best that this matter be kept between us until just before the men leave. Glacon, I think Helen should go with you."

"I'd have asked permission to take her," Glacon responded with a smile.

"And will the others be allowed to take their wives?" Simon questioned.

Judah nodded and called an end to the meeting, but he told Glacon to remain with him after the others had left.

"Do you think Rome will listen?" Judah asked his friend.

"She might, Judah," Glacon answered, "she just might. But you must be prepared to give them something in return for their help."

"In us they'll find a staunch friend," Judah said. "I have nothing else to offer than that. If that won't be enough, then we'll have to find some other way of winning our freedom from the Seleucids. But we must have nothing less, Glacon, or we'll be destroyed in the end. We must have our own soil; we must take back what was taken from us. There's no other way for us to survive. And if we die, Glacon, Yahweh will die too . . . the world will be given over to many gods. But the One, the One who made the Covenant with Abraham and with Moses will be gone forever!"

"I wouldn't have thought you would concern yourself about Yahweh that way," Glacon commented.

"The people are nothing without Him," Judah said. "And if the people need Him, then I'll do everything in my power to let the people keep Him."

"And that includes retaking the land that was once theirs?"

"Yes," Judah answered passionately, "Yes!"

* * *

Not long after Judah's deputation left for Rome by way of Egypt, there was rioting in the streets of Jerusalem, and scores of Seleucid soldiers were killed by bands of well-organized Maccabees.

As his predecessor had done, Alcimus was forced to abandon his quarters in the Temple and seek refuge in the palace, where the Seleucids could protect him.

The deterioration of the situation made Tyropus send a request for help to Demetrius, his king.

In response to this appeal, Nicanor was ordered to Jerusalem. He moved swiftly, and with a force of five thousand men, he went straight south toward the city.

From a hill, Judah and his brothers watched Nicanor and his troops march through the same defile where they had defeated Apollonius some four years before. In a few days, Nicanor and his army would link up with yet another strong force coming from Syria.

That information had been sent to Judah by his spies even before Nicanor had left Antioch. And Judah had decided not to oppose Nicanor's army on its arrival but to wait and see where it intended to join with the second portion of the army.

"We'll harass them," Judah told his brothers, "as much as possible. And when we have the two parts of Nicanor's army in one place, we'll send all of our men against them."

Judah squinted up at the bright sky. Though it was still afternoon and the sky was bright in the west, there was a chill in the air. But spring was already on the land, and soon the burning heat of summer would come. He hoped he would receive some word from Rome before that, something that could be used to rally more people to him. He looked down again at the splendid panoply of the Seleucids and saw the golden, black plumed helmet of Nicanor.

Proud and dignified, the General sat astride a huge white stallion. He rode at the head of his first phalanx.

Remembering what that man had ordered done to Ezra was enough to make Judah gnash his teeth in suppressed rage.

"I wonder if Nicanor knows he's being watched?" Jonathan asked.

"Probably," Judah said tightly, "probably." And he motioned to his brothers to leave the hill. But he remained there a few moments longer to see the last of the Seleucid phalanxes disappear under a cloud of golden dust. Even though Glacon had once told him that a man became a mercenary for money only and not for a cause, he could never understand how men could fight and die for nothing more than a few gold pieces. With a shake of his head, Judah hurried to the base of the hill, where his brothers were waiting for him.

* * *

Nicanor was not given to violent emotions; he believed in the Grecian philosophic doctrine of moderation, and he applied it to every aspect of his life, with the exception of his feelings for Judah. He hated him with a passion that became his reason for living. That Judah was a Jew made him his natural enemy, but that this Jew had routed his army at Emmaus was almost an unendurable truth. That defeat had made him the object of Lysias' displeasure and had forced him to support Demetrius when the young king had made his successful bid for the throne. It had also brought him back to Jerusalem to destroy Judah and his followers forever.

To gain favor with the new king, Nicanor had begged him for the assignment, and he had willingly accepted his lord's admonition, "to destroy only those Jews hostile to my rule and the authority of their priest, Alcimus. Respect their religious practices and do not have your troops despoil their Temple."

Nicanor would have obeyed any order, regardless of how stupid he thought it might be, if it would have given him an opportunity to destroy Judah. If he could accomplish that, where even Lysias and his elephants had failed, he would not only wipe away the disgrace of his past defeat, but he would gain new glory and be given a place at the right hand of the new king.

All of these thoughts passed through Nicanor's mind on the blustery day he led his men out of Jerusalem to link his forces to those phalanxes that had been sent to give added strength to his command.

The wind was biting, and the sky was filled with great plumes of gray clouds. To protect them against the cold, the Seleucids wore their heavy woolen cloaks across their shoulders.

Nicanor and several of his subordinates were on foot in front of the first phalanx. They were especially wary when they started down the road to Beth Horon.

Three days before, at a place called Capharalama, the Maccabees ambushed a phalanx and mauled them so badly that the survivors fled back to Jerusalem. That action further exacerbated Nicanor's hate for Judah and inflamed his desperate need to eliminate him forever. Had he his own way, he would have ordered the execution of every male in the village, but he had his orders from the King and, though he felt bridled by them, he had lacked the self-assurance to disobey them.

The phalanx moved in full battle array. To prevent them from bunching up, in the event of an attack, Nicanor ordered twice the interval of space be kept between each unit. He sent his scouts out in front, and he maintained a cover of light infantry units on his flanks.

"Send a runner to Danas, the commander of the reinforcements," Nicanor told one of his subordinates, "and tell him to join with us at Beth Horon."

"He'll be thankful for that," the officer said. "It's a long march to come up to the city by way of Beth-Zur."

Nicanor agreed, and the officer dropped back to carry out the order.

* * *

Immediately to the north of where Nicanor marched his army, Judah and his men followed it. They kept well out of range of the Seleucid patrols. But from their own scouts they knew not only where Nicanor's phalanxes were, but they were also able to follow the movements of the new units. Eight phalanxes had been dispatched to bolster Nicanor's to a total of four thousand men.

Judah's scouts brought word that the approaching force was making for the pass at Beth Horon. Judah immediately abandoned the shadowing of Nicanor's army. He ordered his own force of twenty-five hundred men to move south, then west, north and finally east. Eventually, it wound up at a place just south of the village of Adasa. Assault positions were set up along the southern edge of the hills and gullies bordering the edge of the main road.

The men huddled close to the earth and wrapped their cloaks around them. Judah and his brothers, with the exception of Johanan, who had been left with several hundred men to guard the camp, each commanded one of the units.

Simon was on Judah's left and Jonathan on his right. Judah motioned to each of them, and he settled down to wait.

The wind had dropped off a bit. But the sky was still full of long, gray clouds, though here and there in the distance toward the west, the spaces between the dark plumes were flecked with sunshine.

To wet his dry throat, Judah sucked on a small gray pebble. Now and then, he flicked his eyes over the men. Not as many had returned, as he had hoped. The number of white stones in the circle was still several thousand. And since the arrival of Nicanor in Jerusalem, none had been shifted to the other circle. Those that had not yet returned were obviously waiting to see how the battle between him and Nicanor would go . . . if Nicanor were to win, then the decision would have been made for them. But if Judah won, they would not hesitate to rejoin him; he was absolutely certain of that.

The familiar sound of the Seleucid marching rhythm trembled through the air and came up through the ground under him. It came from two directions at once. But the thumping beat from the east was closer than from the west. Judah pressed himself against the ground. The absence of Glacon worried him. He knew it also worried the men. In battle, he was Glacon, and Glacon was as close to being him as man could be.

He passed the word to his subordinates to have the men remain very, very quiet.

Trumpets blared and within a short while Nicanor's army came into view. The General and his staff were in front. Behind them was rank after rank of troops. Too many to attack.

Judah motioned his men to fall back.

The Seleucids moved past the Maccabees and some time later they linked up with the Selucid units that had marched all the way from Syria.

Judah ordered his men back to their former positions. It took a while for the Seleucid troops to reorganize themselves and turn around for the march back to Jerusalem.

* * *

Nicanor, now joined by Danas, led the first phalanx. Both men were pleased with the operation. Nicanor was certain that Judah would not dare to attack so large a force. To provide the main body of his army with protection against any such possibility, he sent his patrols to the north, where the Maccabean stronghold was located.

He explained his tactic to Danas and added, "With this force, we can flush the Jews out of their hiding places and, sooner or later, we'll kill all of them."

Danas was new to Judea. His experience had been solely on the eastern frontier of the empire. He had been told by his superiors to avoid becoming involved with Nicanor in any discussion of military tactics.

* * *

From where Judah was hidden, he could see the two men very clearly. Danas was a young man, scarcely more than thirty. Even as Judah made that appraisal, he glanced at the men on either side of him. They were taut with expectation. They were looking at him, waiting for the sight of his raised staff and the single note of the ram's horn. Judah moved his eyes back to the enemy. Nicanor was practically in front of him. Judah raised his staff. The ram's horn sounded. The Maccabees were up and running. Some shouted, "Hear, oh Israel, the Lord is our God, the Lord is One." Others yelled, "Holiness to the Lord!"

Judah was among the first to be at the enemy. With his gold-hilt sword, he cut down two of Danas' guards and then he went at Danas. The two men slashed at each other. Each was wet with sweat. Judah's sword came down on the General's shoulder and broke through the bone.

Nicanor's staff ran to the defense of their General.

But Judah hacked the arm off one man. Thrusting past the shield of another man, he stabbed him in the chest. The others fled.

Nicanor faced Judah and tried to lift his sword. But he was not quick enough.

"For Ezra," Judah shouted. "For Ezra and my brother!" And with a vicious slashing stroke, he sent his sword against the neck of the Seleucid General.

Nicanor screamed; his head rolled from his shoulders; a fountain of blood welled up from the neck; then his body fell to the ground, twitching.

Judah grabbed hold of Nicanor's head. He thrust his sword into its soft bottom; he raised the gory head high above his own and shouted, "Here's your General. Here is Nicanor." He ran toward where the Maccabees and the Seleucids were locked in a life and death struggle.

The Seleucids heard Judah's wild yells and, seeing the bloody head of their General on Judah's sword, lost their will to fight. Many soldiers threw down their arms and begged for mercy.

"Give no quarter," Judah bellowed. "Kill as many as you can. Take no prisoners!"

The Maccabees drove hard into the ranks of their enemy. Shield smashed against shield and sword against sword. Men screamed in terror or shouted in triumph. Then the phalanxes dissolved into smaller units and the Maccabees cut them down.

Finally, the Seleucids turned and began to run.

"Follow them," Judah ordered his men. "Follow them!"

And the Maccabees chased the fleeing Seleucids the rest of the day, and only when they came within sight of the Seleucid fortress of Gazara, did they break off the fight.

The Maccabees lost fifty men.

More than a thousand Seleucids were dead on the field.

Judah left Nicanor's bloody head, with its dull staring eyes and lolling tongue for the vultures and the crows. But even his brothers were shocked at Judah's barbarity. The men who had fought alongside of him there at Adasa, spoke in whispers about what Judah had done to Nicanor's head.

Days later, after Judah had returned to the camp in the Gophna Hills, he received word by special messenger from his two emissaries in Rome that Glacon had been stabbed to death and that his body had been flung on a dung heap. They also said Helen had been killed in a similar manner, though not before she had been raped.

The victory over Nicanor turned to ashes for Judah. The loss of Glacon was an enormous weight that seemed to pull on Judah every time he stood. It was something from which he could not shake free. It was there day and night.

The people whispered that Yahweh took Glacon and his wife to punish Judah for what he had done to Nicanor.

CHAPTER XXV

When Eupolemus and Jason returned to Judah, they brought back with them a bronze tablet inscribed with the following words:

"Success to the Romans and the Jewish Nation by sea and land forever! May sword and foe be far from them! But if war breaks out first against Rome or any of her allies throughout her dominion, then the Jewish Nation shall support them wholeheartedly as occasion may require. To the enemies of Rome or of her allies the Jews shall neither give nor supply provisions, arms, money, or ships; so Rome has decided; and they shall observe their commitments without compensation.

"Similarly, if war breaks out first against the Jewish Nation, then the Romans shall give them hearty support as the occasion may require. To their enemies there shall be given neither provisions, arms, money, nor ships; so Rome has decided. These commitments shall be kept without breach of faith.

"These are the terms of the Agreement which the Romans have made with the Jewish people. But if, hereafter, both parties shall agree to add or to rescind anything, then they shall do as they decide; and any such addition or rescission shall be valid.

"As for the misdeeds which King Demetrius is perpetrating against the Jews, we have written to him as follows: 'Why have you oppressed our friends and allies the Jews so harshly? If they make any further complaint against you, then we shall see that justice is done them, and will make war upon you by land and sea.'"

Judah had Simon read the entire text to all of the people, and when his brother finished, he shouted to his followers, "We are a Nation of Jews. We're a nation among all the other nations of the world!" His words bounded off the surrounding cliffs. He had gotten from Rome more than he had dared to hope for. There were tears in his eyes as he bid his people celebrate the event.

* * *

But Demetrius had learned of the treaty's contents long before Judah, and he had decided to put an end to the new Nation, for fear that the Romans might arm the Jews and send them against him. For this purpose, he dispatched General Bacchides in command of twenty thousand infantry and two thousand cavalry.

* * *

On a clear day, at Elasa, a flat dry place that gave the Seleucids room to maneuver, Judah with no more than three thousand men met Bacchides. Judah would have preferred to fight them in the narrow passes of the Gophna Hills, but Bacchides army was too large, too unwieldy for that kind of combat. Even after the word had been spread to all the Jews in the land that Rome, the most powerful nation in the world, recognized them as a nation, few of the white stones had been moved from their circle to the other one.

When the Maccabees saw the strength of the enemy army, many of them broke and ran, leaving Judah with only eight hundred men. He attacked the right flank of the Seleucid army with the hope that he would be able to cut his way to Bacchides. He could see him sitting astride a big black horse.

For Judah and his men it was bloody work. They were engulfed in a maelstrom of shouting men, metal clanging against metal, the terrible sound of crunching bone, and fearful cries of the dying.

Judah's right shoulder was cut and bleeding profusely. He urged his men to continue fighting.

Quickly, the Maccabees broke through the enemy ranks and were within striking distance of the General, when someone shouted, "Look to the left. The left."

Judah turned and saw the left wing of the Seleucid army running toward them. Instantly he knew it was over; they had lost the battle. He had hoped that this would be their final battle, their final victory. But it was over so quickly. The seven years of struggle vanished in a few moments. It was as if the Almighty had moved His hand across the land and brought with it the shadow of death. "Fall back," he shouted. "Fall back. Save yourselves!" The words sounded like curses. Like obscenities. The next instant an arrow struck him in the chest. He stumbled, fell to his knees and vomited blood.

His brothers ran to him, picked him up and carried him off the field to a safe place among the gullies on the right flank on the battlefield.

Bacchides, content to see his enemy routed, did not order his men after the fleeing Maccabees.

Stretched out on the hard, sun-baked ground, Judah shook his head; he could hardly speak. Blood continually welled up in his throat. He was forced to vomit it out. His vision blurred; the faces of his brothers became grotesquely distorted against the intense blue of the sky.

With great effort, Judah said, "Let Jonathan lead. Take old Eleazar's staff and use it." He paused to spew out scarlet blood. "Jonathan, form a new army and with it . . . with it, Jonathan, build a new nation, our Nation. A Nation for Jews!" He vomited again and, fighting for each breath, he told Simon to be Jonathan's counsel, and to Johanan, he said, "Be to Jonathan what you have always been to me."

Judah fought for a few more moments of life; his face was wet with sweat. More blood poured out of his mouth. Suddenly, he saw his father in his white priestly robes standing in front of him. He started to raise himself and, in a voice strangled by coughing, he shouted, "Hear, oh Israel, the Lord is our God, the Lord is one." An instant later, his body seemed to sink, and a last breath escaped through his lips.

Simon cradled Judah's body in his arms. He wept and, looking at his other brothers, he said, "Judah never walked with Yahweh. But . . ." he sobbed, "but Yahweh always walked with him . . . with *him.*"

EPILOGUE

The Maccabees who survived the battle at Elasa followed Jonathan, their new leader, and Simon into the wilderness of marshes along the west bank of the Jordan River. There they rested, and from there Jonathan staged a series of lightning-like strikes against the superior Seleucid forces.

Bacchides struck Jonathan's camp, and a fierce, bloody struggle followed. When it was over, two thousand Seleucid soldiers lay dead in the marshes. The Maccabean force escaped by swimming across the river to the eastern bank and disappearing into what is now known as the Transjordan.

For the next few years, Jonathan rebuilt his army and kept out of Bacchides way. But destroying the Maccabees had become a "holy cause" for the Seleucid General. And at the village of Beth-Hoglah, he finally surrounded Jonathan's entire army. Under cover of darkness, Jonathan, in command of a small force of men, slipped through the siege lines and attacked Bacchides' army from the rear, while Simon, in command of a suicide force, drove headlong into the Seleucid army and broke the siege.

While Bacchides was trying to subdue the Maccabees, Demetrius was having problems at home, which required him to send for Bacchides and his army.

Bacchides decided it would be better for the Seleucids if they made peace with Jonathan. The fight for the Jewish Nation had finally come to an end. Jonathan was recognized by the Seleucids as its secular and spiritual leader. He soon showed his friends and enemies that he was a consummate diplomat, who was able to take advantage of the dissension that rent the Seleucid Empire. With Simon at his side, Jonathan welded a firm friendship between Judea and Rome. And Judah's vision of a Jewish Nation became a reality.

AUTHOR'S NOTE

Judah died before Rome's recognition of the Jewish Nation. This important alliance was actually forged by Jonathan after Judah's death, but for dramatic purposes and in justice to Judah's role in achieving it, I gave the victory to him.

www.ingramcontent.com/pod-product-compliance
Lightning Source LLC
Chambersburg PA
CBHW070203260626
47160CB00002B/435